The Gra...
Murder

A Victorian Historical
Murder Mystery

Book 3 of
The Field & Greystone Series

Lana Williams

USA Today Bestselling Author

Other Books in The Field & Greystone Series

The Ravenkeeper's Daughter, Book 1
The Mudlark Murders, Book 2
The Gravesend Murder, Book 3
The Rookery Killer, Book 4

Want to make sure you know when my next book is released? Sign up for my newsletter.

Copyright © 2025 by Lana Williams

Ebook ISBN: 979-8-9914769-4-2
Print ISBN: 979-8-9914769-5-9

All rights reserved. NO AI TRAINING permitted.

By payment of required fees, you have been granted the *non*-exclusive, *non*-transferable right to access and read the text of this book. No part of this text may be reproduced, transmitted, downloaded, decompiled, reverse engineered, or stored in or introduced into any information storage and retrieval system, in any form or by any means, whether electronic or mechanical, now known or hereinafter invented without the express written permission of copyright owner.

Please Note:
The reverse engineering, uploading, and/or distributing of this book via the internet or via any other means without the permission of the copyright owner is illegal and punishable by law. Please purchase only authorized electronic editions, and do not participate in or encourage electronic piracy of copyrighted materials. Your support of the author's rights is appreciated.

No part of this book may be reproduced or transmitted in any form or by any electronic or mechanical means, including photocopying, recording or by any information storage and retrieval system, without the written permission of the publisher, except where permitted by law.

Thank you.

Cover Art by The Killion Group

One

Gravesend, England - 1884

Benjamin Norris tightened the muffler around his neck and shivered as he stepped off the train at Gravesend, wishing not for the first time that he lived in London. He grew weary of traveling to his shop each day, especially during the winter months. His back protested from the uncomfortable seats in second-class, and he arched to ease the ache. It was only mid-January, and there were yet still weeks of the dark cold to endure before spring's welcome arrival.

The icy station bustled with passengers both arriving and departing that chilly evening. He clutched his worn leather satchel tighter and peered suspiciously at those jostling past him, determined not to be the victim of theft. As the owner of an import-export shop, he was ever on guard against troublesome thieves.

But of late, that was the least of his problems.

Benjamin attempted to shrug away the tension which had gripped his portly frame these past few days. The new year held promise for his business, partly due to what was in the satchel. He had thought to make a tidy sum from it.

Now he wondered whether the item in question was worth the trouble it could cause.

Unease crept along his spine, and he nearly jumped out of his skin when another passenger pushed past him.

"Sorry, sir," was the hastily murmured response as the other man hurried by.

"Be more careful," Benjamin called after him, more to assure himself than anything else. With another wary glance around, he continued pushing his way out of the station.

Though tempted to take a hansom cab given his aching back and tired feet, home was only four streets from the train station. The exercise would do him good, especially since he was still in his thirties, something his late mother had often told him. The house had felt empty without her these last two years, but her tabby cat, Leopold, would be there to greet him.

The feline was a nuisance more often than not, though Benjamin considered the beast better company than most people. Having worked with the public in his shop for nearly a decade, he held a certain disdain for people in general.

With another shiver as a cold winter breeze sent his coat tails flapping, Benjamin strode toward his destination as if someone more than the cat expected him. His thoughts were a little less direct, drifting between the item tucked inside the case...and the visit from that Scotland Yard Inspector the previous day.

Benjamin had thought Mr. Matthew Greystone's case closed, since the man's killer had never been found. It was terribly unsettling to not only be personally acquainted with a man who'd been murdered, but one who was in the same business.

Still, he didn't appreciate Inspector Field's recent visits to his shop, though Benjamin had been careful not to show it. Having the police stop in even once was bad for business. Worse, it churned the fear in his gut: who else might have noticed the detective's renewed interest?

His fingers tightened around his leather satchel and the item he carried home as he glanced over his shoulder.

Had Inspector Field's visits been connected to Mrs. Greystone coming by last November? In truth, he had been pleased to see her—at the time. She was a delightful woman, one he didn't think Greystone had deserved. The gold coin he'd purchased from her had made him a pretty penny. The objects the mudlarks found while searching the muddy shore of the River Thames intrigued him but were rarely so valuable as that coin, from what he knew.

The farther Benjamin walked the quieter the streets became, the gas lights few and far between on the house-lined street. A warm glow came from most windows as families sat to their dinners and whiled away their evenings. It must have rained earlier, for his shoes made a satisfying slap on the wet pavement, reminding him of boyhood puddle jumping and making him pleased he'd walked.

The air in Gravesend was better than that in London, especially after the rain. He breathed it in as memories took hold. He had spent his early years walking these same streets but moved to London more than a decade earlier. Freedom, excitement, adventure— He had been certain those and more awaited him in the city.

His mother's failing health had forced him to return five years ago. Now she was gone, but Benjamin couldn't bring himself to sell the house, even if living above his shop would be more convenient. He had tenants in those rooms for now. Letting go of the final remnants of his mother and childhood was something he couldn't yet do. It was an escape, albeit a temporary one, to come home to Gravesend each night, though not so much on these cold, dark January evenings.

A sound behind him caught his notice—quiet footsteps sparking his unease. Another person returning from the city, he supposed. Harmless. Yet his heartbeat sped as the footsteps grew closer.

Benjamin quickened his pace and shifted the satchel to clutch it before him with both hands, too easily able to imagine someone snatching it and running off into the night, its precious cargo lost forever.

His breathing grew ragged, a reminder of his failed plan to curtail his habit of third helpings at the start of the new year. To his relief, the familiar outline of home came into view. The tall, stately structure with its sharp peaks and pitched roof was a welcome sight.

Movement in the lit window across the street caught his notice, the twitch of a white lace curtain causing him to scowl. "Blasted nosy woman," he muttered. "Always watching. Doesn't she have better things to do?"

Benjamin hurried around the house to the side door then paused to listen, relieved when the footsteps continued down the street and faded into the night.

"Letting my nerves get the best of me," he told himself as he unlocked the door. His imagination had become too vivid of late.

The faint scent of lemon wax and eucalyptus greeted him when he stepped inside, along with the cat's meow. The creature seemed to berate him for his late arrival.

He locked the door behind him, smiling as the cat wound between his legs. He bent to scratch him behind the ears. "There's a good kitty." His mother had named it after the prince, something she thought highly amusing. "Are you hungry, Leopold? So am I." The brief walk had stirred his appetite, the fleeting urge to reduce his portions easily forgotten.

Benjamin set the satchel on the narrow entry table, his tension already easing. He removed his gloves, muffler, coat, and hat and hung them on the peg by the door, then donned the worn but familiar jumper that awaited him. The house, empty for hours, was always chilly upon his arrival.

With no live-in servants, who would only be underfoot when he returned each evening, he mostly made do for himself. A day maid, who he shared with a neighbor and worked a few hours every other day, cooked several simple meals and left them in the ice box for him to warm on the stove.

He picked up the satchel, struck once again by the immediate unease that filled him whenever it was in his hands. "The bloody thing is probably cursed. Just my luck." At least that would explain the unsettled feeling that had hung over him since its unexpected arrival in his shop.

Benjamin carried it into the sitting room and set it down to light a lamp first, followed by the fire. The cat trailed behind him, its frequent meows suggesting the feline was sharing how its day had progressed.

"Is that right?" he asked as he went about his routine. "And then what happened?" He bent to stroke the cat's soft fur before moving into the kitchen, the tall longcase clock ticking steadily in the hall and lending a pace to his movements.

He lit the kitchen lamps before retrieving what appeared to be a small crock of stew from the ice box. He started the stove and scooped some of the thick beef broth with chunks of meat and vegetables into a waiting pot.

The scent of the cold stew was enough to make Leopold even more vocal, so Benjamin retrieved the cat's bowl and provided a small taste for him as well. "Spoiled cat," he murmured as he watched him devour the treat then fed him his dinner. He made a mental note to ask the maid to waylay the Cats' Meat Man, who sold meat from a barrow in neighborhood.

Soon Benjamin sat at the kitchen table with a steaming bowl of stew and two thick slices of bread covered in drippings before him. He spooned up a bite, blowing on it before eating, savoring the hot broth that helped to warm him from the inside out.

The cat, having finished its own meal, sat near his feet waiting patiently to lick Benjamin's bowl.

"So spoiled. You still miss Mama, don't you? As do I."

Once the simple dinner was finished, of which he hadn't been able to resist a third helping, and the dishes left in the sink for the maid, Benjamin returned to the now warm sitting room. He unlatched the satchel and withdrew a cloth-bound bundle, reverently unwrapping it.

The Egyptian golden scarab gleamed in the firelight, and he carried it to the wingback chair closer to the cheerfully burning fire. Seating himself heavily, his stomach full but churning as he beheld the object which had given him so much worry, Benjamin turned it every which way to examine it more closely. While he sold a few antiques in his shop, this item was different—unique.

There was a difference between old and ancient.

He was no expert in Egyptian artifacts, but he had to think the beetle, fitting perfectly in his palm, was genuine. Some scarabs were seals, others amulets, but because they were fairly common only a few were truly valuable.

But this...this had an unexpected weight to it. The blood red stone in the center glistened, surrounded by intricate gold work with Egyptian markings and yet more gemstones. The piece had a richness that spoke of authenticity.

And it worried him.

Benjamin shouldn't have taken it. He shouldn't have opened the crate, shouldn't have sorted through it when he realized it had been delivered to the wrong address, and certainly shouldn't have kept the scarab when the delivery man returned to collect the crate, mumbling something about the wrong shop.

The scarab was a problem, and in more than one way.

What if it had come from a pharaoh's tomb and bore a terrible curse? He'd heard stories of wording found on tombs in the

Old Kingdom that promised judgment on those who disturbed them. How far did a curse go? To everyone who touched it?

Then there was the matter of that pesky law which forbade Egyptian artifacts from being taken out of the country unless sent through the proper channels. Of course, that didn't prevent treasures from surfacing in London.

The crate had been full of them: a pharaoh's mask, lamps, vessels, a necklace, small figurines, scarabs—all gold. He didn't think taking just one of the scarabs would be a problem, especially when it had been one of the smaller items in the crate.

If only he knew who the objects had been intended for. Something foul was afoot among the nearby import-export businesses, but he'd known that for well over a year. What to do about it, that was the concern. Should he—

Benjamin gasped, heart thumping as a strange sound echoed through the house.

The otherwise unoccupied house.

With a quick movement he stuffed the scarab between the cushion and arm, feeling the thin fabric tear beneath his fingers.

He held his breath as he stared at the empty doorway of the sitting room, listening intently, only to chuckle with relief as Leopold came wandering in imperiously with a meow.

"Up to no good, are you?" The cat rubbed against his leg as Benjamin pressed a hand to his still hammering heart. "Trying to have another go at the bowl in the sink? Shame on you."

He blew out a breath and straightened to stare into the fire, willing his nerves to calm before attempting to retrieve the scarab from the torn fabric.

A sudden gust of cold air had unease creeping along his skin. He stilled as he glanced once more at the empty doorway.

What had been empty was no longer. A tall stranger filled the space dressed in a black coat and hat, his dark eyes as cold as the night.

"W-Who are you?" Benjamin asked, mouth dry as he shifted to the edge of the chair. "How did you get in here?" He was certain he'd locked the door. Hadn't he? "Leave at once!"

"Not only do you have something that belongs to me, but you've been spending far too much time in the company of the police." The confidence in the deep timbre of the man's voice was a threat in itself.

"W-What?" Benjamin jerked to his feet. *Dear heavens.* Hadn't he feared someone would notice the inspector's visits? "I don't know what you are speaking of, whoever you are. Get out!"

"Stirring up the past serves no one." The man drew nearer, the raindrops on his long black coat catching the light of the fire as they dripped onto the floor. "Now, I need you to return what's mine."

"I have nothing of yours!" Benjamin backed up a step, but his legs hit the chair, preventing him from retreating. There was nowhere to go. No way to escape.

"You have one of my scarabs. I want it back."

"I-I don't know w-what you're talking about." Benjamin's thoughts raced as he tried to determine whether it was best to continue the pretense or simply hand it over.

Somehow he didn't think either option would satisfy the man.

Besides, it was the key to a terrible scheme—one he was determined to get to the bottom of. He couldn't do that if—

"Give it to me," the man demanded with a snarl as he took another step forward.

Benjamin's gaze slid inexorably to the satchel, wishing he hadn't brought it home after all.

The stranger followed his gaze and smiled as he reached inside his coat to pull out a pistol. "You leave me no choice."

Benjamin gasped and raised both hands before him, palms up. "Please—n-no—you don't want to do this!"

"Perhaps not, but it is necessary," the stranger said calmly, the grim smile still on his face.

Benjamin could hardly believe this was happening. Dear heavens, could this possibly be the man who'd murdered Greystone? "Wait—there's no need to—"

The blast of the pistol ended his plea.

Two

"The body's through here, sir."

Scotland Yard Inspector Henry Field followed the constable through the modest house in Gravesend, noting the worn but comfortable furnishings and wood paneling in last decade's fashions.

"You said the broken lock on the side door is the only damage?" Henry asked.

Gravesend was not his normal jurisdiction, but the identity of the victim was known to him. Unfortunately he'd questioned Benjamin Norris—again—just two days prior.

With little to show for it.

Whether that unsatisfactory conversation had any bearing on the man's murder remained to be seen, but Henry couldn't deny the knowing sensation in the pit of his stomach. That the hunch was so pervasive in this case concerned him. His hunches were few and far between and rarely this strong.

"Yes, sir. Nothing much else of note."

They passed by the kitchen with dirty dishes in the sink. Norris had at least enjoyed one last meal before his demise.

The constable stepped aside upon entering the sitting room to allow Henry an unobstructed view. The simple room looked like a cozy one in which to relax, small enough to be easily heated by the fireplace that had long since gone cold. Two upended chairs, several lamps, a table in one corner with items strewn over it...and a dead body on the rug.

"How was the victim discovered?" Henry asked as he drew near to examine Benjamin Norris, previous proprietor of an import-export shop, on his back. A significant hole in his temple from a bullet wound had abruptly ended his life, Henry didn't need a report from the surgeon to confirm that. Blood and a powder burn ringed the hole, confirming a close range shot. The exit wound was significantly larger on the opposite side of his head, leaving a grisly spray on the fireplace mantle.

"Just where he is."

Henry turned to glance at the constable, who stared at the scene with a mix of fascination and dread. The man appeared to be in his late twenties, suggesting he had enough experience under his belt to not allow the sight of a body to disturb him—but clearly, he didn't know what to think of it.

Then again, this was Gravesend, a small town a short distance from London. It boasted two train stations and a busy port but little crime these days, though decades ago the road had been notorious for highwaymen. Perhaps the constable didn't come upon murder victims often.

"I meant who found him and how did they know to look for him here?" Henry clarified, trying not to sigh.

"Ah. Yes. Well, it seems his shop clerk became alarmed when Mr. Norris didn't open his establishment this morning and notified a constable, who sent a telegram for us to have a look."

"A conscientious clerk." Henry turned back to study the victim again.

"He expected to be paid his wages today. I suppose that urged him into action."

"When was Norris last at the shop?"

"He and the clerk departed at six o'clock last evening, with Norris locking the door behind them. The place was still shut tight, seemingly undisturbed."

Henry nodded as he surveyed the scene, doing his best to catalog the details. Norris lay between the wingback chair and the fireplace. He wore a brown jumper which had seen better days, and trousers with a few mud spatters along the hem, suggesting he'd worn them home from work and not changed.

"Do you know if he took the train?" Henry couldn't imagine him paying for a hansom cab to bring him from London to Gravesend each evening, and the stagecoach would surely have taken too long.

"The clerk said that was his routine."

"He lived here alone?" Henry glanced around the room again, observing a few feminine touches in this room which mirrored what he'd also noted as they walked through the house.

The constable withdrew a notebook from his pocket and flipped it open. "According to a neighbor, his mother died two years ago after being in poor health for a few years."

Henry already knew Norris was unmarried, he'd mentioned it during one of their…conversations. "Did the neighbor have anything else interesting to add?"

"They didn't see anyone in the area last evening if that's what you mean." The constable studied his notes. "Mr. Norris tended to keep to himself. He wasn't particularly social."

"I suppose that's not surprising, given how much of each day he spent in London at his shop assisting customers."

A faint sound from somewhere in the house had Henry stilling in surprise. He and the constable shared a wary look—clearly the constable wasn't expecting anyone either. Before Henry could investigate, a striped cat ran into the room, meowing.

Henry crouched down as the cat pressed against his trousers and rubbed the friendly creature behind the ears. "Sorry to hear of your master's passing," he told it.

"I will dispose of the cat," the constable said with a frown as he started forward.

"No need." Henry wasn't particularly fond of cats, but he wasn't inclined to take such action just because its owner had died. *Dispose of it, indeed.* "You might try to find it something to eat in the kitchen. It's most likely hungry."

"Hmm. Very well," the constable said with reluctance. "Here, kitty. Follow me." The man's lack of enthusiasm had Henry hiding a smile.

"Perhaps if you find something to feed him, he'll follow you," Henry suggested.

"All right." The man departed, though the feline remained to sniff the body.

How unfortunate it couldn't tell them what had occurred.

Noises emerged from the kitchen, and that was enough for the cat to rush off to investigate, leaving Henry to continue his perusal of the crime scene.

A check of Norris's hands suggested he hadn't put up much of a fight. No broken nails or roughened skin. No bruising. No convenient scraps of fabric. Henry checked the man's pockets but found them empty except for a handkerchief. The jumper had a few stains that seemed to have come from a recent meal, perhaps eaten in haste.

Henry looked around the room again, noting the satchel which had been upended, the contents scattered on the table and the floor. Apparently whoever had shot Norris had been looking for something. The question was: had they found it?

Henry looked over the items, not touching them yet, committing them to memory. Several sheets of paper, more than likely keys to his shop, an antique necklace with scratched gemstones that didn't look particularly valuable, and cards with the name of his shop. Nothing else was in the satchel.

He slowly walked around the room, debating whether Norris would've had time to hide whatever he might have had before being startled by his killer. If he'd been sitting before the fire, the wingback chair was more than likely where he'd sat.

Henry tried to imagine the scene. A simple dinner had been eaten. The dishes left, unwashed. The fire burning in the hearth. Norris and his cat enjoying the warmth and relaxing after a long day. And then...what?

The fact that he hadn't fought back didn't mean much. Norris didn't seem the type to relish physical altercations. Perhaps the killer had been familiar, so Norris hadn't had a reason to fight. Perhaps he'd known why the intruder had come. Then again, the emergence of a weapon might've ended any temptation to fight.

The entire room had been searched, though there wasn't much other than furniture and a few knickknacks in it.

Who had broken in, confronted Norris, then killed him? And did any of this have a connection with Matthew Greystone's unsolved murder?

The question was enough to prompt Henry to re-examine first Norris and then his immediate surroundings, widening his search from the body. He found the bullet embedded into the edge of the mantle amid the spray of blood and brain matter, but would need a tool of some sort to force it out. Norris had to have been standing when shot at close range, more than likely with a small caliber weapon.

Unfortunately the bullet that had killed Greystone had never been recovered. Henry's jaw tightened. And his body had been found several streets away from his shop, not at home. The surgeon had estimated the caliber of the weapon that had killed him—seven to nine millimeter, but it was only an estimate.

Henry sat back on his heels, trying to view the scene objectively without the lens of Greystone's murder over it. He mustn't assume the two were connected until—unless he had evidence to prove it.

As he studied the room, including Norris's body, he couldn't help but wonder if he himself was in some way to blame for the man's death. After all, he had renewed his efforts to investigate Greystone's death, which brought him back not only to Norris's shop but also others in the vicinity of Greystone's. Reviewing previous interviews, speaking again to witnesses or connections to the victim sometimes offered new insights on a case which had gone cold.

Needless to say, this was not the insight Henry had hoped for.

"A dogcart's here, sir," the constable said from the doorway.

"We're going to need assistance to haul him out." Norris's form was generous, and Henry didn't relish the job ahead of them.

"I'll see if the driver can aid us."

"Please do." Henry sighed and stood, moving to the table to record the items in the satchel in his notebook before checking it one more time. *Keys, papers...* He returned to the body and straightened one of the two upended chairs to clear a path to remove Norris from the scene.

The cushions were slit, as if whoever had killed Norris had searched them. For what, Henry couldn't guess. He ran his hand along the cushion and arms but found nothing.

He lifted the next chair, noting the slit in it as well. As he sat it down, he heard an odd clunk.

"A body, you say?"

The unfamiliar voice had Henry turning in response. The constable had returned with the dogcart man in tow. Henry was pleased to see he was big. Perhaps there was hope of getting Norris out of there without a problem.

"I can't say I've ever hauled a body before." The man frowned as he stared at the dead man.

Henry only hoped the driver hadn't known the victim. A second look suggested that wasn't the case.

Deciding it best to have the task over and done, Henry moved to Norris's upper body. "If you'd each take a leg."

"Take—take a leg?" The driver's mouth dropped, his horror obvious.

Henry smothered a smile despite the dark task. Where was Fletcher, his trustworthy sergeant back in London, when he needed him? "*Lift* a leg," he emphasized.

"Ah. Yes, yes of course." The constable nodded as if he'd known that all along. "Here we go." He bent down, and soon the three men were making their way through the house and out the door with their heavy burden.

They got him into the dogcart. Luckily the driver had a canvas tarp to spread over the late Mr. Norris.

"Anything more you need?" the constable asked after the driver had departed for the train station.

Henry had requested the body be taken to St. Thomas' in London since the murder could be connected to another case.

"Yes." Henry had not forgotten the odd clunk he'd heard in the chair. *Was it possible...* "A few more things to check."

The man nodded but glanced down the street as if anxious to go.

"I am happy to lock the house when I'm done," Henry offered, a boon for the poor man and himself. He would prefer to finish on his own without the distraction of the nervous constable.

"Oh. If you're sure?" The constable pulled out a pocket watch to check the time. "I do have other things to see to."

Probably luncheon, Henry thought. But he kept it to himself. "Of course. If you would be sure to find a way to secure the broken door this afternoon?"

"Yes, I will do that."

"We will also need to find a new home for the cat."

"Huh." The man scratched his cheek. "I suppose I can see if that's possible." He frowned at Henry. "If you could bring the key back to the office..."

"I would be happy to. Not sure how long it will all take."

"No rush, of course." The man nodded politely then started down the pavement without a backward glance.

Henry returned to the quiet house, startled again when the cat returned to greet him. "Lonely, are you?" he asked as he bent to give it a scratch.

The cat meowed as if in response.

Returning to the sitting room and the chair it appeared Norris had been seated in, there was one question uppermost in Henry's mind.

What had caused the clunk?

He ran his hand along the cushion without success. Nothing there. But something had made the sound. Had it just been a broken spring or the like?

He tipped the chair forward, hoping to repeat the sound and determine the location. Sure enough, it clunked again. He knelt for a closer look, pushing the cushion away from the arm, and spotted a tear in the fabric. Pulse quickening, with care he reached into the opening, only feeling batting against his fingertips. He pushed deeper, certain there had to be something in there, though of course it might not be related to Norris's murder. Who hadn't lost a coin down the side of a sofa?

His fingers touched a sharp edge. That wasn't a coin.

Further digging allowed him to grip whatever it was. Henry withdrew the item with care, catching it more than once on the fabric before at last pulling it out.

A scarab. The sort one might find in Egypt. Gold, with gems. Rich looking, and much different than the scratched antique necklace. Henry turned it over, certain it was valuable, and quite sure it had to be what the killer had searched fruitlessly for.

Another clue.

Unfortunate, that clues often brought more questions than answers.

Three

"Inspector Field is calling, madam," Fernsby, Amelia Greystone's longtime butler, announced from the doorway of the drawing room where several lamps were lit to hold off the evening's darkness.

Amelia's spirits immediately lifted as Fernsby stepped aside to reveal the unexpected guest. She set aside the book she'd been reading in a chair by the fire and stood with a smile. "Henry. What a pleasant surprise."

"It's good to see you, Mrs. Greystone. Amelia." He dipped his head, still wearing his coat with his hat in hand, an indication he didn't intend to remain long.

His dark hair was brushed neatly to one side, and his brown eyes held on her with a watchfulness to which she was growing accustomed.

Even though she considered Henry a good friend, her heart jolted to hear a man other than her late husband use her given name.

Yet it took no more than a moment to realize something was wrong. Terribly wrong. She knew the inspector well enough by now to discern when something weighed on him. "What is it? What's happened?"

He heaved a quiet sigh as he stepped forward, clearly searching for the fortitude to share bad news. "I am afraid my visit is not...a social one."

Dread crawled along Amelia's spine as she clenched a hand at her side until her nails bit into her palm, bracing herself. She had endured more than her share of unfortunate news and wasn't certain how much more she could take. Grief was already her constant companion.

Her daughter had died of scarlet fever three years earlier, and then a year ago last autumn, her husband had been shot, his murder still unsolved. Inspector Field—Henry had done his best to find who had killed him, to no avail.

And the tragedies had not ended there. Last autumn, Amelia had been embroiled in calamity once again when a ravenkeeper from the Tower of London had been murdered. Though she had only recently met the man to interview him for the periodical she occasionally worked for, his young daughter had sought refuge with Amelia after his death. The girl, deaf, mute, and the sole witness to the murder, had remained with Amelia for a tension-filled week while Henry had tracked down the killers.

Two weeks later, Amelia had been interviewing a barge captain when they'd come upon the body of a mudlark on the bank of the Thames who'd been poisoned. It had taken both Henry and Amelia's efforts to unwind the plot and find the guilty party.

The weeks had slid by, Christmas had been and gone, and she had unconsciously relaxed after yuletide and no more sadness had touched her life. While Amelia would admit to enjoying the challenge of solving a murder case, her own grief resurfaced each time. She could never set it aside completely, nor did she want to. Matthew and Lily would forever be part of her, their memories something she cherished.

But they still hurt.

She couldn't help but think that she was the unlucky link that connected the tragedies shadowing her life. And now…

"Please, have a seat." Amelia gestured to the empty chair near the fire, taking a small measure of comfort in the routine of polite behavior and good manners. She held tight to her patience as she sank onto the edge of the chair and Henry followed suit. "What has happened?" she asked in a whisper, hand still fisted in the folds of her gray skirts.

Henry paused for a moment, his sympathetic gaze holding hers. "Benjamin Norris has been killed."

"Oh." A wave of relief followed quickly by guilt shot through her. She hadn't known the man well and was thankful it wasn't someone she was closer to. Still, the news was unwelcome. Another death, connected to herself. "How?"

Henry's lips pressed tight as if even more reluctant to share the details, which caused her stomach to lurch.

Mr. Norris had been an acquaintance of her late husband's and owned an import-export business not far from Matthew's shop. She had seen him but two months ago when he'd purchased a gold coin that one of the mudlarks had found. He hadn't seemed the type to seek out danger.

"He was shot in his home the last night."

Amelia took a moment to process the news. "Above his shop?"

"No, in Gravesend."

Shot. Just as Matthew had been.

"Did h-he live alone?" She knew he hadn't been married from previous interactions with him but little else.

"Yes."

As terrible as it sounded, she couldn't help but be grateful Matthew's death hadn't been at home with her as a witness. "Murdered."

Though not a question, she waited for Henry to confirm it.

"Yes. It appears so." Henry watched her, as if trying to gauge how she was taking the news, a mixture of regret and sympathy in his expression.

He couldn't like sharing poor news any more than she liked hearing it.

"How awful." She pressed a trembling hand to her mouth, uncertain if she should ask the next question that came to mind.

Henry rose and walked to the sideboard then returned with a finger of whiskey in a glass which he handed to her. "Forgive my boldness. Drink this."

She took the glass with care, surprised by how much her hand shook. Aware of Henry watching, she took a small sip, appreciating the burn of the whiskey as she swallowed.

Seeming satisfied, he returned to his seat, still watching her.

Amelia waited a moment, hoping the liquor would help to steady her, hoping the news wasn't connected to Matthew's death. But she had to ask. She had to know.

She cleared her throat and met Henry's gaze again. "Do you...do you think it could be related to Matthew's murder?"

His hesitation was an answer in itself, but still she waited. "There is a possibility." His expression tightened. "I spoke with

Mr. Norris twice in the past few weeks. Our most recent conversation was only two days ago."

The day before the man's murder. "For what purpose?"

"Investigating your late husband's murder."

Amelia touched a hand against her pounding heart. "Why speak to Mr. Norris?"

He looked away then back at her, his distress obvious—at least, to her. "It is customary in cold cases to interview those involved again if no additional clues come to light. A matter of stirring the pot to see what surfaces."

"And? Did anything surface in your conversation?"

"Not precisely." His gaze shifted to the fire, making her wonder at his thoughts. "Our previous interviews were brief, though I had the impression Norris knew something he didn't want to share. Perhaps something he had learned of late, hence the reason for my second visit." His gaze returned to meet hers. "His death could suggest someone noted that I had spoken with him…and wanted him silenced."

Amelia took another small sip, wishing for calm, but it eluded her. She glanced at the fire, which had felt so warm and cozy only a few minutes before. Now cold had settled into her very bones. She didn't think she'd ever be warm again.

In truth, she wasn't prepared for the details of Matthew's death to be brought forth again. As much as she longed for justice, she also wanted to protect herself from further upset. *How selfish.*

"But you don't know for certain," she suggested slowly. "It might have nothing to do with Matthew's death. It might have been a burglary or the like." She watched Henry closely, hoping he would agree.

"Certainly possible," he agreed, only to then shake his head. "Though unlikely. Nothing seems to have been taken from his home."

"M-Matthew was shot at close range. In the temple." She clutched the glass with both hands to keep from reflexively touching her own. "Was Mr. Norris killed in the same manner?"

"Yes." Henry's eyes darkened, but he didn't say more, his thumb rubbing the wood trim of the chair, surely a sign of his concern. Somehow it was comforting to know she wasn't the only one upset.

Her thoughts reeled as the news sank in, a heaviness settling in her chest that made breathing difficult.

"Amelia, I realize this must be very upsetting to you."

She pressed her lips tight, not bothering to agree. It was more distressing than he could possibly know.

"I fear the investigation will be so as well," he continued. "The same questions, if not more, will be raised."

Amelia nodded. His reminder of the case helped in a way the whiskey hadn't. An investigation meant leads to follow, interviews with others, a puzzle to solve. *Purpose.* That was something she continually longed for since losing her roles of mother and wife. "Did you find any clues at his home?"

Focusing on the case was preferable to giving in to her swirling emotions; a way to hold herself in the present moment rather than dwelling on the painful past or the empty future. Hadn't she been helpful to Henry in solving the last two murders? Assisting with this one, especially given how personal it was, would benefit both her *and* Matthew's memory. And hopefully Henry as well.

"Nothing...conclusive."

She frowned at the vague answer. Did he think whatever it was would upset her—or could he not speak of it because it was an official investigation? After a moment's consideration, she decided perhaps now wasn't the time to ask. She needed time to calm down and find a way to be useful, just as she'd done with the last two investigations.

"Nothing conclusive? That's unfortunate." She attempted a smile. "Solving cases is much easier with clues—or even better, a witness."

Henry's eyes warmed as if he appreciated her attempt at levity. "True. But then everyone would be solving them, and I wouldn't have a job. In this situation, the only witness seems to be Norris's tabby cat."

"Poor thing." Her smile became a little easier. "Despite the lack of a helpful witness, I have faith in your skills. You are an excellent detective."

His expression immediately sobered. What had she said to so perturb him?

"If I were, we wouldn't be having this conversation." He glanced away again only to look back to meet her gaze. "I would have already found your husband's killer."

"As I have said before, I fear Matthew was involved in something unsavory, given the unexpected amount of money in our bank account and the notes I found in his desk." She shook her head. "I only wish I knew what it might've been."

"And I wish I could be certain that looking into the case again hadn't resulted in Mr. Norris's death."

"I don't think for a moment that you speaking with him was to blame," she insisted, not questioning her urge to defend Henry, even to himself. "If that were true, he would've been killed soon after Matthew. You spoke with him back then."

"Perhaps." The twist of Henry's lips suggested he remained unconvinced.

Deciding it best to shift the subject for now, Amelia said, "I suppose the cat was quite distraught by his master's passing."

"It seemed so. Hopefully he will soon find a new home."

The thought of the creature alone in the house had her frowning. Was there someone to take the cat? "I confess that I don't know many details about Mr. Norris, though I remember him mentioning the cat. I believe he called it Leopold. Did he have any relatives?"

"His mother passed away a couple of years ago. He appears to have a cousin or two, though whether they are still living…we are still looking into the matter."

"Did his shop contain any evidence?" she asked, setting aside the glass of whiskey. Better that she focused on action rather than spirits to rein in her emotions.

"A thorough search of it will occur tomorrow." Henry frowned. "I fear it won't be an easy one with so many goods to sort through."

"I noticed that last time I was there, to sell the coin for the mudlarks. Crate upon crate of items yet to be unpacked."

"Yes. He carried a significant inventory."

Amelia nodded, the idea of sorting through it daunting. Perhaps she could be of assistance, since she was familiar with shops like his. "I hope you quickly find a clue. I suppose the shop will be permanently closed and the contents sold?" That was what happened to Matthew's.

"More than likely, unless a relative chooses to continue it." Henry watched her for a long moment. "I'm sorry to ruin your evening with such poor news."

"I appreciate you telling me. I...I would rather hear the facts from you than read speculation in the newspapers." She feared the coming days would be difficult. Already memories of the dark days after Matthew's death swept through her.

How often had she wondered about the circumstances of Matthew's murder? If he had been terrified at the sight of a gun, let alone when it was pointed at him? She briefly closed her eyes to stop the questions.

They wouldn't help him...or her.

This could be the chance to finally bring him justice, and she intended to help Henry seek it in any way she could—regardless of whether he asked for her assistance.

Four

Randolph Locke's shop on Threadneedle Street looked much as Amelia remembered. It was half a dozen doors down from Mr. Norris's, and she hadn't walked by it during her visit to the area two months prior.

She had been curious about the origin of the street's unique name when Matthew had first opened a shop there. Supposedly, Threadneedle Street had been originally known as Three Needle Street, from the needle-makers who'd been located there, though no one knew for certain. As with so many placenames, over time the pronunciation and spelling had changed, and now there were no needle makers left on the busy street.

She drew a breath of the cold air, hoping to clear her head. Sleep had been elusive last night, her thoughts in turmoil, continually circling about how and why Benjamin Norris had been killed—and whether his murder could be related to Matthew's death. It seemed too much of a coincidence to believe otherwise.

The day was a brisk one, and she was pleased to have worn her heavy woolen cloak. Gray clouds covered the sky, a fitting accompaniment for both her mood and purpose.

Investigating death was a grim objective.

A fair number of shoppers walked along the street even this early, all seeming intent on their errands, mainly ladies with a maid or a friend accompanying them, though a few men strode past as well.

As she had before, Amelia was careful not to look in the direction of Matthew's old shop, unwilling to further open the now raw wound. It was no longer his. He was no longer there. It wouldn't be the same, though she wished whoever operated a business in those same walls well. Certainly a better ending than—

No. Do not think of it.

She focused on Mr. Locke's storefront which was just ahead, hoping to see if he could shed any light on Mr. Norris's death. Henry would be busy at Mr. Norris's shop. While she didn't think he would approve of her intent, she was determined to help and hoped her acquaintance with Locke might lend her greater insight.

The brick façade boasted tall windows that offered a tantalizing view of the goods available for sale. Striped awnings shielded the wares from the sun and added a bright note to the shop. A black sign with gold lettering proclaimed the place to be *Importers of Global Wares*.

The sign did not exaggerate. Everything from Asian silks to bolts of American cotton to porcelain dishes from China to lacquered trays from India were stacked in groupings in the window. It was amusing how owning something from another country made one feel more worldly. The Great Exhibition of 1851, which Amelia's parents still spoke of, had started that fashion.

Before Matthew had passed away, they'd dined at the Lockes' home on two occasions and hosted them in return. Amelia had considered Victoria Locke a friend, but the couple had faded from her life after Matthew's death, much like many other friends had.

That was her own fault. She had withdrawn to a solitary existence while trying to gain her bearings, though a few friends had stuck with her, calling on her even though she hadn't returned the courtesy until her grief had eased.

Not the Lockes.

Had they worried their lives were in danger because they knew Matthew? Or did Randolph Locke know something? Henry had spoken with him after Matthew's death, of course, but Amelia had the advantage of actually knowing him.

Now was the perfect time to see what she could discover.

Setting aside thoughts of the past, she took a bolstering breath then reached for the brass handle of the door and pushed it open. A bell tinkled to announce her arrival. She paused as she closed the door behind her to glance around the long, narrow building, curious to see how his business was faring.

Barrels lined the entrance filled with coffee beans in burlap bags, canisters of tea, and tins of spices. Luxury items were located on shelves near the long counter that lined one wall. A mixture of cinnamon and coffee lingered in the air.

"Good morning." A young man dressed smartly in brown trousers and a shop apron with hair parted down the middle walked toward her. "May we help you with something?"

"Is Mr. Locke in?"

"I believe he is. May I say who's inquiring?"

"Mrs. Greystone." Amelia noted the slight widening of his eyes. Had he heard the name?

He dipped his head and moved to the back, leaving Amelia to browse. The goods displayed were similar to those Matthew had carried, though he hadn't offered consumable items. His focus had been on dishes, knickknacks, jewelry, and small furnishings, along with a few antiques.

She pressed a hand to her chest, taken aback by how difficult it was to look over the shop. It wasn't Matthew's but close enough to feel familiar—achingly so.

Perhaps she should have expected this renewed grief. Would the feelings only grow worse if she allowed herself to be drawn into another investigation? Her emotions were something she needed to manage to keep them hidden from Henry. He would be upset when he learned what she was doing, especially if he realized it distressed her.

Better that she focus on her goal rather than emotions.

Footsteps sounded from the rear of the store. "Mrs. Greystone?"

Amelia turned to see Randolph Locke moving toward her and realized she was happy to see him. "Good morning."

"How good to see you." The tall, pleasant looking man stretched both hands toward her to briefly clasp hers, the welcoming smile on his round face echoed in his brown eyes.

"And you. How are you and your family?" Amelia studied him, noting the fine lines around his eyes and a dusting of gray newly visible in his dark hair.

"We are well." He squeezed her hands before releasing them. "Victoria is busy with the children, of course. They are growing quickly, as you can imag—" Regret flashed in his eyes before sympathy tightened his expression.

A pang of loss struck Amelia. *Lily*. She forced a smile. "I'm pleased to hear it."

"And...and what of you?" he asked, shifting his feet.

"I am well. Thank you." With a lift of her chin, she reminded herself that she *was* doing well. She, too, was busy. Just not with the things she'd expected. She gave herself a mental shake, deciding it best if she got straight to the point. "I assume you have heard of Mr. Norris's death."

"I did. How unfortunate." His brow creased, his remorse appearing sincere.

"Had you spoken with him of late?" she asked.

"We saw each other fairly frequently."

"Did he happen to tell you anything of interest, mention any concerns?"

Mr. Locke shook his head. "I might have seen him almost every day but only in passing. He didn't say much." He narrowed his eyes. "Why do you ask?"

Amelia hesitated, wondering what to say. Henry would more than likely question Mr. Locke at some point, but if she could help, she would. It might be best if she made it clear she was acting out of her own curiosity. "In all honesty, I wondered if his death could be connected to Matthew's." That concern would be natural, under the circumstances.

"Surely you cannot believe that." Alarm flickered across his features.

She frowned, unable to understand why he'd say that. "I don't think it's impossible." Though it was on the tip of her tongue to mention how similar the manner of murder had been, she held back. Henry might not be revealing those details. After all, only the killer and the police knew how Mr. Norris had died.

She had to be careful and not overstep her bounds. The last thing she wanted was to hinder the investigation.

"I am very sorry about what happened to Matthew, but that was well over a year ago," Mr. Locke said curtly.

Anger shot through her. Did he think she'd somehow lost track of time since that terrible day? The arrogance of his statement had her drawing a slow breath to hold back her temper. "Yes. I am aware."

He had the grace to look sheepish. "Of course. It's just that it seems as if whatever caused Norris's death—"

"Don't you mean whoever?" Amelia interrupted, puzzled by his odd choice of words.

"Yes, yes." He waved a hand in dismissal. "If whoever killed Mr. Norris also killed Matthew, surely the two deaths would have been closer together. A year is a long time."

It was and it wasn't. When one struggled to get through each day, a year was an eternity. But Amelia did not share that. "Don't you think that the murders of two shop owners in the area are concerning?"

"Quite concerning, yes. I'm not suggesting otherwise."

She waited a moment to see what else he might say, but when he said nothing more, she continued, "You think it's more logical to believe they are unrelated?"

Mr. Locke glanced away with a sigh. "I'm certain this is a matter for the police."

"It is, indeed. You will likely hear from them soon."

"Me?" He looked surprised by the thought. "Why?"

"Well, you knew Mr. Norris, your shop is similar, and it's on the same street." Amelia couldn't believe she needed to say as much. Was the man truly so naïve?

"I didn't have anything to do with his death."

"Surely you want to help find who killed him?" Something dark prickled within her. She was already wondering if that were true.

"Of course." Yet Mr. Locke shook his head, belying his agreement, a ruddy color filling his cheeks. "It's all so shocking."

"Yes. It is." That much she already knew in the depths of her soul. Just as she had with Matthew's death. She allowed a moment of silence to hang in the air before asking, "Did you share some of the same suppliers as Mr. Norris?"

"A few." He shrugged as he stared out the window, a hand tapping against his trouser leg in a restless gesture. "That isn't something normally discussed."

"Oh?" She frowned, realizing she didn't remember Matthew speaking of such things. Then again, she hadn't been involved in the business, too focused on her duties as a mother. Until she wasn't.

"We would prefer to pretend our goods are unique, I suppose."

"I see."

"We need some way to differentiate ourselves from the other businesses on the street, so we try not to carry the same items."

Amelia nodded as she glanced around with fresh eyes, trying to remember what she'd seen in Mr. Norris's shop. Several items were similar, so it made sense that they could have purchased them from the same person. But what did that prove? It wasn't a crime to purchase goods.

The clerk emerged from the rear with a feather duster in hand and began dusting a shelf, moving objects as he went. He glanced in their direction several times, something Mr. Locke appeared to notice with a frown.

"Have you sold any...unique objects of late? Antiques or the like?" Amelia asked. A few of Matthew's regular customers had been interested in antiques from other countries, and Matthew had done his best to find them, occasionally going to great lengths to do so. Those kinds of wealthy customers had made a significant difference to his profit.

"No." Mr. Locke's quick denial had her watching him closely. "Nothing like that." He looked away, not meeting her gaze.

"Truly?" She hoped her voice sounded curious rather than suspicious. "Matthew always had several."

"Oh?" Mr. Locke shook his head, his tone shadowed by disapproval. "I suppose I focus on items I know I can sell daily, rather than risking the unusual."

Amelia didn't argue, wishing she'd paid closer attention when Matthew had been alive. She hadn't visited other shops often, no matter how near to Matthew's they had been. Though friendly with one another, they were competitors of a sort, vying for the same customers. She and Matthew had been friendlier with the Lockes because they were of a similar age, as were their...their children.

Amelia pondered what other questions to ask, disappointed by her lack of progress, though she knew from the previous cases she'd helped with that progress came in fits and starts. Every piece of information mattered, even if it didn't feel like it.

"How has business been?" she asked, wanting to keep him talking, though she knew her visit was nearing its end. Mr. Locke didn't seem inclined to share much.

"Good enough, though we always wish it was better." His fleeting smile was difficult to interpret. Amelia had the impression he felt guilty about the answer, but was that because he didn't want to sound greedy...or something else?

"You have such a nice variety of wares." Amelia turned to feign interest in the items, taking several steps down the aisle.

Mr. Locke was kept from responding by the arrival of a customer, leaving her free to peruse the shop. She watched the shopkeeper interact with an older woman for a moment then continued toward the back, ignoring the watchful gaze of the clerk.

The shelves were tidy with little dust on them, apparently thanks to the assistant, the wares arranged in pleasing symmetry. A narrow curtain hid the rear area from customers' view, but the bottom of the fabric was caught on a wooden crate with foreign markings stamped on the side, along with the name Sable Importers. Amelia paused to look closer, intrigued by what it might contain. The lid had been pried off and was set askew as if the items had been about to be unpacked.

With a careful look at Mr. Locke to see that he still conversed with the customer, she pushed aside the curtain to see a glimmer of gold in the crate amid the straw packing. Interest caught, she leaned down to see the edge of a piece of gold and blue Egyptian jewelry wider than her hand. Chills ran along her skin.

The necklace looked more like something that should be in a museum than a shop.

Yet Locke had denied selling unusual or antique items.

Raised voices calling goodbyes signaled the customer's departure and had her straightening, only to meet the narrowed, menacing eyes of the shop clerk between the open shelves which separated them. He shifted his position as if to better see what she was doing.

Face heating, Amelia quickly tugged the curtain back into place before turning to see Mr. Locke walking toward her. Her heart rattled in her chest. Had he seen her movement—where she had been looking?

"Sorry about that." His smile stiffened as his gaze shifted to the curtain then back to her, brow furrowing.

She followed his gaze to see the fabric still fluttering into place. Her nerves stretched taut as she stared at the swaying fabric, trying desperately to think of an excuse for snooping. All she could do was hope he thought the curtain moved due to a gust of air from the front door closing.

"You must converse with customers, of course." She pointed to a lacquered tray on a nearby shelf. "I was just admiring this lovely tray. Where did it come from?"

When he didn't answer, she looked back at him, his stern expression making her desperate to flee. She held back the urge and reached for the tray, hoping her attempt to feign nonchalance worked.

"India." The one-word answer was less than friendly.

"Very nice." She set it down again, dismayed by the way her hands trembled. "Well, I must be going." Attempting a smile, she forced herself to meet his gaze. "Please give Victoria my best. It's terrible that we've lost touch."

"I will do that." Yet he remained where he was, effectively blocking her path.

Amelia waited, her entire body shaking as she clutched her reticule, wondering if he would move out of her way.

At last, he stepped aside. "Goodbye, Mrs. Greystone."

Holding back the urge to run, she took her leave, grateful to close the door behind her. One thing was clear—Randolph Locke was most definitely selling unusual artifacts, regardless of whether he was willing to admit it.

So what else was the man hiding?

Five

SEVERAL SHOPS DOWN THE street, Inspector Henry Field, along with Sergeant Adam Fletcher and a constable, searched Benjamin Norris's shop. While Henry looked for a clue to the man's killer, not for a moment did he forget what else he hoped for—a connection to Matthew Greystone's murder.

"Any luck?" he asked Fletcher, who he considered his partner in many investigations, as well as someone he called a friend.

The man, who was larger than Henry in both height and weight, shook his head. "Hard to say. I am still unsure what we're looking for."

"As am I." Henry bit back a curse. *It wasn't the sergeant's fault.* The shop's inventory was significant and made finding clues a challenge. Anything could be evidence. Anything could be a distraction. "Whatever doesn't match everything else."

"Humph." Fletcher's impressive moustache twitched, his exasperation obvious, then he returned a decorative vase to a crate. "A bit like looking for a needle in a haystack, except we don't know if we're in the right field. Or actually looking for a needle."

Henry smiled even as frustration snaked up his spine. "True."

He had returned to London the previous afternoon, having taken the keys he found near Norris's satchel, to have a cursory look at the shop and speak with the clerk, a Mr. Andrew Weston, who'd reported him missing. Unfortunately the man had been overcome with emotion and unable to string more than a few words together. Hopefully he had recovered by now and would come to the shop yet this morning.

Fletcher cleared his throat as he perused the shelves before him. "How did Mrs. Greystone take the news?"

"As expected." Henry paused in his search of a cabinet full of knickknacks. "Calmly considering the circumstances."

"Did she see any potential connection to her husband's murder?"

"Yes. Almost immediately." He hadn't needed to spell that out for her, though he wished there wasn't one. It would surely bring her naught but grief.

"How friendly was she with Norris?"

"Not overly so." Henry detested that he once again had brought bad news to Amelia's door. "But she was still upset."

"I'm sure another death so similar resurrects bad memories."

"Agreed." Henry glanced around the shop, wishing for something to point them in a direction, a clue of some sort to pursue. But the goods displayed were much as one would expect. No Egyptian artifacts that matched the scarab. Surely nothing worth murdering a man.

Fletcher heaved a sigh. "Somehow I doubt we will find what we need here." He glanced at Henry. "There was nothing at the house, eh?"

"Only the scarab." He had already told Fletcher about it. Had he missed any clues? That was always a concern when he searched a crime scene—and this death was more complicated than most. Perhaps he only thought that because of the possible connection to Amelia, but still...

"Seems odd that it's been over a year since Greystone's murder and then this happens just down the road, in a shop most similar." Fletcher narrowed his eyes. "You truly believe it's connected?"

Henry hesitated. Answering meant relying on his instincts, something he was reluctant to do. All his training, his experience as an officer of the law, had taught him to prefer cold, hard evidence in his hand. The whisper of instinct that offered possible answers or at least a direction to pursue was unreliable. He feared it sought an easy answer when there wasn't one.

After all, he wasn't a true Field, his name gained through adoption not blood. He had no claim to the effortless and widely respected intuition of his famous grandfather, Charles Field, or that of his father, Thurmond, who had each retired from the police as chief inspectors.

"Connected? Yes." The word escaped before he could halt it; yet he was uncertain enough that he hadn't mentioned the potential connection to his superior, Director Reynolds.

"I wouldn't disagree." Fletcher nodded as he glanced about. "Well, we will keep looking until there's nothing left unturned."

Not for the first time, Henry gave him a look of silent thanks. The man had significant experience with the force and many years in the military before that. He was a sounding board which Henry appreciated. His common sense, logic, and willingness to get his hands dirty were traits he himself tried to emulate. Henry's father and grandfather had shared similar qualities, all of which Henry greatly admired.

Greatly admired, and felt personally lacking.

"Yes, we shall." Henry began sorting through another crate of goods.

The shop was silent for nearly half an hour before the bell above the door chimed, announcing an arrival.

Henry listened while the constable questioned the man, pleased to overhear that the shop clerk, Andrew Weston, had arrived as promised. Perhaps a clue had arrived as well.

"Good morning," Henry said as he walked forward.

The younger man nodded. "My apologies for my upset yesterday. After being employed by Mr. Norris for the past eight months, I...I found the news of his demise extremely upsetting." He glanced around the shop as if expecting to see something different than when he'd last left the premises.

"I appreciate you returning today."

"A terrible ordeal. Simply terrible." The man shook his head. "I hardly know what to think."

Which made Henry wonder what he did think. Was it possible that everyone was hiding something? "You reported Mr. Norris's absence?" he asked, deciding it best to start at the beginning.

"Yes." Mr. Weston gestured to the front of the shop. "I came to work as per usual but found the door locked. I waited, though it was out of character for Mr. Norris to arrive late. After a reasonable time, and with a great deal of uncertainty, I contacted the police who told me they'd notify those in

Gravesend." He shook his head and sniffed, retrieving a handkerchief from his pocket. "I've been beside myself since informed of his death."

"Very upsetting, I'm sure."

"Indeed. Quite. I can't imagine why anyone would want to harm him."

"He was liked by most?" Fletcher asked nonchalantly. "No enemies?"

"None that I knew of. He was always fair in his dealings with customers. In fact, that was something on which he prided himself. It is the best way to keep loyal customers who return again and again. Many asked him to source particular items from various countries. That is the part of the business I find so intriguing."

"Oh?" Henry's interest was piqued. The more the man shared the better. "Did he have many of those customers?"

"Oh, yes. Several wealthy clients were willing to pay a substantial amount for what they wanted." The clerk shook his head again then blew his nose. "You wouldn't believe what some people request or what they are willing to pay for it."

"Is that right?" Henry took care not to show his eagerness to learn more. "Could you give us an example?" He studied the contents of the shop, unable to see any items that appeared to warrant significant funds. Then again, he was no expert in this area.

"Well." Mr. Weston's lips twisted as if he couldn't decide how much to share. "We…we don't normally speak of specifics, but I suppose none of that matters with Mr. Norris's passing. The records he kept are in the desk, as I'm sure you have already seen for yourself."

Henry had looked through the large ledger he'd found in a drawer but only the last few pages thus far. Norris had used abbreviations that were difficult to interpret. "Did you assist with the recordkeeping?"

"No. Mr. Norris preferred to do that himself. I had a look once but couldn't make any sense of it."

Fletcher grimaced, matching Henry's sentiment.

"Italian antiques are highly desired," the man continued. "French as well. We had a shipment of both just last week."

"Italian?" Fletcher again glanced around the shop. "I haven't seen anything that looks Italian, though I couldn't say for certain."

"Mr. Norris acquired them for specific clients, so they weren't placed on the shop floor. You will see them noted somewhere in the ledger, I'm sure. Some collectors were interested in any antiques from a specific country while others were quite particular with their requests. The condition of some of the items was questionable in my eyes, but that didn't seem to matter. The preferences of the nobility, the wealthy, can be quite confusing."

Henry tended to agree but didn't share that sentiment. "Are any of the unique items that Mr. Norris acquired currently here?"

Mr. Weston hesitated, and to Henry, it seemed a calculated pause rather than a natural one. "Not that I can recall."

Why wouldn't the man answer honestly? Henry let the silence grow long before continuing with his questions. "Where were you the night of his death?"

"I already told the constable those details." The man seemed quite put out to be asked again.

"I realize that, sir, but I'm sure you can appreciate our need to be thorough." Henry jotted down the clerk's answers, pleased they matched his original ones.

"My landlady can confirm that I was in my lodgings all evening," Mr. Weston added.

"Good. Someone will drop by to verify that," Henry advised, wanting to make it clear that he remained a suspect. "We may have more questions for you. Don't leave the city unless you advise me first."

Mr. Weston swallowed hard as if unable to believe he was under suspicion but nodded. "Very well."

"If you think of any other details, please send word. It could prove helpful, even if you don't think it's important."

"Of course." The clerk pressed his lips tight. "I don't mean to be crass, inspector, but is there a chance I will be paid the wages due me?"

Henry couldn't blame the man for his concern. Many people in London lived from one payday to the next. Any disruption would cause serious distress. "I couldn't say. Financial matters aren't up to the police."

Mr. Weston sighed. "Understandable." Based on the way his shoulders sagged, he was less than satisfied by the answer. Clearly he needed the money. "Do let me know if I can assist you. Happy to help."

"We appreciate that." Henry nodded. "As a matter of fact, I'd like you to review the ledger with me." He retrieved it from the back of the shop for another look, even if he held limited hope it would offer a true clue. Matthew Greystone's records certainly hadn't provided any leads.

The neat script within the book suggested attention to detail but the limited number of entries regarding the sales of antiques seemed at odds with the clerk's mention of wealthy clients. Only three hinted at more unusual and expensive items, something for which the clerk had no explanation nor knowledge.

While Henry didn't look down upon Norris for making money wherever he could, the lack of records made him wonder whether the goods had been stolen, or if certain transactions had been completed under the table. Taxes were a burden on all classes, and some were better at avoiding them than others. But based on what they knew thus far, there was no reason to assume any illegal activities had occurred.

Mr. Weston soon departed after mentioning his frustration about the pay due to him again. While sympathetic, such issues were out of Henry's hands, but he made a mental note to advise Norris's solicitor.

He looked up from further study of the ledger to glance out the window, startled at the sight of Amelia pausing to glance in the window before continuing on.

Blast it.

He rushed out the door, aware of Fletcher watching in confusion. The sergeant would puzzle out where he was going soon enough.

"Mrs. Greystone."

She halted and turned back, mouth opening and shutting like a fish pulled from the Thames. "Henry. Inspector Field. What a surprise."

"Indeed, it is." He glanced up and down the street, telling himself to ignore the pretty blush covering her cheeks. "And what brings you to the area?"

She blinked several times, glancing at the nearby shops as if they could provide an answer. "Well..."

"Amelia," he murmured as he drew near, sending her a pointed look even though pleasure washed through him from her presence. "This is no coincidence."

"You can't have expected me to remain home given the news you shared."

"I hoped you would. That you would have faith in the police to thoroughly investigate the matter."

"I do." She reached a gloved hand to touch his arm, effortlessly speeding his pulse. "In you, at any rate. But I would also like to provide assistance."

"You would, or did you already?" He glanced over his shoulder at the direction she had come from, wondering where she'd been as no cab was in sight.

Her eyes flashed. Somehow it only endeared her to him. "Did. I visited Randolph Locke's shop just there to see if he knew anything helpful."

Recognizing the name of one of her late husband's friends and a fellow shop owner, Henry heaved a sigh. He should have expected her to do something of the sort. Amelia was determined and resourceful, qualities he admired in addition to her beauty. Perhaps her inquiries would prove helpful—even if he'd rather she didn't take such risks. "And?"

She shook her head, though her furrowed brow suggested something bothered her. "He was less than helpful."

"Any particular reason you chose to visit him?" Henry asked, curious.

"I am—I was acquainted with the Lockes as you may remember from Matthew's investigation. Friends, of a sort." She lifted one shoulder in a half-shrug. "Before he died. But not so much afterward."

His chest tightened at her admission. Her demeanor made him think that hadn't been her choice. How terrible to not only lose one's husband, but friends as well. What made people step back from those who had endured a tragedy? Did they fear it would happen to them—or did bearing witness to another's pain simply make them uncomfortable?

"He is someone with whom I intend to speak." He'd done so after Greystone's death and planned to visit again, not only due to Norris's death but also because he'd renewed his investigation into Greystone's murder. And if they were connected...

Amelia nodded. "I thought as much." She met his gaze, something in her eyes seeming to ask that he accept her need to help. "I hoped he might be willing to tell me more than he would share with you, since we're well acquainted. At least, we were. At one time."

Henry couldn't argue with that. He never failed to be amazed by how tight-lipped some people became when questioned by the police.

Still, he couldn't encourage her in the investigation. The risk was too great and her involvement already too close. How many people had to die for her to take this seriously? "I must ask that you step aside and allow us to do our job."

She lifted a brow, a sparkle in the depth of her brown eyes. "I have complete faith in your abilities. But you cannot possibly think I will sit at home, waiting and wondering what's happening?"

That was indeed what he hoped, even though Henry knew it would be unlikely. "Even if I keep you apprised as much as possible?" He had to try.

She seemed to consider his offer, gaze fixed on something in the distance, though he tended to think the image she saw was not in the street but internal. "I appreciate that, but it doesn't change my mind."

Her stubbornness vexed him even as he admired it. "Amelia—"

She held up a hand to halt his protest. "Henry, I know what you intend to say. But surely you can understand my point of view. Matthew was my husband, and I failed him." She swallowed hard, the emotion in her voice bringing his own to the surface. "I didn't find justice for him."

"That fault is mine, not yours." His heart ached at her obvious upset; at his deep knowing that he was the one who'd failed not just Matthew Greystone but Amelia.

She shook her head gracefully. "You did everything possible. Mr. Norris's death, as tragic as it was, brings a new opportunity for justice. I must see this through. Please don't ask me to do otherwise."

Henry bit back an oath. Who was he to deny her? Though he longed to reach out to offer her physical comfort, he held back. Matthew Greystone's death stood between them, much like a mountain he couldn't summit. Solving it might mean the chance to further his relationship with this woman—and as terrible as it made him feel, he would take assistance from any quarter if it allowed him to become closer to her.

"Very well," he said heavily. "But I will remind you how dangerous this is. You must take every precaution to remain safe." He waited until she lifted those wide brown eyes to his then added, "Please."

Her soft smile was a reward for his agreement. "I will."

Though reluctant to involve her at all, in truth, she already was neck-deep in the case. The desire to protect Amelia made him even more determined to solve the murder quickly so he'd know she was safe.

So that their friendship could perhaps, one day, be more.

Six

AFTER SPENDING THE MORNING searching Norris's shop for clues, Henry and Fletcher took the train to Gravesend. Henry wanted his sergeant to review the crime scene, and he also wanted to speak with the neighbors to ask if they had seen anything unusual. Though the local constable claimed to have done so, Henry held doubts as to how thorough he'd been. The man had seemed all too eager to leave the investigation, in Henry's opinion.

"Nice place." Fletcher eyed the house, helping Henry to view it with fresh eyes. "Appears fairly affluent for a shop owner."

"It was his childhood home," Henry advised.

"I see." Fletcher gestured toward the side of the house. "Why don't we have a look to see if any tracks were left? The recent rain could be on our side."

"Good idea." That was one other task the local constable had completed without success, but Fletcher was far more experienced.

Henry followed the sergeant slowly around the exterior, and within minutes had found a set of footprints near the sitting room window. Unfortunately, grass and fallen leaves prevented the tread from being recognizable. Still, Fletcher measured their length and width as best he could, noting it all down carefully.

As his friend worked, Henry studied the house directly across the street. Movement behind the window and a twitch of a curtain suggested someone was at home, so he made a mental note to call there once he and Fletcher were done viewing the interior of Norris's house.

Henry had stopped by the police station to retrieve the keys and now unlocked the door, the cat's meow greeting them before he and Fletcher had closed the door behind them.

"The cat's still here?" Fletcher asked. "Shouldn't we find him a home?"

Henry frowned. "The local constable said he would do so."

Fletcher bent to rub the striped feline behind the ears. "Aren't you a pretty one, eh?"

"I wasn't aware you had a soft spot for cats." Henry found it amusing to watch the large, gruff sergeant with the creature, which wound about his legs as if it had just found a long-lost friend.

"Had one growing up. I adored that cat. It lived to a ripe, old age." Fletcher straightened and glanced around. "Where was Norris killed?"

"Over here." Henry led him through the house to the sitting room, looking around as they went, still hoping for another clue. Entering the sitting room, he halted near where Norris had been found. "The victim was here on his back. The room had been searched, but whoever did it seemed to be in a rush."

"It clearly wasn't a robbery," Fletcher said as he glanced at the fancy clock on the mantle which had to be worth some money.

"Whoever it was looked for something specific." His sergeant met his gaze. "The scarab."

"That was my thought as well."

"The rest of the house was undisturbed?" Fletcher circled the room, careful not to touch anything, pausing before the blood on the rug.

"Yes. Nothing seems to be missing. Perhaps the killer was interrupted so that was why he didn't search the rest of the house." Henry tried again to imagine the scene. "We believe Norris took the quarter past six train from London to Gravesend, as was his custom at the day's end. He probably walked home from the station, carrying his satchel. The shop clerk confirmed he had it in hand when he departed for home. We can assume Norris had dinner, fed the cat, and returned to the sitting room where he started a fire."

Henry moved to the doorway to study the wood floor. "The footprints are right outside this room, so perhaps the murderer looked through the window and saw Norris. Waterdrop marks are visible in the sitting room doorway, unlikely to be from Norris as his coat hung by the door. So whoever broke in paused in the doorway before entering the room to kill Norris at relatively close range with a small caliber weapon." He gestured toward the mantle where he'd removed the bullet. "The bullet is in the evidence room at the Yard. Probably seven millimeters, though it's distorted so difficult to say for certain."

"Perhaps a Belgian pinfire or the like."

Henry nodded. Those were commonly carried by the criminal class; the weapon was small, easily concealed, and not overly expensive.

Fletcher stepped closer to examine the mantle. "Norris would probably have stood in surprise or greeting, the killer drew closer, and any conversation between them was more than likely brief. The killer wouldn't dally in a neighborhood like this with nearby neighbors."

"Whoever it was might have worried the blast from the weapon would draw attention which would also cause him to be rushed. I would hazard a guess that Norris knew the killer's identity or the reason for his arrival, as there is no sign of him trying to struggle."

"True, though he doesn't sound like the physically active type. Where did you find the scarab?" Fletcher asked.

Henry moved to the wingback chair and showed him the tear. They upended it for a closer look from the bottom, but nothing else was hidden inside it.

"Why didn't Norris simply give the thing to him?" Fletcher asked. "It surely wasn't worth dying over."

"I don't know." The question had been bothering Henry as well. "Perhaps the invader didn't give him the chance. Maybe Norris said something to anger him, or wanted to keep it for himself. Or did the killer think he knew where the scarab was, assuming that was what he came for?"

Henry returned to the doorway, staring at the chair where Norris must have been sitting, then moved forward, trying again to imagine the scene.

Fletcher glanced between Henry's position and the mantle where the bullet had left an indent. "He must've shot him from right about...there."

The pair scoured the floor and surrounding area for any trace of the killer, without success.

"Hmm. It doesn't quite add up," Fletcher said as he straightened.

Henry cleared his throat, hesitant to voice his concern, but holding it in wouldn't change anything. "I have to wonder if someone noted my visits to Norris's shop. That the killer doesn't want Greystone's murder looked into any further."

Fletcher turned to meet his gaze and slowly nodded. "Could be. But it doesn't mean you are at fault—and I don't think we can say with absolute certainty that the two murders are connected."

Henry lifted a brow, a silent question as to whether he truly believed that.

The sergeant heaved a sigh. "But it does seem probable. We should try to keep an open mind."

"Agreed." The weight of guilt on Henry's shoulders didn't lessen, though he was glad to have the concern out.

The cat wandered back in and moved directly toward Fletcher, who smiled in response. "We need to find a home for this one."

"Leopold."

"What?" Fletcher frowned.

"Its name is Leopold, according to Mrs. Greystone." He watched the sergeant pet the cat. "Perhaps you should take him."

"Me?" Fletcher shook his head. "Another mouth to feed? I don't think the missus would agree." Yet the look on his face made Henry think he was considering it.

"Ask your wife. The poor thing needs a home."

"Maybe Mrs. Greystone would take him," his sergeant suggested.

Henry didn't know if she would welcome the cat or if it would be a burden. Perhaps he would ask her.

With that, he gestured toward the door. "Will you check with the neighbors on each side? I'm going to speak to the one across the street."

"Certainly—but first, I will see if there's any food for the cat."

Fletcher fed the feline, ensured it had water, and Henry locked the door behind them. They temporarily parted ways, with Henry crossing the street to knock on the door. It took less than a minute for a maid to answer.

"Inspector Field of Scotland Yard." He showed his warrant card. "Is the gentleman or lady of the house available?"

The maid's eyes widened as she gripped her hands before her, clearly startled to find the police on the doorstep—and from London. "Mrs. Ballard is here. If you'll wait?"

Henry nodded as he stepped inside, and the maid hurried away.

The house appeared to have a similar layout as the one across the street, from what Henry could see. A foyer near the front door. Stairs to one side to go upstairs. Several doors led off the hallway on the main level.

He took the liberty of peeking into the room near the front door to look out the window across the street. Norris's home was clearly visible except for one corner, which was blocked by a tree. There was a chance someone in the house had seen something.

Norris must've arrived home by eight o'clock, though Henry needed to check the train's timetable to be sure. That was close to the end of dinner for many, but someone might have noticed a waiting hansom cab or a person walking down the street. This was a quiet neighborhood, and any unusual activity would draw interest.

"Inspector?"

Henry turned to see a stout woman who appeared to be in her late twenties with brown hair drawn tightly back, wearing a simple navy gown, studying him. "Mrs. Ballard?"

"Yes. Norma Ballard." Her furrowed brow made her concern clear as he showed his warrant card. "What is it? Has something happened to Charles?"

"No." Henry cursed himself for not thinking of that. "No, nothing of the sort. I'm sorry to have alarmed you."

The woman pressed a hand to her heart and drew a relieved breath. "Oh, thank goodness."

"Unfortunately, Mr. Norris across the street has died."

"How terrible." Her mouth gaped as she took in the news. "What happened?"

Henry paused. This part of his job was never easy. "I'm sorry to say he was murdered."

The woman's eyes went wide with alarm. "Murdered?" Her gaze shifted to where the house was visible through her window, then back to Henry, her face pale. "In his home?"

"Yes. We are questioning everyone along the street to see if they noted any unusual activity that night." He found it best to push on with the conversation with the hope of diverting attention from the news to his questions.

"My word. It's...it's just such a shock." She looked around the room, as if trying to get her bearings.

"I'm sure." Henry gave her a moment to collect herself, but his time was not his own. He had to get on. "Did you happen to see or hear anything out of the ordinary two nights ago? Perhaps near eight o'clock on?"

Henry tried to prevent his mind from racing ahead while he waited for her to consider the question. The surgeon, Mr. Taylor, should have finished his examination of the body and his report would provide a better idea of the time of death. He had to get back to London and—

"H-how was he k-killed?"

Mrs. Ballard seemed fixated on the murder, rather than the question. That wasn't unusual. People touched by crime were often fearful when it struck so close to home.

"He was shot." Henry hesitated about whether to say more, not wanting her to worry. Nor did he want to reveal too much, fearing that what he said would be repeated not only to her family but other neighbors as well. Though it was doubtful there was any danger to those who lived nearby, he didn't want to assume. Assumptions had ended more than one career. His grandfather had been adamant against making any. But the potential connection between Matthew Greystone's death and Norris's served as sign of sorts as far as Henry was concerned.

Normally, relying on a hunch went against his personal code, though they'd certainly played a part in the last few cases he'd solved. He preferred physical proof and so did his superior—along with the courts.

"It appears to have been related to his business," he added.

Mrs. Ballard breathed a visible sigh of relief. "I see." She shook her head. "Bringing items here from foreign shores was sure to cause trouble."

As though the foreign element added more danger? Henry masked his impatience at the thought. *Criminals came from every country*. That much he knew for certain. Greed wasn't exclusive to any particular nationality, and England had more than its share.

"Did you note any unusual activities that night?" he asked again, hoping to bring her attention to his question. "A stranger or any odd noises, perhaps?"

"Oh. Well." She glanced away as if finally consulting her mental file. "Eight, you say? We would have been having dinner as that's soon after my husband returns home."

"We?" Henry asked, retrieving his notebook and pencil from his pocket.

"My husband, his mother, and me. Our five-year-old son had already eaten by then."

He jotted notes. "You were all here the entire evening?"

"Yes."

"How many servants?"

"The cook and a maid. Our manservant comes each morning, but he doesn't live in."

"What time does he leave each day?"

"After luncheon, depending on his duties."

The other two servants would probably have been busy in the kitchen serving dinner, so they were unlikely to have seen anything. Henry would speak with them anyway.

"You don't recall seeing any unusual activity across the street?" Henry asked again, almost hopefully.

"I can't say that I did."

"And what do you normally do after dinner?" His thoughts drifted to the peaceful evenings at Amelia's home, spent conversing in the drawing room before the fire. He'd enjoyed several of those, first while helping to guard her and the ravenkeeper's daughter who'd stayed with her, then again when Amelia had aided him with the mudlark case. Their deepening friendship gave him reason to hope for more evenings together.

Amelia had noticed a man watching the house on more than one occasion, the most recent being during the investigation of the ravenkeeper's murder. He could only hope Mrs. Ballard was as observant as Amelia.

"We spend the evenings in the drawing room upstairs." She frowned. "It does overlook the front of the house, but given how dark it is at that hour this time of year, we would've already drawn the curtains for the night."

"Of course." Disappointment speared through him. He waited a moment to see if she added more, but she remained silent. "Could I speak with your husband?"

"He is working in London this week, so won't return until later. He does so about once a month and takes the train."

"Did he ever take the same one as Mr. Norris?"

"Not that he's ever mentioned."

How unfortunate. "I would like to stop by tomorrow evening to speak with him, if that is convenient."

"I'm sure that will be fine."

"What business is your husband in?" Henry asked.

"He works at a bank."

Henry's interest perked further. Just a few months ago, he'd been investigating the apparent death of a bank employee who'd been involved in a lottery drawing scheme. The death was one he still pursued, though the people behind the lottery seemed to have disappeared. "Which one?"

"Hopkins Bank."

He stilled in surprise. Hopkins Bank. The same bank where Adam Spencer, the man who had gone missing and was now assumed dead due to foul play, had worked. Henry didn't remember meeting a Mr. Ballard...but it was a large bank, and it sounded as if the husband didn't always work at the London location. "I would most definitely like to speak with him." At the lady's nod, he added, "Would it be possible to talk to the rest of the household now?"

"I suppose. The maid and the cook are both in the kitchen, if you'd like to question them."

"Excellent. And your mother-in-law?"

"She's resting in her bedchamber at the moment, so that will have to wait."

Impatience threatened, but Henry nodded. He had to return tomorrow evening anyway. "May I go to the kitchen?"

Mrs. Ballard led the way to the back of the house and down the stairs where the smell of baked goods lingered in the air. She paused at the entrance to the room, suggesting the space was the cook's domain.

"Mrs. Anderson?"

A short, stout woman stirred a pot over the stove and turned, the maid nearby. "Yes, madam?"

Mrs. Ballard drew a shaky breath. "There has been a tragedy across the street. Mr. Norris was...m-murdered on Tuesday evening."

The cook's eyes widened as the maid gasped.

"Inspector Field—he would like to ask the two of you a few questions."

Henry stepped forward, notebook in hand. "I wondered if either of you noted unusual activity, say around seven or eight o'clock."

The servants looked at one another. The cook shook her head. "I can't say that I did. I was busy in the kitchen." She gestured toward the small windows at the rear of the house. "The houses across the street aren't visible from here."

"I didn't neither," the maid added. "I was serving dinner in the dining room, and then cleared the table and helped with dishes afterward. I don't think I even looked out the window."

Henry nodded, trying to ignore his groaning stomach caused by the appetizing aroma coming from the stove. When had he last eaten? "What of the past few days? Have you noted any strangers nearby? Any unusual activity?" He glanced at Mrs. Ballard to include her in the question.

Unfortunately, all three women shook their heads.

"No odd deliveries that caught your interest? Visitors to neighboring homes?"

The maid bit her lip, glancing at the other two women, waiting for them to answer first.

"I'm sorry, sir, but no." The cook glanced at the pot she'd been stirring, clearly anxious to return to her task. "I didn't see anything."

Henry looked at the maid, who answered at last. "Nor did I."

"Are you familiar with Mr. Norris's cat?"

The cook glanced at the maid with a frown. "I didn't know he had a cat."

The maid shook her head. "Me neither."

"I did." Mrs. Ballard's lips tightened. "Pesky thing. Is it still at his house?"

"Yes." His hope that one of them might want the animal was dashed. "It will need a new home."

"Just put it out," Mrs. Ballard suggested coldly. "It will find its own way."

Henry didn't bother to argue. "If any of you happen to remember something helpful, no matter how minor it might seem, please notify the local constable. He'll know how to contact me."

"Certainly."

Henry followed Mrs. Ballard back up the stairs to the front door. "As I mentioned, I will return tomorrow evening to speak with Mr. Ballard and his mother, if possible."

The woman nodded. "I will tell them."

"Good. Thank you for your time, Mrs. Ballard."

He stepped out and the door closed behind him, listening to the sound of it being locked. He'd be willing to wager that they would be careful to lock their doors and windows for the next few weeks. It was always the way, but the fear faded. As he studied the houses across the street, Fletcher emerged from one and started toward him.

"Did you have any luck?" Henry asked.

"Other than a new dustman that Mrs. Smythe thinks looks suspicious, no." Fletcher nodded toward the house to which he referred.

Henry sighed. "We will see what the surgeon can tell us about the time of death, but I don't think any delivery or service drivers will be of assistance."

By unspoken agreement, they started walking back to the train station.

"One interesting note," Henry said ponderously. "Mr. Ballard across the street—he works at Hopkins Bank, the same one where Mr. Spencer worked. You remember that lottery scam we investigated last year—Mr. Spencer, who went missing?"

"That is quite a coincidence, though I don't expect him to know the man. Even those who worked in the same room barely did." Fletcher shook his head, clearly as frustrated by that as Henry had been.

"I am returning tomorrow evening to speak with him," Henry advised. They needed a break on that case, and perhaps Mr. Ballard could provide it.

Now they just needed one for both Norris and Greystone.

Seven

"How did your visit with Mr. Locke proceed?" Fernsby asked, taking her scarf when Amelia returned home after a stop at the magazine office to meet with her editor.

Her new assignment was on rare and exotic orchids and those who collected them. Apparently "orchidelirium," which was a term applied to collectors who took their hobby to the point of obsession, had become a craze that risked not only fortunes but lives.

The editor had been pleased with the article she'd written about the mudlarks and their plight and had even suggested they use her interview to help raise additional funds for the children's lodging and education expenses. Amelia was thrilled to hear the praise, and the help for the mudlarks. She dearly hoped the effort was successful.

But as interesting as the meeting had been, her mind remained on the murder investigation.

"Not precisely as I'd expected," she said as she handed the butler her cloak and gloves, thoughts returning once again to her conversation with Randolph Locke.

There was no denying her upset from seeing the shop owner and the memories it brought to the surface. His suspicious behavior bothered her, though she didn't know if she was making more of it than there was.

Had he realized she'd seen the crate of Egyptian items? Would it concern him to know she had? Had she imagined the menacing looks both Mr. Locke and his assistant had given her? "He wasn't particularly...friendly."

The butler frowned. "How unfortunate. I hope you won't have to visit him again."

"I confess that I am not eager to repeat the experience."

The butler offered a silver tray that held two letters. "The afternoon post arrived while you were out."

"Thank you." Amelia took the letters, hiding a smile at the butler's penchant for formality.

"Shall I request tea?" he enquired.

"Yes, please." A cup was just what she needed to settle her nerves.

She climbed the stairs to the drawing room, her thoughts continuing to churn regarding the visit with Mr. Locke, as well as her conversation with Henry.

Whether there was any purpose in sharing how oddly Locke had acted—or the crate of items she'd seen—with Henry remained to be seen. Then again, she should have already done so, but she'd been too out of sorts to tell him earlier. Some detective she made, she thought with a shake of her head.

She would surely see Henry soon and could share the details then, though she hesitated to think they would provide a clue.

She must decide who else she could speak with about Mr. Norris's death. She had to do something.

Henry's concern for her safety was touching, but she already knew she couldn't step away from the investigation when it seemed so closely tied to Matthew.

The idea of finally finding justice for him was tantalizing, though it was surely too soon to know if that was possible. She would be the first to admit that she didn't look forward to dredging up the past and the pain that would accompany it. The next few weeks—or longer—wouldn't be easy.

A glance at the letters she held nearly caused her to take a misstep. One was from Elizabeth Drake.

Chills ran down her spine as her thoughts raced to find a possible reason for the letter. *Elizabeth Drake.*

With a steadying breath, Amelia entered the drawing room and sank into a chair to stare at the neat feminine script, hardly able to believe the woman would have the gall to write.

Amelia had long admired Mrs. Drake, a fellow chemist whose skills far surpassed her own. The woman's work in organic compounds impressed her, as did the fact that the woman excelled in a sphere dominated by men.

Her admiration had been cut short when she and Henry discovered that Mrs. Drake was behind the poisoning of mudlarks. The woman had been testing poison on orphans in a plot to aid certain government officials in eliminating foreign rulers no longer useful to England. She clearly believed the ends justified the means.

It had been a dangerous conclusion to an adventure Amelia had known she should not have embarked on, and it was thanks to Henry that she had escaped it unscathed. Mrs. Drake was now in prison, and the government official she'd been working with had been removed from power.

Amelia's fingers trembled as she reached for a letter opener, trying to guess what the woman had to say or what she could possibly want.

She read the letter, too easily able to hear Mrs. Drake's clipped tones as she read her words.

Dear Mrs. Greystone,

Though we had a difference of opinion on certain matters, I appreciate and respect your knowledge of chemistry. I remain impressed that you were able to determine the details of my work.

As you may remember from one of our conversations, I knew of your involvement with the police thanks to an acquaintance of mine. I recently discovered that he also knew your late husband and was possibly involved in his death.

Amelia gasped, stunned by the information. She read it again to see if she'd misunderstood, dismayed to realize she hadn't.

...knew your late husband...possibly involved in his death...late husband...death

Amelia tried to remember to breathe as her gaze flickered over the remaining lines.

I felt it necessary to warn you, one scientist to another, that this man can be dangerous. Unfortunately, I am unable to reveal his name as doing so would pose a danger to both you and me. However, I would strongly advise you to take precautions and reconsider working with anyone associated with Scotland Yard.

Respectfully,

Elizabeth Drake (chemist)

Amelia stared across the room, hardly knowing what to think. Had Mrs. Drake sent the letter in retaliation for her involvement in the woman's arrest?

Or could she possibly be telling the truth? That she respected Amelia despite their differences and wanted to warn her?

The vagueness of the warning was beyond frustrating, yet she well remembered how uneasy she'd been after Matthew's death. How often she'd felt as if someone watched her. How many times she'd lain awake at night, listening to the house creak and fearing someone was trying to break in. That whoever had killed Matthew wanted her dead as well in case she knew something.

Clearly whoever murdered Matthew was dangerous; that was an understatement. How Mrs. Drake was involved—if that was even true—remained a puzzle.

Amelia's heart was still beating frantically and she placed a hand on her chest as though that could slow it.

Henry had mentioned the woman had ties to London's underworld, and Mrs. Drake's warning seemed to confirm it. Yet she also had ties to wealthy and powerful men involved in the government. Those were opposite ends of the spectrum and Amelia wondered how both could be true.

But all that could wait. The bigger question was: how did Amelia proceed?

Her first impulse was to tell Henry. Would doing so place her in danger? Did she pay Mrs. Drake a visit to try to learn more?

She was still staring across the room, her thoughts in turmoil, when Fernsby arrived with the tea tray.

He paused when he looked at her, worry tightening his features. "Is all well, madam?"

"I received a concerning letter." Not for a moment did she consider holding the news from Fernsby. He served as a confidant and advisor at times, though she often didn't want to overly burden him.

This, however, was a threat upon the entire household—upon them all.

"Oh?" He set the tray on the low table before her and poured, preparing to add milk and sugar to her cup as she preferred in the afternoons. As always, the tray included biscuits and a tiny, frosted cake.

"From Elizabeth Drake."

His movements stilled as he took in the news. "The chemist who was poisoning children?"

"Yes."

"That is troubling." He straightened, not asking what the woman wanted, but rather waiting to give Amelia the space to decide how much she wanted to say.

"She claims she might know who killed Mr. Greystone."

Fernsby nearly tipped over the milk pitcher and quickly set it down. "How—how is that possible?" He frowned, clearly doubtful, though he seemed to be doing his best to hide his reaction. "And if she does know, why wouldn't she simply tell the police? She's already in prison, but if it could soften her surroundings, help with parole—"

"She says telling anyone would put her in mortal danger."

The older man scoffed. "That is a rather selfish outlook, isn't it? Then again, we can't expect more from a murderess."

"No, I suppose we cannot." She met Fernsby's gaze, hesitating whether to say the rest. But if she was at risk, so was the rest of the household and they had a right to know. "Mrs. Drake insists that telling me would put me in danger, too. She went on to advise that I stop working with the police."

"Hmm." He stared across the room for a long moment before saying, "That is terribly upsetting. Such an odd letter. I look forward to hearing what Inspector Field has to say."

A knot of worry deep within Amelia loosened. "You think I should tell him?"

"I do. Show him the letter." He dipped his head toward it, still in her fingertips. "If what the woman says is true, he needs to know. No one can protect you better from a potential threat." Her butler's eyes narrowed as he further considered the matter. "Perhaps whoever she refers to doesn't want you working with the police because he fears he is more likely to be caught. You and Inspector Field have made a formidable team in the past few months."

Amelia smiled, already feeling better. "Yes, we have."

"Will there be anything else, madam?" Fernsby asked as if they hadn't just had a conversation about murder and mayhem that could affect his very life.

"No, thank you, Fernsby. I appreciate your wise counsel as always." She was so lucky to be surrounded by such a supportive staff.

"The pleasure is mine, madam." With a slight bow, the butler departed, leaving Amelia to her thoughts and her tea.

She didn't, couldn't trust Mrs. Drake—but what if she told the truth? Could the woman help solve Matthew's murder?

Eight

Arthur Taylor, the surgeon at St. Thomas' who performed postmortems, raised a scalpel in greeting. "Afternoon, Henry."

"Arthur. I hope the day finds you well." He didn't know how well it could be, given the blood covering the surgeon's hands from the body spread open on the cold marble slab before him—though he appreciated the friendly welcome.

He and the surgeon had fallen into using their given names just before Christmas. Perhaps the coming of the holiday had eased the previous formality between them and helped bond their friendship.

A lock of dark blond wavy hair fell onto the surgeon's forehead as he looked back at the body. "Nearly done here. Give me a moment, and we will have a proper chat."

Henry had previously stopped by for the preliminary findings on Norris's death but had a few more questions. He enjoyed his conversations with Arthur and had put forth more effort into the few friends he had after seeing a reflection of his own solitary existence while investigating the missing Mr. Spencer.

The victim's lack of relationships, both at work and on a personal level, had been uncomfortably familiar to Henry. He didn't want that for himself. Spending time with Amelia helped him see there could be more to his life than only work. He knew having connections with others provided much-needed support, especially during difficult times. Friends and family eased burdens, no matter how big or small. Better to cultivate them before they were truly needed and feel less alone in the world.

As usual, a medical student served as assistant and stood by the surgeon's side, taking notes. It was rarely the same young man. Whether that meant they quickly learned what they needed before moving on in their studies or found they didn't have the stomach they needed for the job, Henry didn't know. He had never wanted to ask.

The victim before Arthur—a male—was too slender to be Norris. Several metal dishes were near Arthur's side, holding organs Henry had no urge to look at closely. It was an odd thing to know those same items were in his own body, necessary to keep one alive and functioning.

"*There* we are." Arthur plucked something from inside the chest cavity and set it in a dish then stepped back, arching his back and stretching before setting down the scalpel. "You can close him up, Mr. Clarke," he told his assistant.

"Yes, sir." The young man quickly set aside the board clip and moved to wash his hands, seeming eager to lend his aid.

Arthur crossed to the sink and, after waiting for his assistant to step aside, washed thoroughly before removing the leather apron that protected his clothing and hanging it on a nearby hook. "What brings you by?" he asked Henry as he rolled down his shirtsleeves and fastened the cuffs. "Not another murder, I hope."

"No, thank goodness. I think Norris's death could be connected to another case and hoped you could confirm it."

"Which case are you thinking of?" Arthur led the way to his office.

"Matthew Greystone, age two and thirty, killed fourteen months ago by a single bullet in the temple at close range. Unsolved, as of yet." The description fell short in many ways.

It didn't mention the extra money in the man's bank account, the lack of clues for Henry to follow, the similar trades the men shared, that the men knew each other...or Greystone's widow, who'd shown incredible strength throughout the investigation despite her grief.

Nor did it include the sense of failure that weighed heavily on Henry, especially since he and Amelia had come to better know one another over the past few months. That feeling of lack had worsened once he realized how attracted he was to her.

The dinner they'd shared at his parents' home before Christmas had been...well, delightful. It had been the first time he'd invited a lady to meet them. His mother had enjoyed Amelia's company, and he hadn't missed the light of curiosity in her eyes as she looked between him and Amelia. His father had seemed equally enamored of her, especially when he learned of her interest in chemistry.

But as wonderful as the evening had been, there was no hope of a future with her late husband's unsolved murder standing between them. He had to hope that if he found the killer, the crevasse between them would narrow enough to at least build a bridge.

Only time would tell.

He didn't share any of that with Arthur. Apparently he still had much work to do on his friendship skills. The idea of sharing such personal thoughts made him more than a little uncomfortable.

The surgeon sank into his chair by his desk with a grateful sigh and gestured to the empty one. "I'm sure we could both use a little time off our feet. What was the other victim's occupation?"

"The same. Owner of an import-export shop."

"Interesting. Same occupation, same method of murder." Arthur opened a drawer and sorted through a small stack of files. "I like to keep some details of unsolved murders on hand, in the event that new information arises."

"Good idea." Henry waited, appreciating how it didn't take long for Arthur to find what he was looking for.

"Here it is. Matthew Greystone." He opened the file and reviewed the notes within, though Henry was fairly certain the man already knew what they said. The surgeon had an excellent memory.

"Not many clues for the case, if I remember correctly."

"No, there weren't." That hadn't lessened Henry's guilt for not solving it.

"We deemed the caliber of the weapon to be relatively small, but neither the bullet nor the weapon was found."

"Correct."

Arthur glanced up at Henry. "Nothing of interest at the crime scene?"

"No." They had scoured the alley where the body had been found for clues without success—something that rankled, even now.

"The method—in the temple at close range—suggests a certain type of criminal, does it not?"

"One with experience. A deliberate killing. Possibly completed at the end of a conversation with unsatisfactory results." The last was conjecture, but made sense to Henry.

"You know there was another, similar case not long prior to that." Arthur's eyes narrowed as if he consulted a mental file this time.

"Oh?" Why hadn't Henry heard of it?

"Another inspector was involved. Perdy, I believe."

Frustration shot through Henry at the name. The man was useless, as far as he was concerned.

"I don't believe he made much effort to pursue the killer as the man who died had been imprisoned several times. Perdy seemed to believe he got what he deserved and let it go."

"That's not how the law works," Henry protested. "Perdy knows that."

"Hmm. Well, between you and me, I don't think he is especially ambitious. Or honorable."

"No. Avoiding the more difficult parts of investigations seems to be his routine." Henry knew he sounded bitter, but the man had nearly foiled two of Henry's recent cases—on purpose. "Much of his time is spent at the Yard rather than on the streets to pursue leads."

"I thought that might be the situation. I came across my notes on it when I was looking for something else last week, otherwise I don't know that I would have remembered it. Too many victims to remember them all, unfortunately. I have a few details on the case here somewhere." Arthur sorted through more files and pulled out one. "Here we are."

Henry resisted the urge to take it to read for himself. The surgeon often used abbreviations that only he understood. Better that he interpreted his own notes.

"The victim was a Douglas Grant, though I couldn't say what he'd been arrested for. He was killed by a small caliber in the temple as well, much like Greystone. Such different men, of course, so I suppose that's why I didn't put the two together until now."

"Normally that is the job of the police. Perdy." Henry's frustration with the man was quickly growing.

"True," Arthur readily agreed. He turned the notes to show them to Henry. "I don't have much more to share, but here is the location where the body was discovered."

Henry frowned as he tried to place the street. If he remembered correctly, it was in Whitechapel on the outskirts of the East End. A rookery—a slum occupied by the poor and frequented by criminals. That wasn't so far from where both Greystone's and Norris's shops were, though miles apart in other ways. "Interesting."

What did the men have in common that would cause potentially the same killer to act? While neither Greystone nor Norris had carried items in their shops that appeared to be worth murder, they both seemed to have sold special antiques for private collectors.

Private collectors who didn't care how they came by their beloved objects.

That practice could explain the extra funds Amelia had discovered in the bank account. The thought reminded Henry to look into Norris's bank records as well, though there was always the chance he'd hidden such profits to avoid paying taxes.

They hadn't found evidence of cash during the two searches conducted in Norris's residence or his shop, which had a small desk in the back.

"I can see the wheels turning in your head," Arthur said with a smile. "Do you think they could be related, all three cases?"

"It is certainly possible. I will check our records on Mr. Grant to see what else was known about him." Henry lifted a brow. "Can you think of any others that match the same scenario?"

"Not to my recollection." Arthur stared across the small space for a moment then shook his head. "I will certainly give it more consideration, though. A dangerous man, if indeed he has killed all three."

"Thank you. You still think Norris's time of death was between nine and eleven o'clock that evening?"

"Yes." Arthur had provided Henry with the basic information but had not yet sent the formal report to the Yard. He pulled another paper from a pile on his desk to review. "I'll send this over later today, but nothing else was unusual. Stew for his last meal, no alcohol or anything that would slow him down. No other wounds, so no sign of a struggle."

"Not a surprise. Norris didn't strike me as the type to defend himself, though he might have been taken by surprise."

Arthur tapped his notes with a finger even as he shook his head. "I wish I had more to offer."

"As do I." Henry stood with a smile. "Thanks as always, Arthur."

The surgeon nodded. "I'm sure I will see you soon."

Henry strode out the door and quickly walked the short distance to Scotland Yard. He nodded at several associates who were coming and going as he entered then walked directly toward Sergeant Johnson, who manned the front desk.

"Can you locate a file on a murder case for Douglas Grant?" Henry provided the date Arthur had given him and hoped the man had recalled the rough time correctly.

"Of course. I'll request it brought to you."

Files from old cases were kept in a nearby room, so it wouldn't take long to retrieve. Henry didn't hold out much hope the file would be particularly helpful, given Perdy had worked on the case.

Though tempted to confront Perdy, he wanted to wait until he knew more, even if a mixture of frustration and anger brewed within him at the idea that he could have had a true lead on Greystone's case months ago.

Greystone's case. Amelia's case.

How could Perdy not have connected the similarities between the two investigations and mentioned them? The inspector had been quick to frequently prod Henry for not having found Greystone's killer.

Then again, the man latched onto anything that showed Henry in a poor light. Perdy resented his quick rise through the ranks of the Metropolitan Police Department, and Henry knew he wasn't the only one to question it. He'd heard the snide comments about his father and grandfather being the reason Henry was already an inspector. Only Perdy was so blatant about voicing that opinion, at least while Henry was within hearing.

Henry was tempted to mention the Grant case to Director Reynolds, but doing so before he had any facts would only sound like sour grapes. Reynolds already knew there was no love lost between the two men.

To Henry's dismay, Perdy was at at his desk, three down from Henry's. Henry ignored him, though he did greet a few others. Most inspectors were rarely in the Yard, spending the majority of their time in the field questioning suspects and pursuing leads.

Not Perdy. The man was there more often than the other inspectors put together.

Henry sank into his chair, unsurprised to find a new case on his desk, this one a theft. Whether he would have the time to look into it himself was doubtful, but he read through the report then jotted down several items for a constable to look into. Sometimes all that was needed was to point them in the right direction.

That done, he returned his attention to the Norris case. Nothing of particular interest had been found in the shop thus far. His time would be better spent speaking with nearby shop owners—the same ones he'd spoken to after Greystone's death. He still wondered if his conversations with Norris had contributed to the man's murder. If that had been the case, why hadn't another death occurred soon after Matthew Greystone's?

Still, he intended to tread carefully even though he didn't yet know what might have caused the murderer to strike again. He didn't want another death on his hands.

Nine

THE FOLLOWING MORNING, HENRY looked up and down Threadneedle Street, debating with whom to speak next, but as if deciding of their own accord, his feet carried him toward Locke's shop. Though he knew it was because Amelia had been there the day before, he needed to talk to the man anyway. Sooner was better than later, something his mother often told him, especially when it came to unpleasant tasks.

It bothered him that Amelia had appeared upset after the visit. Was that due to memories surfacing or Locke himself?

His last visit with Randolph Locke was eight or nine months ago, and the man had been visibly distressed by Matthew Greystone's murder. To Henry, his upset had appeared to be a result of his friendship with the victim rather than guilt.

Whether that would prove true this time remained to be seen.

Upon opening the door, a bell announced his arrival. Mr. Locke emerged from the rear of the shop carrying a crate, which he set on the nearby counter. "How can we be of assistance?"

Henry loosened his muffler and waited a moment before responding, wondering if the shop owner would remember him.

"Inspector Field of Scotland Yard." He showed him his warrant card even as recognition slowly crossed the man's face.

"Ah, yes." Mr. Locke offered a polite smile, barely glancing at the card. "You're looking into Mr. Norris's death, I presume?"

"I am." Henry glanced around the shop, noting little seemed to have changed from his last visit.

"I hope you have better luck with this case."

His dry tone had Henry studying the man again, trying to decide if he meant the remark as an insult. "As do I." He withdrew his notebook. "When was the last time you saw Mr. Norris?"

"I saw him most days, though we didn't always speak."

"Oh?" The answer had an undertone. Would the man offer more?

"I'm sure someone probably mentioned it to you, but we crossed paths the day of his death." He shrugged one shoulder as if to suggest it was nothing. "We both said hello and continued on our way."

No one had as of yet, but the fact that Mr. Locke had bothered to mention it made Henry think there had been more to the conversation—or perhaps more to the reason that little else had been said. "He didn't say anything particular?"

"No."

"Did he seem distracted or act unusual in any way?"

"Not that I noticed."

"Were you friends?"

"More acquaintances, I would say." Mr. Locke's smile had Henry studying him again.

Despite the smile, his behavior almost suggested he was...anxious. "I'm sure it's difficult to be friends with someone who is also a competitor," Henry suggested, keeping his tone casual.

"True," Mr. Locke quickly agreed. Too quickly.

"But you were friends with Matthew Greystone, and he was also a competitor, am I right?"

"I suppose Matthew and I had more in common."

"I see." Henry nodded. "Similar in age."

"Yes, and we were both married with children." Mr. Locke glanced away, clearly uncomfortable with the topic. "Unfortunate that his daughter died."

'Unfortunate' was an understatement, but somehow Henry didn't think Lily's death was the reason for the man's unease. "You and Mr. Norris didn't share any interests, aside from antiquities?"

"No." The abrupt answer had Henry lifting a brow in response.

Mr. Locke shook his head. "We didn't agree on a few business matters, especially as of late."

"Such as?" As the silence drew long, Henry began to think he wouldn't answer.

The shop owner's lips twisted as he eventually said, "The quality of some of his wares for one."

"I see. Did any of your...disagreements become physical?"

Mr. Locke's eyes went wide with alarm. "Of course not." His mouth gaped before he closed it. "Am I to be a suspect simply because we disagreed about how to run our respective shops?"

Henry waited a beat. "Everyone is a suspect until ruled out. Where were you the night of Norris's death?"

"I-I was at home." Locke's face reddened, clearly distressed at the direct question.

"Can anyone verify that?"

"My wife—surely you don't intend to drag her into this."

"Asking her a few questions won't cause any harm." Unless she couldn't substantiate her husband's claim.

"I beg to differ." His chin lifted. "We have two young children, and she has enough on her mind without something like this."

"I will take care not to upset her. This is my job, sir."

Mr. Locke appeared less than reassured, but Henry was starting not to care. He didn't appreciate the man's attitude. A human had died, for God's sake.

"What was the nature of your last conversation with Norris?" Henry asked. Something felt off, and he was determined to do his best to discover what.

"I couldn't say."

Now that was hard to believe. "Try to remember. Was it before or after Christmas? Was it a discussion, as you say, about business practices?"

Mr. Locke pulled a rag from his apron and wiped the nearby counter, his movements jerky as if he'd rather be doing anything except having this conversation. "More...more of an argument, I would say. I discovered we had the same supplier for a few items and wasn't happy about it."

A glance around the shop suggested it was more than a few. Many of his goods appeared similar to those displayed in Norris's establishment.

"What was Mr. Norris's response to your concern?"

"He laughed, which I did not appreciate. He suggested I find a different supplier because he didn't intend to."

"That must have been frustrating." The question was how frustrating. Enough for Locke to take action? Enough for murder?

"We agreed years ago to take care to avoid such issues, and Norris—Mr. Norris had completely disregarded that."

"Were any other shop owners involved in the agreement?" Henry asked. It would make sense; there were several similar shops on the street, not to mention at other locations throughout London.

"Matthew, of course. Norris. Myself. One or two others as well." He reluctantly listed them, and Henry wrote them down. Leads. People to question. People to demand answers from.

"Do you own any firearms?" Henry asked.

Mr. Locke's face went pale, his gaze darting about. "No, I certainly do not."

The fact that he didn't ask if Norris had been shot didn't bode well. Usually, those acquainted with the victim wanted to know the details. Did that mean the man already knew?

Henry asked several more questions, but they didn't seem to cause the man the same unease.

At last, he tucked away the notebook and looked about. "How has business been?" No one had entered since Henry's arrival.

"January is always slow. Customers make purchases for the holiday, making purse strings tighter for a few weeks after the first of the year."

Henry continued his perusal, a collection of what appeared to be Egyptian items catching his eye. "These are interesting." He walked closer, only to realize they were rather cheaply made replicas of amulets, jars, and other items depicting pharaohs.

"Yes, those have been quite popular." Mr. Locke moved toward a display case in the opposite direction, and Henry had the oddest feeling he was trying to distract him. "These Chinese vases have also sold well."

Henry joined him to look at the small, painted vases that looked much like the ones Norris had in his shop. "Very nice." "But these are even more intriguing." He returned to the Egyptian items and could practically feel the shopkeeper's tension rise.

He didn't know much about such things, but they didn't compare to the scarab he'd found in Norris's chair. They looked as if they'd merely been painted to look old—a common enough trick, though not a crime he frequently dealt with.

Why did his presence near this case make the shop owner nervous? Or was it only Henry looking at them that caused him concern?

After advising Mr. Locke that he might return with additional questions, Henry continued down the street, spending time speaking with other shop owners to see if anyone had witnessed Locke and Norris arguing. Unfortunately, none had noticed anything, though two admitted to also having a disagreement with the victim regarding suppliers. Another praised Mr. Norris for his kindness. Still another seemed to barely know him. Each had an alibi, which Henry intended to verify. No one knew of any reason someone would want the man dead.

By the end of the morning, Henry was no further along in the investigation—but he wasn't ready to eliminate Locke as a potential suspect and wanted to hear Amelia's thoughts on the man. That would have to wait until later, as he was meeting with Norris's solicitor and visiting his bank that afternoon.

Why was it that the first few places he looked so rarely provided a clue? It was proving to be one of those days where he had to remind himself that he liked his job.

"Henry, I'm so pleased you called." Amelia's smile was rather strained as she shared a look with Fernsby, her butler. "We were just speaking about you earlier and wondering if you might come by."

"Oh? I hope the remarks were positive," Henry teased. In fact, he very much hoped that they were.

"Of course they were." She gestured toward his customary chair near the fire in the drawing room as Fernsby departed. "Please warm yourself. The wind was terribly cold today."

"Very much so." January was always a long month. The cold, damp air didn't make his job any easier when much of his time was spent going from one place to another. Most unfortunately, the weather didn't seem to slow down criminal activity.

"May I offer you a drink?" she asked. "Perhaps you'd care for some hot tea?"

"Unfortunately, I can't stay but thank you." He dearly wanted to, but he couldn't make a habit of joining her daily. Matters were still…unsettled between them, and nothing except finding her husband's killer would calm them.

"Oh." Her expression fell, something that helped to warm him more than the fire. "I suppose you have more work ahead of you." She glanced out the window as if to gauge the time of day.

"I do." He had to return to Gravesend to speak with Mr. Ballard and couldn't linger if he wanted to catch the train. He intended to retrieve the key to Norris's home from the Gravesend police station so he could check to see whether the constable had made good on his promise to find the cat a new home. Another look around the crime scene might stir an idea.

Amelia sank into the chair, hands folded on her lap, back straight. "I don't envy you your work during these colder months."

"I confess to questioning it myself when the temperature drops." He watched her for a moment, her tension palpable. *Something had happened.* "Is something amiss?"

She pressed her lips together, clearly reluctant to speak of it. "That remains to be seen." With a sigh, she reached for a piece of paper on the nearby table and handed it to him. "I received an unsettling letter yesterday."

Henry glanced at the signature, alarm filling him as he met her gaze. "Mrs. Drake?" He quickly read it then did so a second time more slowly as his pulse quickened. "This is quite curious."

He shared a worried look with her before further studying the letter. His thoughts raced as to what it might mean, conscious of the weight of Amelia's regard, aware she was waiting for his response.

Then awareness struck.

He held her gaze, more touched than he could say. "You—you told me about it, despite the warning it contains."

She blinked. "Yes, of course." As if it were only logical.

Her trust tightened his chest, and Henry hardly knew what to say. "I appreciate your faith in me."

Given his failure to solve her husband's murder and the danger she'd faced when assisting him with two of his previous cases, he had to admit himself surprised.

"And I appreciate yours in me," she replied, the warmth in her brown eyes making him smile.

Well, it was true. He trusted her as well, and that wasn't something he gave easily.

He glanced at the letter, trying to gather his thoughts, wanting to be careful with his words. This was a delicate situation.

After clearing his throat, he said, "I have to wonder if she is telling the truth—that she might know who killed your late husband." He lifted his gaze to meet Amelia's, the pain in them twisting his heart.

"I agree. It is worth looking into." Despite her obvious upset, there was no denying the determination in her words. "How shall we proceed?"

"I will visit the prison tomorrow and speak with her," Henry began, already considering what he could say to convince Mrs. Drake to share the name of the person she suspected. What leverage could he find that—

"Then she'll know I told you." She slowly shook her head. "If she is telling the truth, that revelation could endanger both of us."

"Not if she provides a name and we can make an arrest." Yet doubt sent a cold chill along his skin. He couldn't promise an immediate arrest any more than he could promise Amelia the moon, and he wished to give her both.

"What if she doesn't? It can't be forced from her. And in all honesty, I don't think she would feel compelled to tell you."

Henry shifted in his seat. Amelia was right. Clearly she'd spent a significant amount of time thinking through the situation since receiving the letter.

"My priority is to ensure your safety." He wanted to make that clear.

"I appreciate that. Very much." She lifted her chin. "However, *my* priority is to discover who killed my husband."

A ding dented the fragile shield of his confidence. She wouldn't feel that way if he'd done his job. If he'd solved the case over a year ago, they wouldn't be in this perilous situation that involved a murderess.

But he wouldn't take back his words. Her safety was his top concern and not just because of how much he cared for her. She was alive, while her husband was dead. There was nothing he could do to save the man. While he wanted to find justice for Greystone, he wouldn't do so at the cost of Amelia's life.

But what was the best way to both protect Amelia and find the killer?

"I propose that I visit Mrs. Drake," Amelia said, determination in her eye. "There is every chance she will tell me what she knows, based on what she wrote."

Henry shook his head, hating the idea. "That might be her plan. To bring you to the prison and place you in danger."

"The thought crossed my mind, but why would she do that when she already took the time to warn me? Whoever killed Matthew must know that I don't have any information, or they would've attempted to silence me a year ago."

That truth only slightly calmed Henry's upset as he stared into the fire, his thoughts on the memory of Mrs. Drake's coldness as she spoke of poisoning the mudlarks and how she had been doing the city a favor by taking their lives. How could they trust such a woman?

"Elizabeth Drake is stirring a hornet's nest," he said at last. "Perhaps just for her own personal amusement. I don't want you anywhere near her." He knew he spoke out of turn but couldn't help himself. The very idea that—

"Henry." Amelia's quiet tone had him meeting her gaze again. "You may be right, but what if she does know and I can convince her to tell me?"

He smothered a curse, wanting to deny the possibility, yet he couldn't. Amelia's courage was something he'd admired since their very first meeting. Ironic that now he wished she weren't quite so brave.

Mrs. Drake wouldn't be able to harm Amelia physically, a guard would be present during any visit, but he worried about the emotional hurt she might cause. There was only so much he could do to protect this woman from that.

"Are you certain you want to do this?" he asked, willing her to say no. *Say no.*

"Yes." No hesitation. No uncertainty.

Damn if he didn't admire her even more. Her determination left him no choice except to agree. However, he would do all in his power to protect and prepare her for the visit.

"Very well. Here is what you need to know…"

Ten

Henry's obvious reluctance to agree to the visit with Mrs. Drake touched Amelia deeply, his protectiveness warming a place in her heart which had been frozen since…since losing her husband and daughter. However, her mind was made up, and nothing he could say would change it.

Her guest cleared his throat as he stared into the fire. "Prisons are primarily built by men for men. The authorities are still trying to understand how to hold women in the system. Holloway is one of only a few prisons that even house women. Though Mrs. Drake's deeds were horrendous, chances are she will face the same process as lesser female criminals once sentenced, unless she receives the death penalty."

The thought was a sobering one, but then so was poisoning children. "What is the process?" Amelia asked.

She didn't know anyone, let alone another woman, who'd ever been imprisoned. What better way to manage the stress of the situation than with curiosity?

"It is thought that women should have the opportunity to be returned to their ideal place in Society, one of motherhood and domesticity. The theory is that they should be saved first from their criminal endeavors, then a second time from deviating from what is considered normal female behavior."

Amelia frowned. "And how precisely are men saved from their crimes?"

"With hard labor." Henry shook his head as if unsure whether it was effective. "Women are put to work as well, of course. I can't say that any methods have had impressive results to successfully rehabilitate behavior, but that is a discussion for another day."

"Interesting." She wondered if it could be a topic for an article for the magazine. Perhaps it would be worth mentioning to her editor.

"The authorities seem to believe it is more shocking for a woman to behave out of character than it is for a man. In most prisons, depending on the crime, women are placed in confinement away from others where they eat, sleep, and work. Once a solitary period is completed, they are allowed to be with others. Finally, they are transferred to an establishment with other women and trained in a skill such as domestic work."

"But Mrs. Drake is a well-respected chemist." Amelia couldn't imagine her being treated in the same manner. Taught domestic work—what, to embroider a cushion or bake a cake?

"One who committed murder," Henry reminded her as he held her gaze.

Amelia sat back in her chair, uncomfortably aware that he was right. Mrs. Drake had spoken about the mudlarks as if they were of little importance, that harming them didn't matter.

Having lost a child of her own, Amelia couldn't understand how anyone, even someone who had devoted her life to science, could be so uncaring about another human life.

"Of course, she has not yet been convicted," Henry continued, "and there is every chance she will face the death penalty if found guilty. In that case, the question of 'saving' her will not much matter."

Mrs. Drake hadn't seemed willing to admit to any wrongdoing. Unless she did so, the chance of being rehabilitated seemed out of the question. "Do you think she is aware she could be facing the death sentence? Could that be the reason she wrote to me?"

He paused, seeming to consider the possibility, one finger idly tapping on the chair arm. "She is intelligent, if misguided, and I'm certain her barrister advised her of it—perhaps to weaken the evidence, should it come to that. I suppose she would want to communicate with others while she has the opportunity, especially if she feels there is unfinished business between the two of you."

"I wouldn't have said there is any, when I made it clear what I thought of her actions. That's why I was so surprised she wrote to me. But she made mention during my first visit to her home that she knew I worked with the police." The memory was disturbing, and Amelia rubbed her arms to ward off the sudden chill that washed over her.

Henry nodded. "I remember you asking me if I had told anyone about you assisting with the cases. I did mention it in passing to Director Reynolds, and Sergeant Fletcher knows about it as well, of course. I don't think anyone else is aware."

"Then surely it's likely that she truly knows something about who killed Matthew..."

The idea of being given a name which could provide justice for her late husband was enough for Amelia to rise early the next morning. As much as she dreaded the visit with Mrs. Drake, she was eager for it.

Henry had wanted to go with her, repeating his offer as he had left when darkness was falling, but Amelia had refused, certain it was safer for both her and Mrs. Drake to pretend she hadn't told him of the letter. The information he'd provided, including a description of the prison and the procedure to enter it, had nonetheless helped to relieve her anxiety.

It seemed unlikely that anyone was watching her or her house to see if she communicated with the police, so Henry's visit the previous evening shouldn't matter. He was a frequent visitor anyway, and there was no reason to suspect that she had shared any information with him. Nevertheless, she did not regret that she'd shown him the letter.

After a light breakfast in the kitchen, as was her habit, she requested Fernsby to send for a cab then returned upstairs for her things. When she returned to the foyer, she found Fernsby with his coat and gloves on, hat in hand, along with a walking stick.

"What is this?" she asked as her steps slowed on the bottom stairs.

"I am accompanying you." When she opened her mouth to protest, he dipped his head, effectively halting her. "I insist. No one will look twice at a servant by a woman's side." He lifted the stick. "I may be growing older, but I am capable of wielding a weapon if needed."

Amelia was touched and relieved. She should have expected it of him. Unless… "Did Inspector Field ask you, by any chance?"

"The inspector may have mentioned it on his way out last evening. However, I already planned on accompanying you since I had the feeling you would be visiting Mrs. Drake to hear what she has to say."

She smiled. "You know me so well. I am grateful you will be nearby if anything untoward occurs."

"Then shall we be off?" the butler asked primly, evidently raring to go.

"Yes. I look forward to returning home for luncheon." Amelia had learned to manage difficult tasks over the years by focusing on a pleasant one that followed. Looking to the near future had a way of easing the challenge directly ahead.

"As do I." Fernsby reached for the door. "I believe Mrs. Appleton is preparing a hearty beef soup since we will be out in the cold for a time."

"How kind of her."

They continued their inconsequential chatter as they stepped into the waiting hansom cab. The driver balked at the mention of the prison which Fernsby supplied as their destination but reluctantly agreed when Amelia promised a significant tip.

The drive was shorter than Amelia expected, taking less than a half hour even with traffic. But it was an entirely different world in appearance, which made it shocking that it was so near to home.

She was doubly grateful for Fernsby's solid, steady presence beside her as the prison came into view. The foreboding place, with its Gothic architecture, resembled a medieval fortress. Tall brick walls lined the entire prison. The imposing entrance consisted of a large arched gatehouse, complete with guards, and had Amelia drawing a slow breath. Its bleak appearance surely discouraged anyone who'd seen it from a life of crime.

"Oh, my." Already she could feel the crushing weight of the place as if a hundred hopeless souls were housed within. Thank goodness Henry had already described the prison, or it would've been an even bigger shock.

"Indeed, madam," Fernsby agreed as he followed her gaze, his expression grim. "Remember, we are only here for a brief visit."

"Thank goodness." How did Mrs. Drake bear to be within those walls? Then again, she didn't have a choice—and the woman's actions made it impossible for Amelia to feel any sympathy.

The cab soon rolled to a halt, and they alighted, requesting the driver to wait.

"Fer how long?" the driver asked, clearly reluctant to remain there any longer.

"It won't take us much time," Amelia advised, though she didn't know for certain. Would they have to wait before being allowed to see Mrs. Drake? She should have inquired of Henry about those specifics.

Fernsby sent the man a stern look. "Any criminals nearby are already imprisoned, so you needn't fear for your safety, especially not with so many police in the vicinity. Your time shall be compensated."

The driver nodded, though he wore a disgruntled look.

Amelia had donned her most obvious widow's attire, including a heavy woolen gown with black braid trim, a matching cloak, and a hat with a generous veil. With a nod to Fernsby, she rolled down the veil to cover her face before they walked toward the gate. There, Fernsby stated their purpose to the guard. Several long minutes passed before they were allowed through. They waited briefly at the heavy metal doors before those were opened as well.

The sound of them clanking shut behind them was enough to send chills down Amelia's spine. How terrible it would be to enter, knowing it would be months, perhaps even years, before one could leave.

If ever...

The netting covering her face slightly restricted her view, but it also allowed her the chance to look around more freely. The place was austere and dark, with a stone floor and walls, and was eerily quiet. A uniformed warden sat at a wooden desk on a raised platform and sternly eyed them from head to toe. "The purpose of your visit?"

"To speak with Mrs. Elizabeth Drake," Fernsby advised.

"What is your relationship to the prisoner?"

The butler hesitated briefly. "Acquaintance."

If asked for more details, what could Amelia say? That she had been involved in the woman's arrest? That she thought Mrs. Drake might know who killed her husband?

Luckily, they weren't asked for more information.

"Names?" The guard reached for a pen and pulled a list close, adding their names and address to it. Then he checked a pocket watch sitting on the desk and noted the time. "Wait over there."

Amelia turned in the direction of the tip of his head to a small room with a wooden bench along one wall.

"Comfy," she murmured as she and Fernsby took a seat in the cold, stark space.

"I suppose they don't want anyone to linger unnecessarily."

Amelia smiled, relieved once again that the older man had accompanied her. Damp cold seeped from the stone walls, permeating the air. While pleased she'd worn warm clothing, they would both soon be chilled to the bone if they waited long.

Well over a quarter of an hour passed before the sound of a door opening caught their notice. Nerves tightened Amelia's stomach, but she didn't rise, waiting instead to see if they would be summoned.

"Mrs. Greystone and Mr. Fernsby," the guard at the desk called.

"As if we aren't the only ones here," Fernsby murmured with a smile.

Amelia appreciated his humor as they returned to the desk to find a second man there.

"The guard will show you in."

"This way." The guard glanced at them both, and Amelia had the impression he was deciding if they could cause any trouble. "Leave the stick," he ordered.

"I require it to aid in walking," Fernsby countered, much to Amelia's surprise, when she knew that was far from the truth.

The butler climbed the stairs at home more times each day than she cared to count. "I am no longer young in years."

The guard's lips pressed tight with disapproval, but at last, he nodded. "Very well." He reached for a ring of keys on his belt and unlocked the tall, steel door then held it for them to enter. "You are to stay with me at all times. Remain quiet. Keep your hands to yourself. Is that understood?"

"Yes," they both agreed solemnly.

As they stepped through, once again Amelia was grateful for how much Henry had described. They walked down a long dark hallway, the smell of unwashed bodies and stale urine greeting them. Raised voices could be heard in the distance, though Amelia couldn't make out what was being said—and was rather glad of it.

They passed several closed doors before the guard paused to unlock one and opened it. "Wait in here."

Amelia stepped into the room with a simple wooden table, four chairs, and no windows. The sound of the guard locking the door behind him had Amelia looking at Fernsby in alarm, only to remember he couldn't see her face.

"I can't say I care for that," she whispered.

"Nor do I, madam. I suppose they don't want us wandering about on our own."

"It still makes me a mite uncomfortable." Amelia sighed as she approached the table. "Shall we sit?"

"Why don't I remain standing behind you along the wall?" Fernsby asked. "That way she won't pay me any mind."

"Very well." Amelia patted his arm. "Will you listen closely to what she says? I'm not certain I will remember everything." She worried that once Matthew's name was mentioned, her feelings would get the best of her. Though it had been well over a year since his death, her unruly emotions didn't always grasp that.

"Absolutely." He lifted the walking stick. "And remember, I am prepared to use this if necessary."

The image of Mrs. Drake attempting to physically harm her seemed improbable; it was the emotional damage Amelia worried about. Henry's concern that the woman intended to set a trap of some sort echoed in her mind.

Mrs. Drake was a brilliant scientist but clearly lacked understanding in other areas of life, including proper behavior, societal expectations, and a basic moral compass. Amelia need only remember how the woman had invited her to tea but failed to serve it, not to mention how surprised Mrs. Drake had been to realize Henry and Amelia hadn't shared her disregard for the mudlarks' lives. Never mind that she hadn't batted an eye at poisoning children.

Amelia hoped her own intelligence would serve her now, and she could prevent Mrs. Drake from causing her further distress. Amelia lifted the veil, wanting a clear view of the woman while they spoke.

The thick stone walls of the room served to deaden sounds, and the creak of a key in the lock startled both her and Fernsby.

The door opened, revealing Mrs. Drake in a drab, gray gown. "Mrs. Greystone. How kind of you to call."

The woman's pleased smile, as if she'd just made a clever move on a chessboard from which there was no hope of recovery, made Amelia's skin crawl.

Had this visit been a mistake after all?

Eleven

THE MORNING DRAGGED BY as though on square wheels for Henry. He could hardly focus, his thoughts solely on Amelia as he and Fletcher made their way to the docks.

His concern that he should have insisted on going with her had kept him awake much of the night. Yet she was right—his presence might endanger her further. He only hoped she hadn't refused Fernsby's company. As loyal as the butler was to her, Henry had no doubt he'd defend her with his very life.

Yet somehow, that was of little assurance.

His meeting the previous evening with Mr. Ballard proved interesting, though not with regards to Norris's murder. The man hadn't seen anything noteworthy and seemed surprised Henry had bothered to make the trip all the way from London to ask.

"I think my wife has already told you everything about that evening. I'm sorry to say we didn't realize anything was amiss," he said, gesturing to a chair in his small study. An appetizing aroma lingered in the air, suggesting dinner had recently been eaten. Henry's stomach grumbled in response, a reminder he hadn't yet eaten. Again.

Though disappointed by the answer, he wasn't surprised. However, that was only one of the questions he had for Mr. Ballard.

The sound of a child's laughter echoed in the house, causing the man to smile. "My son prolongs his bedtime as long as possible every night."

Henry nodded in understanding. "I remember doing the same as a boy." He cleared his throat, eager to get on with the questions before the night grew any longer. "Your wife also mentioned you are employed at Hopkins Bank."

"Yes, for nearly five years now. Originally I worked at the London branch but was transferred to Gravesend a year ago."

"Were you by any chance acquainted with a Mr. Adam Spencer, the employee of the London location who went missing in November?"

The man's eyes widened in surprise at the question. "Why, yes. I knew him. Such a tragedy to learn that he's believed dead." He shook his head.

Henry regretted that his body hadn't been discovered, but that didn't prevent him from pursuing the investigation.

"I am—or rather, I was actually the reason he worked at the bank," Mr. Ballard added. "I knew his late father. When his mother wrote to say Adam was looking for work, I offered him a position. He was smart as a lad and good with numbers. I knew he'd catch on quickly."

"How were you acquainted with his father?"

"My family lived in the same village." Mr. Ballard's eyes narrowed. "Has more been discovered about his disappearance?"

"No. That is, not as much as I'd like." Henry hesitated. How much could he say? It was an ongoing investigation, and therefore they didn't normally share details. However, in this situation, given the lack of leads and evidence, what harm could it cause?

They needed a break in the case to pursue it further—to find the missing man.

"This is all in confidence, of course," Henry said, watching to gauge Mr. Ballard's reaction. Surely a man in banking would be accustomed to keeping certain matters private.

"I understand."

Henry liked to think he could be trusted. "We discovered Mr. Spencer bought lottery tickets on occasion."

The man's brows shot up, clearly surprised. "Oh? I wouldn't have guessed that he liked to gamble."

"He may have become involved in one that was more of a scheme than a true game of chance. We have reason to suspect that, due to his accounting background, he realized something was amiss with the expenses versus the prize monies, and he may have mentioned it to the wrong person."

Mr. Ballard's jaw dropped. "And that was sufficient to potentially get him killed?"

"Schemes like that one provide a substantial sum for those fiddling the books. Numerous people are involved, and it is a complicated, multi-layered operation run by professional criminals." Henry and Fletcher had only worked through the first layer before those behind it disappeared, but he had no doubt another would soon emerge to take its place. The police had seen that pattern time and again.

"How distressing. I had no idea." Mr. Ballard shook his head.

"You weren't aware of any of this? He didn't mention it to you?"

"No, though I would've been surprised if he did. He would surely know I don't approve of gambling in any form. Besides, he worked in a different department, and I only venture to the London offices once a month or so now. Our contact was quite limited."

Hope was quickly slipping from Henry's grasp, but he pressed on. "Do you know of any friends he had in London? We spoke with his direct colleagues but didn't discover much."

"Adam kept to himself, for the most part, a quiet man. Much like his father. But he has—had—a childhood friend from the same village who now lives in London. I believe they saw each other on a regular basis."

"Do you know his name?"

"Gregory Palmer. He works as a clerk at a warehouse near the docks." Mr. Ballard glanced away as if searching his memory. "I believe he's employed by Blue Star Shipping—Blue Star? Star Royal? I could have that wrong."

Henry jotted down the information, relieved to have a clue no matter how small. "That is helpful, thank you. Can you think of other details? Other acquaintances, perhaps? Any places you know he liked to frequent?"

"No, I'm sorry. I wish I could be of more help."

"Thank you for your time." The information wasn't much, but more than they'd learned in some time. Henry was pleased he'd made the trip to Gravesend.

The cat had been pleased as well, meowing and carrying on the moment Henry entered Norris's house. He fed it the last of the beef stew from the ice box and filled its water bowl, resolving to return with a cage to transport it to London the next day. Clearly, the constable hadn't bothered to find Leopold a home, nor had any member of the family claimed him.

Henry was pulled from his thoughts of the previous evening when Fletcher slowed his pace to point to a building across the street. "There it is. Blue Star Shipping."

They had ventured to the dock with the hope of learning more about Mr. Spencer's friend, Mr. Palmer. Though Henry was anxious to locate him, he was even more anxious to know how Amelia fared. Unfortunately, it would be hours before he could call on her to find out.

Fletcher didn't remark on Henry's distracted demeanor, after their hurried conversation on their way to the docks about the risk the widow was taking. Henry knew Fletcher was concerned as well. All she had to do was ask a few questions, get the name, and leave...

The sergeant opened the door of the shipping office, and they stepped inside. After a brief look around, Henry followed as Fletcher strode toward two men wearing plain suits who stood talking nearby.

"We are looking for a Mr. Gregory Palmer," Fletcher said courteously. "We were told he works here."

"Palmer?" One of the men pointed to a door. "Should be just through there."

They opened the door to find a large room with three rows of desks and nearly a dozen clerks busily working with stacks of papers and ledgers before them.

"Can I help you?" the nearest one asked.

"Gregory Palmer, please," Fletcher said.

The man's eyes widened as he looked between them, taking in Fletcher's uniform. "That would be me."

"We would like a word," Henry advised, glancing around to see everyone staring at them. "Is there a place we can speak in private?"

"Certainly." Mr. Palmer stood, seeming a little unnerved by Fletcher's uniformed presence. He gestured toward another man at a nearby desk. "Please allow me to advise my manager."

A moment later, he led the way back out the door and through another into a small room with a single empty desk then turned to face them. "What is it?"

"We understand you were friends with Adam Spencer." Henry retrieved his notebook.

"I was." Mr. Palmer's expression tightened. "For years. I thought he might be the reason you are here."

"You were advised of his apparent passing?"

"Yes, his mother wrote to tell me." He shook his head. "I could hardly believe he just up and disappeared like that. What's the world coming to when you leave for work one morning and never arrive?"

The man's genuine upset had Henry pausing to give him a moment to gather his thoughts. "You saw each other often?"

"Usually once or twice a month. Both of us work long days, and we lived far enough apart that we only connected on Saturdays."

"Did he mention purchasing lottery tickets?"

"Yes, we both did it on occasion. More as a lark than thinking we'd win—but who doesn't dream of coming into some money?"

"True enough," Fletcher added, which seemed to help put the man further at ease.

Much like his conversation with Mr. Ballard the previous night, Henry shared what they thought might have happened, hoping Palmer could provide additional information.

"Unbelievable. I told him not to tell anyone when he mentioned the numbers didn't make sense." Again, Mr. Palmer shook his head. "But he could be a stubborn one. He had a strong sense of right and wrong that wouldn't be denied."

"Do you have any idea who he might have told?"

"No. The last time I saw him, he only talked about doing it. I thought for sure I had convinced him not to. That it would be far too dangerous." He paused, brow furrowing. "There was one man who helped sell tickets that Spencer spoke with several times...Richards was his name. He has a scar near the corner of his eye. The man gave me the chills. I hope Spencer didn't tell him, as I could see him killing someone without a second thought."

Henry took notes as Palmer shared where and when they had last purchased tickets together, along with the other details he remembered.

"I should have come forward and shared this before." The man shook his head, clearly feeling guilty. "But I didn't have any evidence, only suspicions, and I didn't know for sure…"

"Yes, you should have." Henry couldn't help but think of the wasted hours he and Fletcher had spent. "If something like this occurs again, I strongly encourage you to do so."

"Do you think I'm in danger?" Palmer asked, clearly concerned by the thought. "We were together at the drawings more often than not and came to know a few of the regulars who frequented the pub."

"I would avoid returning to any places where the tickets were sold," Henry advised, "but no, I don't think you are." The man would've surely been harmed by now, if those running the scheme had suspected him.

He glanced at Fletcher to see if he had any further questions, but the sergeant shook his head.

"I hope you find who killed him if that's truly what happened," Mr. Palmer added.

Henry paused. "Do you have any reason to believe he's still alive?"

The clerk considered the question for a long moment, only to sigh. "It's nothing more than wishful thinking on my part that he might suddenly reappear."

Henry and Fletcher thanked the man for his time then took their leave.

"That's the most information we've had since the start of the case. If only he had reported all that sooner." Fletcher lifted a brow. "Shall I stop by the pub where Palmer last saw Spencer and see if I can find this Richards person?"

"No, it's too dangerous. I'm not sure a uniformed policeman asking questions will help us—not when the last time we ventured there, I was threatened with a knife, and I wasn't even in uniform."

"More than threatened," Fletcher corrected as he adjusted his hat. "So what do you suggest?"

Henry glanced around the street as he considered their options. Trying to find a single person behind Spencer's death was proving difficult when it seemed an entire criminal organization might be involved. But it could prove worthwhile to question Richards, the man with the scar—if they could find him.

A man hurrying across the street a short distance away caught Henry's attention. Something about him seemed familiar. As the man passed another person, he tipped his head down, holding the brim of his hat as if to hide his face.

Fletcher followed Henry's gaze, watching as the man nervously glanced over his shoulder. "Now what is he trying to hide?"

"Good question." Henry started toward him, Fletcher at his side. "He looks familiar."

"I can't say that I recognize him. He's certainly acting oddly, though."

The street was lined with wood and brick buildings. Some were warehouses, based on the pulleys and ropes hanging from upper levels. Others were offices of one sort or another. A pub stood on the street corner, though only a few customers ventured inside at this hour of the day. Smoke hung in the air courtesy of a nearby factory, smudging the horizon and stinging his nose. Traffic was moderate, though enough carts and wagons rolled past to make it relatively easy to hide their pursuit of the man from the opposite side of the street.

The man turned to look around again, and this time Henry had a good look at his face. "Randolph Locke."

"Who?"

"One of the shopkeepers near Norris's establishment. I spoke with him yesterday."

"Any reason to suspect him, other than today's suspicious behavior?" Fletcher kept his attention across the street.

"Possibly. He acted rather nervous when I spoke with him then, too. He and Norris had a falling out a few weeks ago. I'd like to know what he's up to." Henry paused. "Apparently he and his wife were friends with Mr. and Mrs. Greystone." How that played into the situation, he had yet to determine.

"If he's trying to avoid detection, he's doing a poor job of it." Fletcher watched him a moment longer. "It would make sense that he has reason to be in this area given that he has an import-export business, but why act as if he doesn't want anyone to recognize him?"

"Good question."

"Shall I catch him?" Fletcher asked once they drew closer. "Just say the word."

"Let's see where he's going first."

They kept their distance as they followed him, using the traffic to shield themselves. They had nearly reached the corner when he paused again to briefly study a building as if uncertain he was in the right place. A moment later, he stepped inside.

"Curious." Henry didn't see any sign proclaiming what the business was. "We will wait a moment to see what happens."

"Hopefully we won't have to wait too long." Fletcher stomped his feet. "I am already weary of the cold. Can't say that I miss the days of making rounds as a constable in this weather."

"Nor do I," Henry agreed as he turned up the collar of his jacket.

"Shall I ask the business next door to see what they can tell us?" Fletcher suggested as he studied the neighboring building.

"Please do." Anything to soon be out of the cold. "I'll keep watch for Locke."

Fletcher crossed the street, pausing to allow a cart to pass, and soon entered the building next door.

Henry shivered, moving to keep the cold from settling in too much. The thought of luncheon at a warm pub was enticing but too far off to bring relief.

His thoughts returned once again to Amelia, and worry took hold. Would Mrs. Drake be helpful, or had she simply intended to torment Amelia with that letter? Somehow he didn't expect her to give them a name. Nothing was ever that easy.

Within minutes, Fletcher exited the building and returned to Henry. "It is the office of a shipping company. They moved in about a month ago."

Henry scowled, disappointed by the news. "No reason to worry over that."

"Except the man I spoke with said there is something shady about the place. They keep odd hours, and rumor has it that not everything they ship is legal. He also said they use several different business names."

"Now that's interesting. Let us see what Locke is up to."

With a grin, Fletcher nodded. "I'm sure he'll be happy to see you."

They crossed the street and entered the building to find Mr. Locke standing before a desk, his back to them as he spoke to a man. "The shipment is late. I want to know what you intend to do about it."

The man at the desk glanced at them, which had the shopkeeper turning to follow his gaze. The shock on his face nearly made Henry smile. Clearly, he wasn't pleased.

"Mr. Locke." Henry dipped his head in greeting.

"Inspector Field." He glanced between Henry and Fletcher, clearly uncertain what to say. "What brings you here?"

"We happened to see you walk in and wanted to follow up with you on some questions."

The man behind the desk stood, his expression darkening. He didn't look pleased to have the police there either.

Henry lifted a brow as he met the man's gaze. "What is the name of this business? I didn't see a sign outside."

He hesitated. "Sable Importers."

Henry shared a look with Fletcher. "I don't think I have heard of it before."

"Nor have I," Fletcher agreed, amusement flashing in his eyes.

"It's a relatively new company." Mr. Locke turned hurriedly to the man. "Isn't that right?"

"Yes." His stiff posture suggested he was very uncomfortable with the situation.

"I see." Henry nodded as he looked around the spartan office, before staring at the closed door behind the desk. "Is it a large operation?"

"Large enough." Mr. Locke licked his lips as he turned back to the man. "I must be going, but please send word when I can expect the shipment."

"New wares coming in from abroad?" Henry asked, planting both feet to make it clear he wasn't in any hurry to leave.

Mr. Locke turned but didn't meet Henry's gaze. "Yes."

"From where?" *Egypt?*

"Various places." Mr. Locke straightened his shoulders. "As you may have noticed while perusing my shop, I carry items from numerous countries."

"Fascinating. What kind of items are you expecting?"

Despite the relatively innocent line of questioning, Mr. Locke's face reddened. "I'm sorry to say, Inspector, that I am in a rush. Unless you have a specific question regarding the investigation—"

"What investigation?" the man behind the desk asked.

Mr. Locke visibly trembled as if realizing he shouldn't have mentioned it.

"The murder of an import-export shop owner. Perhaps he was one of your customers. Mr. Benjamin Norris," Henry supplied.

"Never heard of him," the man said, though a flicker of what appeared to be recognition crossed his face.

Mr. Locke moved toward the door, forced to step around Fletcher and Henry to reach it. "I really must be going. Good day."

Fletcher lifted a brow to ask if he should stop him, but Henry shook his head. He had rattled the man enough for now. Instead he looked back at the remaining man and pulled out his warrant card. "Inspector Field of Scotland Yard. We have a few questions about your business."

Twelve

"Mrs. Drake." Amelia inclined her head in greeting, doing her best to hold on tight to her emotions. "I would ask if you are well, but I believe I already know the answer." She glanced around the stark room to make her point, determined not to allow the woman to have the upper hand.

Yet Amelia couldn't deny feeling she was at Mrs. Drake's mercy, and desperation threatened—but she swallowed it back. She would not plead for information regarding Matthew's death. Not when she had yet to be convinced that Mrs. Drake knew what had truly happened.

Prison had not been kind to the woman, based on her appearance. She seemed to have aged several years, though it had only been two months since Amelia had last seen her. She'd lost weight, her hair was dull and untidy, and her skin sallow. The simple gown she wore hung on her thin frame, and her eyes glittered with a strange light that Amelia had yet to interpret.

"I received your letter," Amelia said, refusing to allow herself to feel any sympathy. She need only think of Nora and Charlie, the two mudlarks Mrs. Drake had callously murdered, to quell it. "I assume you have a few more details to share than what it contained."

With a glare at the guard as if to warn him to keep his distance, Mrs. Drake walked slowly to the table and sank almost gratefully into a chair. "I might. Then again, it would be unwise to do so, much as I stated in my letter."

"If your only intent was to worry me, then I will be going." Amelia made to rise—only to have the other woman place a hand on the table to halt her.

"I already know you are not easily frightened," Mrs. Drake said quietly.

Amelia wished that were true, yet since the woman's letter had arrived, already her habit of looking out the window to see if someone watched the house had returned. Luckily, she hadn't seen anyone thus far.

"The situation is complicated." Mrs. Drake shifted in her chair, but her eyes held steadily on Amelia. "Moving forward could place us both in danger."

"From whom?"

"A name would serve no purpose to you."

Amelia masked her impatience. "Then what harm could it cause if you shared it?"

Mrs. Drake glanced momentarily at Fernsby before returning her attention to Amelia. "Do not make me repeat myself."

"And do not waste my time. I will ask you again. Do you know who was behind my husband's death?"

The guard frowned as he looked between them, but Amelia ignored him, breath hitching in her lungs. *Just breathe. All you have to do is breathe.*

"I have a very good guess."

And now Amelia's breath caught, her chest tight, making it difficult to inhale. It was impossible to hide her reaction to the news, so she didn't bother to try. "I would like to know."

Mrs. Drake studied her. "I'm sure you would." She shook her head. "Telling you now would be a mistake. You might feel inclined to share it with the police—and as I said, that would get us both killed."

The fleeting hope building inside Amelia subsided, but she wasn't prepared to give up yet, not after coming all this way. Perhaps a different angle of approach would provide results. "Why? Why was my—was Matthew killed?" She detested the tremble of emotion in her voice when she had no wish to reveal it to this woman. "Can you at least share that much?"

A smug smile returned to Mrs. Drake's lips. "You don't know?"

"No." Guilt speared through her at the single syllable admission. As his wife, she should. That was what the voice in her head whispered to her in the middle of the night. That she had failed him by not paying attention; by not understanding what he was involved in, what he was doing with the business, with whom he was working.

"Tsk. Tsk. What kind of wife were you?" Mrs. Drake feigned almost pantomime disapproval. "How could you be unaware of what your husband was up to when you lived in the same house and shared the same bed?"

A mix of anger and guilt swirled in Amelia, but she did her best to mask it. "Was your marriage a close one?"

Asking a question to avoid answering another was something Henry had taught her. The thought of him and his steadying presence was welcome, and she latched onto it. Only then was it clear that he had become her rock. A shelter from the storm.

She wasn't alone in this odd situation—Henry was with her in spirit and Fernsby in body, and that gave her courage.

"I was never married." Mrs. Drake lifted her chin, seeming to take pride in the statement. "I played the part of a widow to further my career. It is difficult enough to gain respect as a woman, but it is even harder if unmarried. Men tend to think you require their assistance, regardless of whether you want it. I did not."

"The gentleman who assisted you, Mr. Allard—he didn't mind the farce?" Amelia already guessed as much as the man had seemed more than prepared to do her bidding, no matter how terrible the deed was.

The tinkle of her laughter sent shivers along Amelia's skin, the sound unpleasant, not inviting one to join in. "Heavens, no. He was my lover. One of them, anyway."

"I see." Amelia realized how brazen the woman was, to have forged a place in the field of chemistry, pretended widowhood, and taken lovers... "What an...interesting life you've led." One she couldn't admire.

"It has been." The woman heaved a sigh. "Though I fear it will soon come to an end."

"Do you think your sentence will be so severe?" It should be for taking two innocent lives, if not more. Yet a part of her lamented that the woman's other talents, ones that might find cures and save lives, would never be realized.

Henry's explanation of the process women criminals went through came to mind. Somehow, Amelia didn't think Mrs. Drake could be "saved" by the system.

"It is not the law I fear."

"Then what—or who?" Amelia leaned forward, holding her gaze. "If it's the same man who killed Matthew, give me his name, and I will do everything in my power to protect you and have him arrested."

Mrs. Drake's smile was tight. "So naïve, though I appreciate your enthusiasm. I think we could've done wonders together in a laboratory, but now we'll never have the chance to experience that."

"Based on what I know about your more recent experiments, I tend to think our philosophies wouldn't have meshed." Amelia's thoughts raced, wondering how she could convince her to share specifics, anything. "Is the same man who killed my husband behind Mr. Norris's death?"

"Who is—"

"Time is up." The guard's curt words startled Amelia. One glance at his unyielding expression as he reached for the heavy keys on his belt suggested it was not possible to request more time.

No, I need more—

Mrs. Drake pushed back from the table, and desperation speared through Amelia. To be this close to an answer and not have it was unbearable.

"I must be going," the woman said. "A shame. I have enjoyed our conversation."

Amelia jerked to her feet, panic loosening the grip on her emotions. "Please. Won't you tell me who killed my husband?"

No sign of softening showed in Mrs. Drake's face.

Tears filled Amelia's eyes. She couldn't let it go. Not finding justice for Matthew tore at her. "If not his name, then something else, anything that might help."

The other woman hesitated, seemingly torn. "I can't. M-My—" She pressed a shaking hand to her mouth as if startled, then shook her head. "I-I can only say your husband wasn't completely innocent in the situation. He chose to cross the wrong man."

"Who?"

"Let it be, Mrs. Greystone. For both our sakes." Then she hurried to the door, the guard barely opening it before she was gone.

A terrible, heavy silence descended, and Amelia braced herself against the table as she continued to stare at the empty doorway.

The feel of a gentle hand on her elbow had her stiffening in surprise. She'd nearly forgotten Fernsby's presence. To think that he'd heard the entire exchange had her briefly closing her eyes in a combination of regret and relief—but then again, he probably hadn't learned anything he and his wife didn't already know.

People who employed servants might like to pretend their workers were invisible, but they were not. They heard and saw more than their employers wanted them to.

Mr. and Mrs. Fernsby must have known that all was not well between Amelia and Matthew well before his death. Besides, worrying about what Fernsby thought was the least of her concerns. Though they could have decided to give notice, he and his wife had remained with Amelia and provided ongoing support these last few, difficult years. She had no reason to think this meeting would change that.

Not after what they'd already endured.

"Shall we depart, madam?" Fernsby asked quietly.

"Please." Amelia lowered the netting on her hat, more than ready to leave.

They stepped into the empty hallway as another guard hurried forward to escort them back to the front desk. Several more minutes passed as the warden noted the time of their departure on his list, the cold causing Amelia to shiver despite her layers, and then they were allowed to leave.

She breathed in the frigid, but fresh air the moment they stepped out of doors, hoping to dispel the prison smells from her lungs. She remained silent as they returned to the hansom cab and settled inside.

Only then did Amelia realize she was trembling; a combination of nerves and cold, she supposed.

"Thank you again for accompanying me." She met Fernsby's eyes at last, relieved to find no judgment there.

"My pleasure." He dipped his head and glanced out the window, clearly giving her permission to keep her silence if she wished.

"I confess, I was hoping she'd share something more." Better that she speak of it so she could move her thoughts—and energies—elsewhere. "Something...helpful."

There had been a moment when Amelia thought she'd say his name, but she'd only said 'My'. As in 'my lover'? My what? Clearly whoever it was had power over her.

"As was I. Perhaps Inspector Field will be able to shed some light on her statements."

"I look forward to finding out." Maybe he would come by that evening, even stay for dinner. She didn't relish being alone after the morning's events, but she didn't want to impose when he was deeply involved in another case. Working evenings was too often a regular part of his schedule.

Though tempted to send a message to Scotland Yard for him to call, she had retained her faculties sufficiently to know that would be unwise. There was always the chance Mrs. Drake had spoken truthfully, and Amelia's involvement with the police was a problem—a danger, even. While she didn't intend to stop, she would certainly do her best to hide it for the time being. She wouldn't seek out notice.

As they neared home, she deliberately perused the street out the cab window in search of anyone or anything out of place. It would be wise to remain on guard for the foreseeable future.

She prayed that didn't mean forever.

Thirteen

HENRY PUSHED BACK FROM his desk at Scotland Yard, relieved to be done with the day so he could give in to the urge to call on Amelia. While he hadn't expected a message from her and would've been displeased to receive one, given Mrs. Drake's stark warning, he still wished she had sent word so he knew she was well. He shook his head at his illogical and conflicting thoughts, his movements rushed as he prepared to leave, anxious to see her.

He'd received a telegram from the police at Gravesend, advising that Norris's home had been broken into again and searched, though nothing seemed to have been taken. The news was concerning, but there was little Henry could do about it. No doubt whoever it was had been looking for the scarab.

Sergeant Johnson had finally found the Douglas Grant file, whose murder did indeed resemble those of Norris and Greystone. Apparently, it had been mislabeled and so had taken time to locate—a little suspicious, in Henry's mind, but he was pleased to have it at last.

He donned his coat and tucked the file under his arm to take it home to look over. He didn't intend to do so at work when Perdy might come upon him and start asking idiotic questions.

"Field?"

His chest tightened as he looked over to see Director Reynolds wave him into his office. He did his best to push away his impatience and strode toward the director's doorway where he remained standing with the hope the conversation wouldn't take long. "Yes, sir?"

"What do you have on the Norris case thus far?"

"I am becoming more and more convinced of a possible tie between his death and Matthew Greystone's. The method of murder and caliber of weapon are similar, as was the wound placement, which was confirmed by the surgeon. And they were in the same type of business—import-export."

"Interesting." Reynolds lifted his glasses to rub the bridge of his nose, clearly weary. "Any motive?"

"More than likely, the killer wanted the gold Egyptian scarab I told you about earlier, found in the torn chair arm. It appeared whoever it was searched the room but not the furniture in any great detail, nor the rest of the house."

"So many of those kinds of things are forgeries these days. Have you confirmed that what you found is a true artifact?"

"Not yet, but I will."

"Any suspects?"

Henry's jaw tightened. "One of the other shop owners on the street is the primary one based on what we have learned, but I need proof. He had a disagreement with the victim before his death and might be dealing in illicit antiquities."

"That sounds promising—but not without evidence." Reynolds sent him a pointed look.

Henry nodded, well aware. "We spoke with the surrounding neighbors in Gravesend, but no one noticed anything unusual that evening. Mr. Taylor estimates the time of death to be between nine and eleven o'clock—"

"A time when the street is dark, and most are settled inside for the night."

"Yes." Unfortunately. "By happenstance, one neighbor is employed at the same bank that our missing-person-turned-murder victim was." Henry shared the relevant details of his conversation with Mr. Ballard as well as the one they'd had with Spencer's friend, Mr. Palmer.

"Disappointing that Mr. Palmer didn't share those details sooner." Reynolds heaved a sigh. "We must pursue that closely with the hope it gains results."

"Yes, sir."

"What is your next step on the Spencer case?"

"I propose we monitor the pub where Palmer last saw Spencer. When they start selling lottery tickets there again, and they will, we raid the place to catch those involved in the scheme, hopefully including the man with the scar that Palmer told us about. That would allow us to question him to see if he had anything to do with Spencer's absence—or rather, apparent death."

"Aggressive. I like it. Let me know more as the plans come along." Reynolds' gaze dropped to the file Henry held. "Taking work home again?"

Henry smiled even as he tensed. "I hoped for some quiet time to review a case."

Reynolds nodded. "Your hard work is appreciated. Have a good evening, Field."

"And you, sir." Henry breathed a sigh of relief that his superior hadn't asked what file he was taking. Looking over another inspector's work without permission was not forbidden, not exactly, but frowned upon. Yet if what Arthur Taylor had told him was true, that Perdy had done little to pursue the case, Henry would most definitely be raising the issue with Reynolds.

A hint of daylight lingered on the horizon as he left Scotland Yard, a reminder that the days were slowly lengthening. It was a welcome sight. The darkness within himself—the doubt and worry ever whispering in his ear—was easier to battle in the light of day.

Deciding he needed to clear his mind and save the cab fare for another day, he walked to Amelia's, taking the time to pause several times to look around to ensure he wasn't being followed. While he'd reassured himself throughout the day that nothing could happen to her at the prison as she'd be surrounded by guards with the loyal Fernsby at her side, he would feel better once he saw her for himself.

And it had nothing to do with any burgeoning feelings. Not at all.

The chances of Mrs. Drake providing the name of who had killed Greystone seemed unlikely, but Henry understood why Amelia had to pursue it. He would've done the same in her shoes.

Still, he didn't like it. Mrs. Drake was a complicated person with illogical and criminal motivations, which made her actions difficult to anticipate. The risk she presented wasn't at an end merely because she was behind bars.

Soon he knocked on Amelia's door, pleased when Fernsby quickly answered it. The walk had helped to settle his thoughts but chilled him in turn.

"Come in, Inspector. We had hoped you would stop by."

"All is well?" Henry had to ask, trying to keep the urgency from his voice.

"It is. Mrs. Greystone awaits you in the drawing room." The butler reached for the file and Henry's things, though he didn't intend to remain long. He didn't want to impose.

He quickly climbed the stairs, anxious to hear the details of the meeting. The sight of Amelia, reading in her usual chair by the fire, had him pausing to admire her. The cozy scene pulled at him, as always. She wore a gray gown, an unwelcome reminder of her widowhood, even if it didn't detract from her appearance. Her dark hair was loosely drawn in a bun at the back of her head.

She was an attractive woman, one he had long admired for a multitude of reasons. He hoped he hadn't imagined the growing...awareness between them, though he knew it would be some time before he could act on it.

Only a moment passed before she noted his arrival, and Amelia quickly set aside the book and rose, a welcoming smile on her face. "Henry. I'm so pleased you're here, I was hoping you would stop by."

He briefly wished that her apparent pleasure at seeing him had more to do with the two of them and less with where she'd been earlier in the day. But such thoughts would have to wait until he discovered who'd murdered her husband.

"I hope your day wasn't too taxing?" he asked as he held her gaze, rubbing his hands to warm them.

She hesitated, seeming to debate her answer. "Actually, it was quite distressing."

His chest tightened in sympathy at the admission, but he wouldn't deny that he was touched she'd given him an honest answer. "I am sorry for that."

"Thank you." She absently gestured to his usual chair as she moved to the sideboard to pour them drinks.

He moved to stand by the chair and waited until she joined him. After thanking her for the whiskey he sat, taking a moment to appreciate the drink, the fire...but most of all, her company.

"I am anxious to hear the details." Henry took a sip, pleased to see her do the same of her sherry. If she were still upset, the drink might do her good.

"There isn't much to tell." Amelia shook her head. "She spoke in circles, really, for the surprisingly short time we had together. Of course she didn't provide a name or even a hint of the person behind Matthew's murder. I asked if the same person had killed Mr. Norris, but she didn't seem to know what I was talking about, and I am inclined to believe her."

Henry waited, certain there was more, but allowed the elegant woman to share the story as she saw fit.

She stared into the fire for a long moment then met his gaze again. "She says she thinks she knows who shot Matthew but again said that telling me would place us both in danger." Her brow furrowed. "And she said that Matthew was not innocent in the situation."

"Oh?" Henry asked, puzzled by the remark. *How would the woman know?*

"I'm not sure exactly what she meant." Amelia pressed two fingers to her temple as if to calm her racing thoughts. "Then again, I suspected as much, given the unexpected funds in our account."

The information was no surprise; she'd shared it with him near the beginning of the investigation. That was one of the reasons she'd been fearful after her husband's death—worried the killer would want the money returned and confront her about it.

Or worse...

It might be wrong, but he was somewhat relieved Mrs. Drake hadn't given a name or said much more. He didn't like seeing Amelia upset, but he especially didn't want her in danger.

"She said he'd crossed the wrong man."

Henry released a quiet sigh, wishing he knew who that was.

Before he could reply, Amelia scoffed. "She isn't even a missus."

"I'm sorry?"

"She was never married. Apparently she's had several lovers, including Mr. Allard. Then she had the gall to lament how much we might've accomplished if we'd worked together in a laboratory."

"Hmm. I do believe her idea of conducting experiments differs from yours."

"My thoughts exactly."

She continued to share snippets of the conversation until Henry had most of it.

"There was one moment when I thought she slipped and nearly said the killer's name." She shook her head slowly. "I am sure that must have only been wishful thinking. She said 'my' but that could have been 'my' anything."

Henry pondered the information. "Unless it was the beginning of a name."

Amelia shrugged. "If so, it wasn't enough to be helpful."

"I confess that I am tempted to visit with her, too," he admitted as he finished his drink and set aside the glass, telling himself he should leave. A man should never overstay his welcome. "Perhaps she would tell me if I pressed hard enough."

"Maybe, but she had nothing good to say about the police prior to meeting you." She shared a smile with him. "She more than likely has even less admiration after you arrested her."

He almost chuckled. "True."

"Henry," Amelia began, running a hand along her skirt as if nervous, "I know you're quite busy with the case, and others I'm sure, but I don't suppose you could stay for dinner? I-I would like the company. Yours in particular."

The uncertainty in her expression warmed him along with her words. He would be hard-pressed to refuse her anything, especially when she asked like that. "I would be pleased to, if it's not too much trouble."

"Not at all. Fernsby set an extra place just in case."

"Thank you." Deciding she must be more than ready to speak of something other than Mrs. Drake, he cleared his throat. "I saw Mr. Locke earlier."

"Oh?"

"Fletcher and I were following a lead on another case near the docks and saw him at a shipping business. He acted strangely as if doing his best not to be seen."

"What could that have been about?" Amelia's eyes narrowed as she seemed to search for her own explanation.

"As we entered, he was asking about a late shipment. Is visiting a shipping company normal in that line of work?"

"Matthew worked with certain ones and trusted some more than others, though he rarely went to their offices, from what I knew. Do you think he went to one less than reputable?"

"I will have to find out."

Her eyes widened, and she gasped. "Henry—do you know the name of the shipping company?"

"Sable Importers." He lifted a brow in surprise when she said the name with him.

"I should have told you sooner, but the letter from Mrs. Drake completely distracted me. When I went to his shop, there was a crate that looked to contain Egyptian artifacts on the floor. I might not have paid much attention, but he had just told me he wasn't selling anything unusual or special. There's a chance the one I saw wasn't real, but the crate was stamped with foreign markings—and it also said Sable Importers."

"Egyptian artifacts?" Henry's pulse thrummed at the news. He hadn't mentioned the scarab to her, so it could not be a coincidence... "Such as what?"

"A wide gold necklace for one." She held her hands near her neck to show the size. "I saw glimpses of more gold, but everything was packed in straw, so I couldn't say what they were." She shook her head. "It might have been my imagination, but Mr. Locke wasn't pleased to find me looking in that area, though I tend to think he didn't know for certain if I saw the crate."

"That is very interesting." He hesitated, thinking over the situation. His questions at Sable Importers hadn't resulted in any clues, nor had he uncovered any evidence of wrongdoing. He couldn't take a closer look without cause, but was this enough? "I suppose I shouldn't tell you this, being that this is an ongoing investigation, but you are already involved. I found a gold Egyptian scarab near Norris's body."

"Oh my." Amelia's gaze held on him, her eyes wide. "Do you think Locke killed Norris?"

"It seems possible. But I need proof." He leaned forward in eagerness, reluctant to ask questions but needing her expertise. "Did your—Mr. Greystone verify the authenticity of the genuine antiques he sold?"

"Yes, he did. He knew a man associated with a museum who would examine some of the more unusual items for a small fee." She frowned. "I don't recall his name, but I believe it is noted on some of Matthew's papers still in his desk."

"That might be helpful if you come upon it."

Fernsby announced that dinner was served, but that didn't stop their conversation. Henry greatly appreciated better insight into how shops like Norris's and Locke's operated. Most of the import-export shops on Threadneedle Street sold moderately priced items that the middle class enjoyed. However, a few also dabbled in antiques and artifacts, though laws on importing such items from foreign countries had become stricter in the last few years.

"The days of digging in Egypt and simply piling items one pulls from a tomb into a crate to ship back to England to sell are gone," Amelia advised with a small smile. "That was one of the reasons a couple of shops in the area closed."

"Change can be challenging for us all." Henry savored a bite of roast beef with gravy, one of his favorite meals. "Delicious, as always." So delicious that the meals his landlady served paled in comparison.

"Mrs. Appleton has a way with food, does she not?" Amelia ate sparingly, her fork trailing a line in the gravy, leaving Henry to wonder if she was still upset from the meeting with Mrs. Drake.

"I should have mentioned the crate in Locke's shop to you sooner." She sent him a worried look.

He realized his attempt to shift the conversation away from the investigation had failed, though he could hardly blame her. "You had no way of knowing it could be connected to the case."

"I am no expert..." Her voice trailed off as if she wasn't certain whether to share her thoughts.

"But?" he prompted, eager to hear her opinion no matter what it regarded.

"It rather seems as if Matthew's death caused a rift between some of the shop owners. They used to be closer, almost friendly, despite being competitors."

"Locke mentioned an unwritten agreement to avoid carrying the same items."

"Understandable, I remember Matthew mentioning it too. They believed it was to their benefit to avoid duplication with the hope variety would bring more customers to the street to shop."

Whether a falling out resulted in Locke killing Norris remained to be seen. Locke had supplied an alibi for Greystone's death, which had been verified, so it seemed unlikely that he had killed him. And then there was the file downstairs of a third murder...

Fernsby arrived to clear the table and soon returned with an apple tart which had Henry sighing in appreciation. Despite feeling stuffed, there was no way he would refuse such a dessert. "I shall have to walk home after this fine meal."

Amelia smiled. "I'm pleased you've enjoyed it."

"How is your aunt faring?" he asked. The woman had stayed with her for several weeks last November before moving to a home of her own, and was a memorable person. Henry needed to leave soon but didn't want to end the night with talk of her late husband or ongoing investigations.

"She is well. Much happier I believe since becoming involved in the church near the mudflats. Their efforts to aid the mudlarks have already made a difference in the children's lives, though she did mention Carl stopped by the church to complain about the difficulty of finding mudlarks to search for him."

Henry could imagine the conversation and shook his head in amusement. He cleared his throat, debating the wisdom of raising the next subject. "We are trying to find a new home for Leopold. And by 'we' I mean me."

"Mr. Norris's cat? Poor thing." Amelia paused, tapping a finger on the stem of her wine glass as if thinking. "Doesn't someone in the family want him?"

"Norris's solicitor is doubtful they will." Henry shook his head. "I convinced my landlady to allow it in my room for a day or two by telling her it was a potential witness."

Amelia's eyes widened with surprise before she burst into laughter, the sound loosening a tightness in his chest he hadn't realized was there. She had barely smiled since his arrival, let alone laughed, and hearing her do so made him long to hear it again.

"I can easily imagine the conversation." She drew a breath only to start laughing again, and he couldn't help but join her. "How amusing."

"It wasn't at the time, but I can certainly see the humor now." He held her gaze, hoping his next words would cause her to laugh even more. "Carrying it on the train, though it was in a cage, was no easy task. Deciding what ticket to purchase for him, for a start."

Amelia laughed again. "I'm sure it was difficult." She pressed a hand to her chest as she tried to catch her breath. "Forgive me," she said with a sympathetic smile. "I have no doubt that it was no easy feat."

"Let us say that Leopold was not enamored with me in the least. He refused to emerge from the cage once we made it past the landlady at my flat and has remained ensconced there."

"Poor Leopold. It sounds as if he was thoroughly traumatized." She bit her lip. "I wouldn't mind having him here, but I shall have to check with Mr. and Mrs. Fernsby."

Henry allowed the topic to pass, noting that Amelia didn't mention it to the butler when he returned to clear the dessert dishes. Better that she had time to think about it before discussing it with her staff.

He eased back from the table, reluctant to leave. "I am sorry to say that I must be going. I have an early morning ahead of me."

"The work of an inspector is never over." Amelia smiled with a sympathetic look.

"No, but evenings like this make the long hours bearable."

"I'm pleased to hear it. Thank you for staying, Henry. It helped me more than you know. Sharing my conversation with Mrs. Drake allowed me to clear it from my mind."

"Good." He only hoped the woman left Amelia in peace. If she wasn't going to be helpful, then she should remain silent.

Yet somehow, he feared that wouldn't be the case.

Fourteen

Amelia slept better than she had expected, and knew Henry was to thank for it. Having someone to speak to about the day's events had helped tremendously, and Henry already knew the story, which made his presence even more comforting.

And that was as much as she was willing to admit as to how she felt about him at the moment.

She gave herself a mental shake. How could she possibly feel anything more than friendship for Henry when a good portion of the evening had been spent speaking of her late husband? *What must Henry think?*

She sighed at the thought. She'd practically begged him to stay for dinner so she wouldn't have to be alone. It would be a surprise if he came by again after what must've been an odd, or even uncomfortable, evening.

Yet part of her wanted to think he had enjoyed their conversation in addition to the meal. Was it possible...

At the very least, she owed him information in exchange for him keeping her company last evening—the name of the man whom Matthew had consulted for his opinion on antiques. Amelia knew he worked at a museum but couldn't remember the place nor his name, having never met him herself. But hadn't she seen the name written somewhere not long ago while working in the study?

After her maid Yvette assisted her to dress, she had a light breakfast in the kitchen then attended church as she did most Sundays. After luncheon, she settled into the study to begin her search, the perfect task for a Sunday afternoon.

She had yet to claim the room as her own. It still held many of Matthew's things, from the desk itself to the ornate brass inkwell to most of the books on the shelves. There was little of her in the room at all.

In truth, she was more comfortable in her laboratory than the study. The reasons for that were varied, but all of them led back to Matthew. The study had been where he spent much of his time when home, his private retreat from the world, and it was still a masculine space.

The room was a good size, and the light streaming in through the windows helped to make it more welcoming. Perhaps she would make a few changes after finding the name. After all, it was one thing to honor Matthew's memory and quite another to be continually reminded of his absence. Unfortunately she had yet to discover where the balance was. Did other widows feel the same?

She'd been through the desk on numerous occasions in search of a clue that might lead to his killer, or at the very least, a reason for his death. Henry had been through it as well, along with a nameless constable. To her dismay, none of the papers Matthew had left behind had proven helpful.

She opened the top right drawer, relieved to feel only traces of grief and guilt at the sight of his familiar handwriting. With her goal uppermost in mind, she sorted through the papers, skimming each one for the name. Receipts, inventory lists, business correspondence with suppliers, reminders to himself of tasks yet to be done...all were stored in the drawer.

It didn't take long for her to find what she was looking for. Mr. Oscar Powell, of the Wexley House Museum. Pleased to locate it so swiftly, Amelia set aside the paper but continued to sort and organize two additional drawers. Most of the items could be put in storage in case they were needed at some future point in time—she was hardly going to get rid of them, with his murder still unsolved. One never knew what might suddenly be helpful—no matter that she'd studied every piece of paper in the desk numerous times but hadn't found a clue.

Soon Amelia had a stack on the desk which could be boxed and placed in the attic. She moved on to the other side of the desk to empty those drawers, adding to the stack. But the center drawer didn't open smoothly, no matter how many times she attempted it.

"Fernsby?" she called, wondering if he might be nearby.

Only a few moments later, the butler appeared in the doorway. "You called, madam?"

"This drawer is being stubborn." She tugged on it again, unable to pull it out completely. "Do you have any suggestions?"

"Allow me to have a look."

She stood and pushed back the chair to give him room. "It's never been particularly smooth, but it seems to be even worse."

He pulled on it several times, frowning as it stuck. "It is a stubborn one indeed. Something seems to be catching on the slide." He knelt to peer under the desk. "There's a piece of paper lodged in it. I believe we need something to force it out—a letter opener perhaps," he suggested. "Preferably one that you wouldn't mind being damaged."

She swiftly retrieved an old one that already had its share of scratches. "How's this?"

"That should do it." It took several tries before he was able to remove the paper. Then he opened and closed the drawer a few times with ease. "Much better."

"Thank you." She reached for the paper and unfolded it to see not Matthew's, but unfamiliar handwriting. It appeared to be a list of artifacts with prices noted alongside them. The amount of two in particular, several thousand pounds each, had her taking a closer look.

"Is all well, madam?" Fernsby asked.

"Yes," she murmured, thoughts swirling. "I...I just haven't seen this before."

"It must have been stuck in the drawer for some time." He waited a moment longer before adding, "If there's nothing else, I'll continue with my other duties."

"Thank you, Fernsby."

She sank into the desk chair, pondering what the list could mean. The items weren't ones Matthew normally carried in the shop, nor had he carried any in that price range.

Not as far as she had known, anyway.

Were these antiques he had sold to particular customers but never placed on the shop floor? If he'd been selling items like these, at such high prices, it would explain the unexpected funds in their bank account.

Mrs. Drake's words ran through her mind. "...your husband wasn't completely innocent in the situation. He chose to cross the wrong man."

The wrong man.

Amelia sighed as worry filled her. "Matthew, what were you doing? And who were you doing it with?"

Silence was her only answer.

Henry and Fletcher headed toward Threadneedle Street after meeting bright and early at Scotland Yard. Henry had spent the previous day, Sunday, with his parents, as well as entertaining Leopold. The cat had seemed restless, perhaps used to having more space to roam than in Henry's small rooms. He could only hope Amelia decided to take the cat.

He had already shared the basic details of Amelia's meeting with Mrs. Drake with the sergeant, who had felt much like Henry—unsurprised but still disappointed.

"I read through the notes on the Grant case last night," Henry advised him as they walked.

"And? Was Mr. Taylor correct in his assumption that Perdy didn't do much in the way of investigating the man's murder?"

"It seems so—that, or else he didn't take adequate notes. He interviewed a few potential witnesses, as well as family, then let it go." Henry sighed. "I suppose since the man was a repeat offender, those who were part of his life might have been of the same ilk. His murder took place in a rookery, not an easy place to conduct an investigation. Those would be the only excuses for not further pursuing the case and could explain the dearth of people willing to speak to the force."

"Then why not note those observations? That is what you would have done."

Since Perdy seemed to go out of his way to avoid any more effort than required into his cases, it didn't come as a surprise that the man hadn't bothered to write a full report on any issues he'd come up against. Henry doubted whether Reynolds had reviewed the case—the director couldn't read every file in the place, he'd never get anything else done. Then there was the question of why the file had been stuck inside another...

Henry was careful what he said to Fletcher though, as he didn't want his own poor opinion of Perdy to worsen his friend's, even if he doubted that was possible. Fletcher had witnessed first-hand how Perdy worked, and had been forced to help clean up the mess Perdy had made in the ravenkeeper's case when he'd allowed their only witness to be taken from Amelia's home. They were hardly bosom companions.

Perdy had never shown remorse for that failure, nor had he apologized. Yet he continued to poke at Henry for any supposed flaw he saw, frequently suggesting the tired old routine: that Henry had only been promoted because of the legacy of his father and grandfather.

Though Henry had grown accustomed to such remarks because of his quick rise through the ranks, something which a few people in the department insisted was only because of his last name, Perdy in particular grated on Henry's last nerve.

Henry had known from a young age that he wanted to be a policeman just like his grandfather and father. Learning the true circumstances of his birth hadn't changed his mind about what career he wanted; he only wished he were better at it. Not even his recent successes on a few cases had eliminated his doubt as to his abilities.

He would never have his grandfather's blithe assurance or compelling presence, nor his father's keen instincts and easy manner. Henry's best hope was to investigate each case using a methodical process, paying close attention to details. Relying solely on hunches was not for him, not when he didn't know where he came from.

Any ideas about who might be guilty and why needed to be backed by evidence—or ignored.

"How do you intend to proceed?" Fletcher asked, glancing about, ever watchful and observant. Those were only some of the reasons Henry liked to work with him. He was logical, thorough, and suspicious. Henry valued those traits, especially the latter.

"I have not yet decided." Raising his questions on the Grant case to Reynolds at this point would force Henry to admit he had reviewed the file, and spark more problems than solutions. "It might be better to see what we can uncover with the Norris investigation. If the two are related, someone might recognize Grant's name."

Fletcher nodded, though his grimace suggested he was reluctant to agree. "I'd rather confront Perdy next time we see him and demand to know what he was about by shoving the sluggard against a wall, but I understand your point."

Tempting, but Henry preferred not to become an even bigger target than he already was for the other inspector, and admitting that he'd reviewed one of his cases would certainly do that.

"The similarities in the manner of death for the three victims is undeniable. But that seems to be the extent of it from what we know thus far. It seems doubtful that Grant was in the import and export business, though the file didn't note his employment."

"Unless it was the unsavory sort, as in stolen and illegal antiques."

That had crossed Henry's mind as well, and he was pleased Fletcher had also spotted the possibility. He couldn't forget the extra funds Greystone had managed to obtain nor the crate Amelia had seen in Locke's shop. Sable Importers. Those made him suspect a criminal element tainted some of the shops on Threadneedle Street. How the Egyptian scarab he'd found in Norris's chair fit in remained to be seen.

As always, he needed proof.

He hoped Amelia located the name of the expert her late husband had used soon, but Henry intended to ask another's opinion on the scarab as well. There was always the chance Greystone's contact had criminal ties, if the former had been selling illicit antiquities.

"A nice change of pace to have the sun out today, eh?" Fletcher asked as he glanced upward, squinting.

"It hasn't improved the temperature much, but I appreciate it all the same." He'd made a point to wear his muffler again today to ward off the cold, damp air and was pleased he had.

"I can't seem to keep Locke's behavior yesterday out of my mind," Fletcher said after a lengthy silence, their feet taking them several streets farther.

"Nor can I. Clearly the late shipment upset him. Another visit with him is in order—and I want to speak with the other shop owners again, along with a few more." As Reynolds had said, someone had to know something.

Soon they arrived on Threadneedle Street and entered a shop, asking similar questions to what they'd asked everyone before.

How well did they know Mr. Norris? When did they last see him? Had they noticed anything unusual in the days prior to his death? And more importantly, where precisely were they the evening of his death?

Another round of inquiries might shake something loose.

Little came of questions at the first shop or the next one either. Henry paid more attention to the variety of goods offered at each. Some appeared more upscale than others. Some sold wares from a variety of countries and others focused on only one region. Neither the shop owners nor their clerks appeared anxious by the presence of the police. While they were obviously concerned about what had happened to Mr. Norris, the fact that it had taken place at his home in Gravesend rather than his shop seemed to create enough distance between them and the murder to provide them with a moderate sense of safety.

Even if it were merely an illusion.

"Must have been a personal matter, don't you think?" one man suggested. "Since it happened at home."

"Perhaps. We are making inquiries on all fronts," Henry advised.

"Did you notice—no sign of Egyptian artifacts at any of the shops," Fletcher remarked once they stepped outside again. "This is quite the puzzle. Where to next?"

"Let us see what our good friend Mr. Locke has to say for himself today." The man hadn't done anything illegal, and as far as they knew, the shipping company he'd visited near the docks hadn't either. But his secretive behavior was enough to warrant additional questions.

"This should be interesting," Fletcher said with a smile.

"We will press him a bit, watch his reaction." The man acted guilty of something.

Perhaps it was murder.

It came as no surprise that Mr. Locke was less than happy to see Henry again, let alone with a uniformed officer at his side.

"Inspector Field." Mr. Locke scowled. "Back again?"

Luckily, no customers were in the shop, and his assistant was absent, making it easier to speak with him.

"We have a few more questions for you." Henry retrieved his notebook from his pocket and flipped through the pages laboriously—not that he needed them to refresh his memory. "You mentioned a disagreement with Mr. Norris. How long ago was that?"

The man huffed. "I don't remember. Before Christmas, I suppose."

"Can you be more specific?"

After a beleaguered sigh, he gave the question further thought. "Mid-December, I think."

Henry nodded, noting the rough date. "And did you feel threatened by Mr. Norris? Did he say or do anything that concerned you?"

"Our difference of opinion made interactions uncomfortable, but it was no more than that." The man's gaze shifted to Fletcher who was walking around the shop, pausing near the rear curtain to look back at them. Mr. Locke frowned in response.

"Can you think of anyone else who had an argument with him? A supplier, perhaps?"

The shop owner narrowed his eyes as if considering the question, though Henry couldn't help but think it was only an act. The movement felt feigned, as if he did what he thought would appease Henry. What the police would expect.

"Can't say that any come to mind. Of course, we didn't share all the same suppliers and even when we did, we usually bought different items from them."

"Of course." Henry nodded. "Do you know if Mr. Norris and Mr. Greystone were friendly toward one another?"

Though the movement was subtle, the man's face tightened, alarm flashing in his eyes. "They certainly knew one another. I don't remember any altercations between them."

"I see." Henry jotted that down in his notebook, taking his time to see if the man would become uncomfortable as the interview drew long.

"Any other questions?" Mr. Locke asked and gestured toward the bare counter. "I have some rather urgent issues to attend to."

"Of course. We won't take much more of your time." Henry shared a look with Fletcher who returned to his side before facing their suspect again. "Were you able to straighten out the issue with the shipping company?"

Mr. Locke shifted impatiently, clearly annoyed by the question—or perhaps the fact that Henry and Fletcher had seen him at the place at all. "They sent a message to say they're working on the problem."

"That must be frustrating," Fletcher suggested lightly.

"It is, yes. Unfortunately it sometimes happens."

"What sort of items are in the shipment you're expecting?" Henry asked, keeping his tone friendly as if he was just curious.

"Vases. From the Far East," Mr. Locke said after a moment's pause.

Had he needed time to come up with an answer, Henry wondered.

"Is that all you needed?" the shopkeeper asked as he took a step toward the counter, clearly anxious to be done.

While nervous and edgy, it was difficult to know if guilt was behind his behavior. Perhaps he simply didn't like the police. He would hardly be alone in that regard.

"Yes. I hope the shipment arrives soon, sir." Henry closed his notebook and put it away. "Thank you for your time."

"Of course. I'm pleased to help. Such a tragedy." Mr. Locke moved toward the counter.

Henry turned partially away only to turn back, his pulse quickening as his voice remained steady. "Oh, I do have one more question. Were you acquainted with Douglas Grant?"

Locke stilled as his body stiffened. A long moment passed before he slowly turned on his heels to face them. "I don't believe so. The name's not familiar. Should it be?"

Henry offered a polite smile. "Just thought I would ask." He dipped his head. "Thank you for your time."

He and Fletcher departed, but when Henry glanced back, the shopkeeper hadn't moved.

"That was an interesting reaction," Fletcher murmured as soon as they moved down the street. "I would say he did know him and was shocked you brought it up."

"Agreed." Henry nodded. "The question is, how do we confirm a connection between them?"

Something was definitely amiss with Locke, and the man remained at the top of Henry's list of suspects...though admittedly it was a very short list.

Fifteen

RANDOLPH AND VICTORIA LOCKE resided in a stately three-story home in Wigmore Place with a mansard roof and dormer windows. Amelia had visited a few times with Matthew but hadn't since his death.

She had not been invited to do so.

After requesting the hansom cab driver to wait, she walked up the steps and knocked on the door. With luck, Mrs. Locke would be at home, and her husband wouldn't. Having given what Henry had shared the previous evening much further consideration, Amelia had to think Randolph Locke was up to something. Whether it imitated what Matthew had been involved in was one question Amelia dearly wanted to know the answer to.

A visit with Victoria might provide details to aid both Matthew's and Benjamin Norris's investigations. Perhaps Victoria would allow a few details to slip out during their conversation.

Of course, there was always the chance she didn't know what her husband was doing, much like Amelia.

She shrugged away guilt at her lack as a wife and handed her card to the maid who answered the door, and waited patiently to see if the lady of the house was receiving.

A glance around the foyer had Amelia taking a second look. The furnishings, from the Persian rug to an elegant vase on an equally elegant Chippendale entry table beneath a gilt-framed looking glass, hadn't been there when Amelia had last visited. From the foyer alone, it seemed clear the Locke business was doing well.

"This way please, Mrs. Greystone," the maid said when she returned and led the way to the drawing room.

This space also looked much different from the last time Amelia had been there. The fringed paisley drapes, patterned wallpaper, and other furnishings were a significant improvement from the past décor—not that Amelia would be so impolite to mention this.

Victoria Locke rose from a chair near the window, an embroidery hoop nearby, and walked forward to greet her with both hands outstretched. "Amelia. It has been too long. What a lovely surprise this is."

Amelia took them with a smile, though puzzled by the warm greeting. Victoria hadn't once called on her since Matthew's death, leaving Amelia to believe they hadn't been as close as she'd thought. Perhaps the fault was her own; she hadn't reached out to Victoria either.

"It's good to see you, Victoria. I hope you've been well."

Victoria Locke was an attractive woman with an oval face, even features, and thick brown hair. She had always taken care with her appearance and that didn't seem to have changed.

In truth, Amelia didn't know if they still shared any interests. She was no longer a wife or a mother, two roles that Victoria took great delight in. The thought was unsettling, and Amelia sincerely hoped they could rekindle their friendship.

"I have been well, very well. And you?" Victoria released her hands and stepped back to gesture toward the chairs for them to sit.

Her friend's green gown had a brocaded velvet bodice and followed the latest fashion of a small bustle, which emphasized the back. It had a high neck, tight sleeves, and white braided trim. She wore a ruby pendant the size of a small bird's egg that Amelia guessed was real.

Clearly, business was even better than she had suspected.

"I am well, thank you." Amelia sank onto the edge of the chair, slightly uncomfortable and already vowing not to stay long. Her own gray gown felt dowdy by comparison, but she hadn't been willing to shed the role of a widow for this visit.

"When Randolph told me you had stopped by the shop, I was so happy to hear word of you." Victoria's smile held as her gaze swept over Amelia, leaving her to wonder what the other woman saw.

A hint of pity darkened Victoria's brown eyes and had Amelia lifting her chin. She should be accustomed to the reaction. Victoria wasn't the first to pity her, nor would she be the last. But pity made her feel lesser, and that was something she refused to allow.

"It was good to see him, and it made me anxious to visit with you as well," Amelia said. Well, that much was true. "The children must be growing quickly." She ignored the pain in her own heart at what it must be like to have the privilege of watching them do so.

"They are." Victoria's gaze dropped to the floor, suggesting she was uncomfortable with the topic and uncertain what more to say.

"Wonderful. They change so quickly, don't they? How old are they now?" Amelia didn't want the other woman to feel awkward when talking about the children, since much of her life revolved around them. It was not her fault that Amelia was now childless.

Victoria's expression eased as she shared a few details about her daughter's talent for drawing and her son excelling in his classes at school.

As the conversation slowed, Amelia couldn't resist glancing over the new furnishings before running a gloved hand over the arm of the chair. "The new décor in here is lovely."

"Thank you. I finally convinced Randolph to change a few things."

"How nice. Did you do the entire house?" If so, then it made Amelia even more suspicious of the business.

"Much of it." Victoria's face lit up. "Doing so was a challenge, but we hired a designer to assist with some of the selections." She glanced around the room, which allowed Amelia to do so again without drawing notice.

All of the furnishings were of the highest quality, from what Amelia could tell. The cost must've been substantial if they'd done most of the house in the last year alone. "Impressive."

"Thank you." Victoria beamed, obviously proud of their home.

Had it been paid for at least in part by the sale of ill-gotten gains? *If only she could ask.* "Business must be very good. Has Mr. Locke opened a second shop?"

"Oh, no." Victoria bit her lower lip, her hesitation obvious, yet her enthusiasm overcoming her nerves. "Suffice it to say that he has several loyal customers willing to pay for...special items."

"How interesting. Antiques or artifacts?" Amelia's mouth went dry, and her stomach tightened in anticipation. *This was exactly what she wanted to know.*

"Some are archaeological items." She smiled, a gleam of amusement shining in her eyes. "Not everyone bothers about the provenance of cultural artifacts. What point is there in leaving them in places, I think, where so few can enjoy them?"

Amelia managed a polite smile as her thoughts raced. What point was there in one person owning them when no one else could view them? Was this what Matthew had been involved in? She had to think that might be the case given the extra funds, the list of items she'd found that morning, and Mrs. Drake's comments. The idea was disturbing, an unpleasant reminder—as though she needed another—that she hadn't known her husband as well as she thought. "That sounds rather...dangerous."

"Perhaps." Victoria lifted a brow, and Amelia couldn't help but wonder if the other woman's thoughts were on Matthew as well. "Randolph is *very* careful though."

Was she suggesting Matthew hadn't been? Amelia wished she knew, the tension within her making it impossible to think clearly. "I'm relieved to hear that. I suppose he is being doubly so after Mr. Norris's death."

"That was terribly shocking," Victoria exclaimed, fingering her ruby necklace. Again, she hesitated, then added, "I suppose it was even more so because he and Randolph had a disagreement not long before that."

"Oh?" Amelia could hardly stand the suspense.

"Something about artifacts, though Randolph didn't want to speak of it. He was very angry with Mr. Norris. That much was clear."

"How unfortunate."

Victoria shook her head, sympathy in her expression. "Who could have killed the poor man in his own home?"

"I am sure the police will soon discover who was behind it." Henry was doing everything in his power to find the killer. Not for the first time, Amelia wondered if Mr. Locke had been involved. He and his circumstances certainly seemed to have changed in the last year.

Victoria's lips pressed into a tight line, a hardness glinting in her eyes. "Do you think so? I mean, after..." She paused, clearly uncertain how to continue with her point. "I don't wish to cause offense, my dear, but since poor Mr. Greystone's case remains unsolved, one has to wonder if they will."

Amelia adjusted her position on the chair, not appreciating the reminder. Guilt rose each time she was confronted with that truth, as if she were somehow to blame. Being a widow was one thing, but being the widow of a murdered man carried a certain stigma, especially at moments like this—with women like Victoria.

Perhaps that was the reason the woman she'd thought a friend wasn't any longer.

Amelia was determined to do all she could to help find who had killed Mr. Norris for it might help solve Matthew's murder—but she decided against pointing out a possible connection between them, especially when Mr. Locke could somehow be involved.

"I suppose only time will tell." She studied Victoria, deciding with a heavy heart that it was unlikely they could return to their former friendship.

Amelia was a different person now after going through so much. Grief had taken a toll, and she'd come to see that what her friends thought important didn't matter as much to her anymore. Fashion, furnishings, and gossip no longer played much of a role in her life. She couldn't imagine telling Victoria of her work in the laboratory or her position as a correspondent for a periodical.

Perhaps that would change in time…but perhaps it wouldn't. Still, she was proud of herself for finding new interests, including assisting Henry with his police investigations.

She could only imagine Victoria's reaction if she mentioned that new hobby.

Since her host didn't ring for tea, it seemed clear the visit had come to an end. A pang of regret filled Amelia at the reminder that she no longer belonged in certain social circles like this one.

That was quite all right, she reassured herself. She'd discovered as much as she could hope to, which had been the purpose of her visit, and so shifted to the edge of the chair. "It was delightful to see you, but I should be on my way." She rose, unsurprised that Victoria stood as well, signaling that she, too, felt the conversation was over.

"I am so pleased you had the chance to visit. It's been too long." The woman's smile appeared genuine. Maybe Amelia was reading too much into the situation, but she still could not shake the sense that she'd lost yet another friend due to the turns her life had taken.

Turns she had never asked for.

"I wish you well, Victoria." Amelia dipped her head and turned toward the doorway.

"Thank you for calling. I will hope to see you soon," Victoria said as she walked her to the top of the stairs.

Amelia was soon settled in the hansom cab, sadness momentarily sweeping over her. Her entire life had been upended by both Lily and Matthew's passings, and she continued to mourn for what had been and what would never be.

She rubbed a hand over her chest at the tightness there, knowing she needed to shift her focus to her new future.

If only she knew what that might be.

With a sigh, she decided that would have to wait until tomorrow. For now, she would send a message to Henry's boarding house with the hope anyone watching her movements wouldn't pay attention. That was surely safer than sending one to Scotland Yard.

The new furnishings in the Locke house could mean something, along with the argument between Locke and Norris. The more clues she could help gather, the better chance of solving the murders.

All of them.

Sixteen

It took far longer than Henry would've liked to find someone reputed to be an expert in Egyptian artifacts at the British Museum that afternoon. It took far less time for Henry to realize he didn't like the 'expert' or his demeanor.

"I am quite busy this afternoon." Professor Carter, a short, bespectacled man who'd been summoned to the lobby, looked Henry over and seemed to find him lacking. "You will need to make an appointment."

Fletcher was spending some time taking a closer look at Sable Importers, the shipping office where they'd seen Locke, while Henry had ventured alone to the museum, giving his sergeant instructions to watch to see who came in and out, and ask other businesses in the area what they knew of the company.

There were so many moving parts to this case that it was difficult to know which thread to pull to find the one leading to the killer.

But they needed to remember that it only took one tug.

Verifying the authenticity of the scarab was one of those threads, though Henry felt certain it was genuine *and* valuable. If only he knew how it had come to England and why Norris had it stuffed in his chair.

And for that, he would need the cooperation of Professor Carter.

"I am sure you are very busy, but I am afraid this is police business and cannot wait," Henry advised politely. Though tempted to order the man to have a look, he dug deep to find patience as he showed his warrant card. "A murder investigation is underway. I'm quite certain that with your level of famed expertise, it won't take much of your valuable time." A little flattery often went a long way.

"Murder." The man adjusted his glasses, his distaste obvious. "What does that have to do with an artifact?"

Henry had wasted enough time waiting for the man's arrival and didn't intend to waste more by explaining the details. "I'm not at liberty to say, it's an ongoing investigation."

"Humph." Professor Carter waved a hand in the air with a dramatic flair. "How can I offer an opinion without knowing the details?"

"Our question is only whether the item involved is genuine. Is there somewhere we can speak privately?"

With a poor attempt at hiding his displeasure, the man gestured toward a door behind the front desk. "In here, I suppose."

The moment the door shut behind them, Henry pulled the bundle from his coat pocket and unfolded the handkerchief to reveal the contents.

"A scarab..."

As Henry had hoped, the man's focus immediately shifted, his interest heightened and reverence in his tone.

Professor Carter reached out to take the piece and turned it over to study it from every angle. "Interesting."

Remaining silent, Henry gave him time to examine it.

"Where did you find it?" the professor asked.

"I can't say," Henry responded. Better not to share details of finding it stuffed in the torn fabric of an armchair, when the tale might startle him.

"As I'm sure you know, it is no longer permitted for such items to be taken from Egypt without going through the proper channels."

"I am aware. How it arrived in London is not in question at this point in time. Does that mean you think it is real?"

"I don't 'think'. I know." Professor Carter lifted his nose, a snootiness coloring his tone. "But there are those, of course, who would argue that it should be returned to Egypt. A travesty, in my opinion. The object can be better preserved and studied here."

"That will have to wait until the investigation is completed." Henry politely retrieved the scarab from the man's hand before he decided to keep it.

The professor huffed in response.

"So you believe it is old? How valuable is it?" Henry carefully wrapped it back in the cloth, well aware of the man's watchful and disapproving gaze.

"Quite valuable. What bearing does that have on the case?"

"Would it be in the hundreds or thousands?" What level of criminal were they dealing with?

The professor stared at the bundle in Henry's hand. "Thousands—it's most unusual. The quality of the workmanship is impressive. The gold and gemstones are valuable in themselves, let alone in this unique form. I can't say I've seen one exactly like it."

"Thank you. That is helpful. I appreciate your time, Professor Carter."

Henry departed, a sense of unease taking hold. Given the value of the object the killer clearly sought, the stakes were even higher. Ordinary criminals rarely got their hands on artifacts of this sort. Had they not realized what they had—was that how it had ended up in Norris's hands? Or were they fully aware, and Norris had claimed it with the hope of selling it to a wealthy collector?

Those were only a couple of the possible scenarios.

Then there was the question of what had gone wrong. Had the killer realized he'd made a mistake by allowing Norris to have it and so came to take it back? Or had Norris stolen it, possibly from Locke? Was that why they'd argued? But if that was true, why had there been a delay between the argument and Norris's death?

It seemed logical to assume the Egyptian scarab had arrived illegally in London and doubtful that it was the only one, especially given the crate Amelia had seen. Would selling one or two artifacts be profitable? Perhaps, but selling several crates of them would be even more so. If that was the case, it meant a large operation.

He had to determine who in London's underworld dealt with illegal Egyptian artifacts. Surely there weren't many who dipped their toe in such an unusual trade. At least, he hoped not.

A few questions with some of his acquaintances in the East End might prove helpful. It wasn't the best place to go alone, but if he waited for Fletcher, he could lose the rest of the day.

As always, time was of the essence.

Henry glanced at the sky as he walked, which suggested he had at least a couple of hours remaining before darkness took hold. He would need to leave the East End before that if he wanted to ensure his safety.

First, he had to return to Scotland Yard and put the scarab back in the evidence room, making sure it was safely locked away. He managed that as quickly as possible, then took a hansom cab close to Spitalfields.

It had been several weeks since he had last spoken to his contacts in the area—a man couldn't pursue every case all the time. Though it seemed doubtful they would know of someone trying to sell illegal Egyptian artifacts, it took manpower to move crates of goods from a ship to a building and even more men to guard the wares. Those men would more than likely be hired from the area and had family and friends there who knew about their jobs. One of those could be a contact of his.

Henry alighted, paid the driver who was quick to leave, then walked the rest of the way, looking around as he went.

Spitalfields was often the first stop for newcomers arriving in London. The market, which Henry had once read started in the thirteenth century in a field next to a priory, sold produce and other goods.

French Protestants of the Georgian era had claimed a portion of the area as their own the previous century, when their religion was no longer welcome, bringing their skills in silk weaving with them. The changing production style of textiles, especially in Northern England, had apparently significantly decreased their business in recent years, and changed the people who lived here. Henry spotted a kosher shop with two men wearing yarmulkes chatting away happily outside, as a woman with a strong Irish accent scolded a small child hanging to her skirts.

Henry surveyed the bustling street as he walked, keeping a wary eye around him. A young woman with a basket on her arm shopped nearby. Two older gentlemen in well-worn jackets and patched elbows stood on the corner visiting. Children of all hues shrieked as they played with a stick and ball in the street until a passing cart forced them aside, their cries adding to the fabric of the scene. Numerous languages were spoken here, and accents varied greatly.

Henry might be English, at least as far as he knew, but he was clearly a minority in Spitalfields. He paused to allow a young couple to pass before entering a Georgian townhouse with a sign above the door that read *J. Tremblay & Sons - Fine Silks*.

Jacques Tremblay, who ran the family business, smiled in greeting and stood to walk around his desk to shake Henry's hand. The small room displayed everything from bright scarves to simple ribbons to bolts of silk in a variety of temptingly tactile patterns. "Inspector Field. Good to zee you."

"And you, Mr. Tremblay—and how is business?" Henry glanced around the shop, amazed as always to think the fabric was woven just upstairs where tall windows let in the light so vital for the intricate work. The rhythmic clatter of the looms echoed through the place, worked by his family. He'd had the pleasure of watching them once.

"Busy enough." The man's strong accent could be a challenge to understand, even though he'd been born in England. "You?" His blue eyes sparkled with humor.

Henry chuckled. "Too busy."

He had helped Tremblay recover stolen bolts of fabric a few years ago, and the man remained grateful enough to pass him information when he had it. Those who lived and worked in the area were wise to keep their wits about them, and Tremblay did just that.

Many of the somewhat affluent families had moved away, allowing the poor and desperate to move in. Tremblay was one of the few silk weavers who remained, insisting that if the place had been good enough for his father, and his father, it was good enough for him.

"Have you finally come to purchase silk for a lady?" Tremblay wiggled his brows up and down suggestively. "I 'ave new colors you will like." He gestured toward one of the bolts in a vibrant red.

An image of Amelia dressed in such a gown filled Henry's mind. She would look stunning in the color. Odd to think that, considering he'd only seen her in mourning attire for the past year—with the exception of the day he'd called on her to advise her that her husband had been killed. Of late, she had worn a deep purple gown twice, including the dinner at his parents, a color considered acceptable for widows.

He hoped...no, wished she would eventually do that more often.

"No, sorry," Henry quickly refused even as he reached out to touch the smooth fabric. The conversation was a familiar one that always ended the same.

"Perhaps one day, eh?" The man's grin had Henry smiling in return. "Soon, I 'ope."

"Perhaps," Henry acknowledged as he stuffed his hand in his pocket. "I came by to ask a couple of questions."

Tremblay heaved a beleaguered sigh. "Of course you 'ave. Who are you looking for now?"

"Someone with stolen artifacts. Most likely from Egyptian tombs."

"Illicit antiquities? That's an unusual one. Sounds dangerous." The man leaned against the desk, arms folded over his chest as if prepared to settle in for a chat.

"I have reason to think this person could have numerous items," said Henry carefully. Just enough detail, but not too much. "Possibly crates of them. They are more than likely storing them in the area and would have hired men to guard the place. Have you noticed any unusual activity that might match such a scenario?"

Tremblay shook his head, his expression resigned. "There is always suspicious activity of some sort 'ere. It is better not to look too closely at those involved, *n'est-ce pas*?"

Though disappointed, Henry understood. "If you happen to hear anything, I would be grateful if you would let me know."

"Of course." The man's eyes narrowed as if he'd remembered something. "Several men were standing outside a building near the end of Booth Street the other day when I passed by. They looked rather suspicious. I didn't look long as zat's a place I prefer to avoid. I can't say whether it concerns your case, but one never knows." He shrugged.

"Thank you. I'll have a look."

"Not upon leaving 'ere, I 'ope. I'd rather not have it noted zat I told you of it."

"No. I have another stop or two to make." Henry turned to go, only to pause. "Is the name Douglas Grant familiar?"

Tremblay pondered the question but shook his head. "No."

Henry touched the brim of his hat in farewell. "I will wish you a good afternoon then."

"I 'ope you find both the thieves and the artifacts. Be on guard, Inspector, and take care. *Au revoir.*"

"I will—and you as well." Henry departed for his next stop.

The shoemaker's tiny shop was difficult to find unless one knew where to look. A grimy window and an equally grimy door surely didn't encourage passing trade. A bell clanked to announce Henry's arrival, the sound muffled. The interior was neat and tidy, the smell of leather lingering in the air. A gaslight above the workbench didn't seem like enough light to Henry.

The older gentleman at the bench looked up from his work but only briefly. His loyalty didn't run as deep as Tremblay's, and he had no interest in idle chatter. "What brings you by, Inspector?"

Henry shared what he was looking for, but the man quickly shook his head. "Can't help you with that one."

"Did you know a Douglas Grant? He died nearly two years ago. Lived in the area." He almost felt ridiculous asking about the man, given how long it had been.

"No." The curt answer offered no invitation to chitchat, and had Henry moving on.

He asked the same two questions at the grocers stand.

The stout man with a moustache even bigger than Fletcher's frowned. "Grant? I had a second cousin wid a friend by the name. He got hisself shot a couple of years ago."

Henry stilled in surprise at the unexpected response. "That sounds like him. Do you know what he did for work?"

The man grimaced then leaned closer, his onion-scented breath causing Henry to hold his own. "He worked for *Edgarton*. I told my cousin no good could come from that and he should steer clear of 'im."

"Edgarton?" The name wasn't familiar, a rarity for Henry.

The man reached to straighten several turnips in his cart before looking back at Henry. "Many aroun' here know 'im. He has a finger in lots of different pies, none of 'em legal."

"How can I find him?"

The man shook his head. "Ye can't. Nor do ye want to. I don't know any more than that."

A name was more than Henry had before, and there was surely a chance someone at Scotland Yard would recognize it.

Though the afternoon was waning, and he needed to leave soon if he wanted to be gone before nightfall, Henry couldn't resist meandering vaguely toward Booth Street, since Tremblay had mentioned activity there. It wouldn't do to venture too close as he was by himself, but he wanted to see if it was worth further investigation.

He walked at a moderate pace, not wanting to draw attention by going too fast or slow. There was little point in trying to fit in with those on the street when so many people, especially in this area, tended to recognize the police no matter what they wore. Luckily, there was a mixture of others walking past that he liked to think he didn't stand out overly much.

Once he neared Booth Street, he kept his head down and his brim pulled low, hoping to suggest that he was merely walking through the area and not there to study it. He reached the corner and slowed his stride, waiting for the traffic to clear to cross the street. A subtle glance around revealed precisely what he had been looking for; two men lingering outside a brick building.

If not for Tremblay's mention of it, Henry wasn't sure he would've noticed the place. Yet the men's watchful air suggested they could be guarding it. Henry didn't recognize them or the building. No other activity hinted at what might be happening inside.

Since there didn't seem to be any possibility of getting a closer look without drawing notice, Henry continued on his way. Perhaps the constable who patrolled the area might know more. Worth a few questions, at least.

He flexed his gloved hands and shivered, the temperature dropping. It was definitely time to end the day. He found a cab stand several streets away, relieved to put the East End behind him. The place had a menacing feel, but maybe that was only because of his position with the police.

His thoughts shifted to the next day and how to best make use of his time. A few questions for fellow inspectors might provide information on Edgarton—and he would find out which constable was familiar with the area. Hopefully, Fletcher had discovered more about Sable Importers. Henry would like to know who operated the business, and what and where they imported from. The employee they'd questioned previously had offered less-than-satisfactory answers.

There was little to be done on missing-murdered Spencer's case until they found a place selling lottery tickets. Not finding a body put them at a distinct disadvantage. However, Henry intended to continue pursuing it until he'd followed every clue to the end, just as he did all his cases.

If only that guaranteed success.

He smiled at the thought of Leopold greeting him upon his return to his flat. Already the cat made evenings less lonely, but he still hoped Amelia decided to take him. The creature deserved more frequent and better company than Henry could offer.

How ridiculous was it that one of the reasons he hoped Amelia wanted the cat was because it would provide an excuse to see her again?

Seventeen

Henry woke early and, after feeding Leopold, made his way to Scotland Yard to see if anyone there had heard of Edgarton. Duncan, an inspector several years older than Henry, was the only one who could offer a smidgeon of information.

"Edgarton is a bad egg." Duncan shook his head, a wary look in his eyes. "He's got more businesses than you can imagine, nearly all illegal."

"And how do I find him?"

The older inspector grimaced. "I wish I knew. He's a slippery one—he has a large operation filled with loyal men, mainly because he kills any who dare to cross him. He dabbles in everything from selling stolen goods to selling girls. Made a fortune in opium early on and moved on to other ventures."

It sounded promising. "All that and no arrests?"

"Never been able to charge him with anything since we have no evidence or witnesses. He's careful to bury any proof that could be used against him, including evidence and witnesses. All we have are rumors and hearsay."

"Do you have a description?"

"Thought to be in his forties, brown hair and eyes, though I've heard different at times."

"Thank you," Henry said, wishing he had more.

"Field, if you dig into that one, take care," Duncan warned sharply. "He's dangerous."

"I will." Henry nodded, frustrated by what felt like a dead end.

He departed for Amelia's, hoping it wasn't too early to call. A message from her had awaited him when he returned to his flat the previous evening, though it had been far too late to justify a visit. It hadn't offered any details, only requested him to come by when he could, making him think the matter wasn't urgent. She must have found the name of the expert her late husband had used—or perhaps she had made a decision about the cat.

Though he'd been more than tempted to call on her last night, further consideration kept him at his flat. Better that he avoid the temptation of spending another evening in her company. Such visits were becoming too much of a habit.

As whatever she had to share more than likely involved their case, he didn't feel too guilty about taking time out of his workday to call on her, and the walk to her house allowed him time to organize his thoughts regarding Norris's murder.

Despite a night of tossing and turning as he considered all the information they'd gathered, Randolph Locke remained the primary suspect. No others Henry had spoken to seemed as likely to have killed Norris. His behavior during Henry's questioning, the crate with the gold necklace which Amelia had seen in his shop, and his disagreement with Norris—it all weighed against him, not to mention his suspicious behavior at Sable Importers.

Henry needed to determine a motive or find evidence to know for certain and be able to make an arrest. He'd already sent word to Norris's assistant to meet him at the shop later that morning. Learning more about the argument between Norris and Locke would hopefully be helpful. Perhaps the man had overheard the argument, or Norris had mentioned it—something.

Unfortunately, Fletcher hadn't discovered much after watching Sable Importers the previous afternoon. Few people had gone in and out, and the neighboring businesses either didn't know anything about it or weren't willing to speculate. Perhaps the company didn't have anything to do with the case after all, but the crate with their name on it at Locke's shop said otherwise.

He knocked on Amelia's door and Fernsby soon greeted him. "Mrs. Greystone is working in her laboratory this morning, Inspector. Perhaps you would like to join her?" he asked politely. "She was hoping you would call and so is expecting you."

Henry climbed the stairs, pleased at the prospect of seeing Amelia and even more so to see her working. Her interest in chemistry fascinated him, especially given how much of it she had taught herself of her own accord. To conduct experiments she'd learned from a book, such as the one she'd done for him to test for arsenic last year, had impressed him.

The door to the lab was open and he paused in the doorway to watch her. Morning light streamed in from the windows at the opposite side of the room, giving the space—and her—a warm glow. She stood before the long, tall table with gloves on and an apron over her gray gown. A row of beakers stood in a line before her, along with a row of small clay pots. A notebook and pencil sat nearby.

He wished he could simply watch her for a time, but the weight of the investigations pressed on him, the clock ticking. As so often was the case, time was the one commodity of which he had very little.

He tapped lightly on the doorframe so as not to startle her. "Good morning."

"Henry." His chest tightened at the welcome in her tone and on her face. "I'm so pleased to see you." She removed her gloves and set them aside.

"It's nice to see you as well." *Nice*? The word lacked vibrancy in every possible way. He walked closer, forcing his focus from her to the worktable. "What are you working on?"

"Testing a few types of fertilizer to see if we can improve the health of both the indoor and outdoor plants. Mrs. Appleton keeps a small herb and vegetable garden, so I hope to lend assistance with the task."

"How interesting." He peered into the pots to see soil in each one and seeds nearby. Eggshells in water stood in a jar next to another container with a white powder and another with what looked like dried tea leaves.

She tapped a pot with one finger. "Adding nitrogen to the soil can aid growth, but finding a natural way to do so would be preferable."

"A worthy endeavor." He pointed toward the seeds, which looked familiar. "Are those peas?"

"They are." She smiled, seeming delighted that he recognized them. "Did you have a vegetable garden growing up?"

He nodded as warm memories of helping to tend it filled him. "Mother still does. She spends many pleasurable hours in her garden."

"It will take some time before I have results, but I would be happy to share them with her—if you think she would be interested."

He stilled at the simple offer, struck by the promise it held. It meant time spent together in not just the coming days, but the coming months. Perhaps when an investigation wasn't the reason for them seeing one another. He did his best to mask his reaction, not wanting to make too much of her remark. There was always the chance she hadn't meant it that way. The way he so eagerly wanted.

Forcing back his happiness, Henry cleared his throat. "I know she would not only appreciate that but enjoy it."

"Good. As would I." Amelia drew a quiet breath and touched a finger to the scale, sending it rocking. "I paid a call on Victoria Locke, Randolph's wife, yesterday."

"Oh?" As was often true with her efforts involving cases, he couldn't decide whether to be grateful or worried by the admission. She was not a woman to be held back.

Emotions flashed across her face, gone before he could interpret them, one quickly replaced by another. Clearly, the visit with Mrs. Locke hadn't been easy. But she was a friend—why?

Her gaze met his. "Based on the changes in the furnishings and décor, it is clear the Lockes have had a significant improvement in their financial success over the past year."

"Interesting." That snippet only added to his belief that Locke might be their man.

"Victoria said they redecorated most of the house and even hired a designer to help them. That must have been quite expensive based on the furnishings I saw. She was dressed well, with a large ruby necklace. She also mentioned that her husband had certain customers willing to pay significant sums for artifacts, regardless of how they were acquired."

Henry nodded, thoughts churning. That description matched the scarab and could possibly tie Locke to the crime. Of course, he needed evidence, but now he knew what he was looking for and it could change the whole course of the investigation.

"Egyptian?" he asked quietly.

"She didn't say, nor did she offer specifics. I wish I had more details to share."

"That is more than enough. Thank you." He hesitated, trying to guess her feelings on the matter. "You and Mrs. Locke are well acquainted?" If so, Amelia's loyalty to her friend must be torn. Perhaps that was the tension he sensed.

"We were." She offered a smile, though it was at odds with the shadows in her brown eyes. "I suppose we...we no longer have much in common."

Those words pained him, causing a heavy weight to settle within him. He could guess the reason—the loss of her daughter, then her husband. Their deaths had shifted everything in her world, including friendships. Life wasn't fair.

"I'm sorry." The words were inadequate, but he had no others.

"So am I." She drew a visible breath as if to refill herself. "But life marches on."

"It does."

"I also have the name of Matthew's expert if you want it." Her brow furrowed. "Actually, I have something else to show you as well. Do you have a moment to join me in the study?"

"Of course." He stepped back to allow her to lead the way.

"One of the drawers in the desk was most irritatingly sticking," she explained as they made their way down the stairs. "I noticed it before, but it had grown worse. Fernsby managed to fix it—in an unexpected way."

Henry was familiar with the desk; she had allowed him to search it soon after her late husband's death. What a stuck drawer had to do with anything, he wasn't sure.

She opened the study door and walked to the desk to pick up two slips of paper. "Here's the expert's name and the museum where he works."

"Thank you." Henry glanced at it, but neither was familiar. It certainly wasn't the mildly unhelpful Professor Carter.

"And this is what was stuck in the drawer." She handed him a creased piece of paper.

"An inventory list?" He skimmed it without much thought—then took a second look.

"It appears to be. That is not Matthew's handwriting, and those weren't the normal type of wares he carried." Amelia pressed her lips tight, whether in indecision or disapproval, he didn't know. "If those are items he sold and the amounts next to them reflect their prices, it might explain the surplus funds in our account."

Henry turned the paper over, but maddeningly, nothing was on the back. "Do you have any idea where he would've acquired them?"

"No. I'm not even sure if he did have them or what exactly they are."

"May I take this?" he asked, curiosity rising.

"Of course."

The case was growing more interesting by the moment. "Thank you for these." He slipped the papers into his pocket.

"I hope they help."

"Everything we learn does."

She nodded. "One more piece of the puzzle."

"Exactly."

"Oh, and I spoke to the Fernsbys about Leopold, and they are agreeable that we take him."

Henry smiled. "I'm pleased to hear it. He will be as well, along with my long-suffering landlady."

"Good. You can bring him by whenever it is convenient."

With reluctance, but sadly no greater excuse to stay, Henry bid Amelia goodbye and went on to Threadneedle Street.

By the time he arrived at Norris's shop, Andrew Weston was waiting by the door. The hopeful look on the man's face made Henry wonder what he thought he might hear.

"Good morning, sir." Mr. Weston dipped his head, rubbing his hands briskly together before tugging up the collar of his coat. "Cold this morning, eh?"

"It is." Henry unlocked the shop. The keys had been kept in the evidence room while they awaited the new owner. Apparently, a distant cousin was the closest relative and was expected to decide what to do with the shop, once his claim had been formally established.

"Thank you for meeting me here." Henry closed the door behind them and glanced around the shop with fresh eyes. "I have a few more questions I'm hoping you can help me with."

"I will do my best." Mr. Weston's gaze swept the shop, a hint of melancholy in his expression.

Henry had to wonder if he missed working there—and precisely what employment had occupied him since the murder. "Have you been in touch with Mr. Norris's cousin?"

"I sent a letter with an inquiry but have yet to receive a reply. I would like to keep my position, if I could."

"Being that you're familiar with the business, he might very well appreciate your help if he intends to keep the place open."

"That is my hope, but we shall see. I have been forced to apply for other positions in the meantime, as I don't know what will happen. Funds are tight without employment."

"Understandable. I did mention your overdue wages to the solicitor, though I can make no promises."

The gratitude on the man's face was undeniable. "I appreciate that. Very much."

Henry retrieved his notebook. "We discussed Italian and other items during our last conversation, but did Mr. Norris carry any Egyptian wares?"

"A few, yes." He moved toward a shelf and gestured toward it. "We have a variety of perfumes and oils which come in decorative bottles. Jasmine is always popular, as are frankincense and myrrh. Incense burners. Small sculptures and vases carved from alabaster that look like the sands of Egypt all sold well."

He moved farther into the store to point toward a pile of rugs on the floor. "These rugs are considered Egyptian art."

"What about more expensive items?"

"The rugs can be expensive, depending on the pattern, quality, size. We also have copperware and brass, some of which were engraved that could also be expensive, along with hand-painted clay plates."

"Anything made of gold?"

"Some jewelry, of course. Otherwise, little else."

Henry nodded. That still wasn't what he was looking for. "Did you sell *any* gold artifacts?"

The man looked blank. "I'm not sure what you mean."

Neither was Henry. "Statues or pharaoh's masks? Staffs or any items that look as if they could've come from a tomb?"

"No—not since I started here."

That suggested he hadn't seen the scarab, if it had ever been here. Henry glanced around the shop. "What is the most expensive item you carry?"

"Probably the imported rugs. The jewelry we have is fairly modest in price."

Rugs. Rugs were not worth killing over.

Time for a new line of questioning. "How well do you know the other shop owners in the area?"

"Well enough to greet them on the street, I suppose." He shrugged. "As friendly as competitors can be."

"How did Mr. Norris get on with them? Were there any he mentioned that he didn't like?"

"He and Mr. Locke had a rather heated argument—oh, about a month ago. Mr. Norris passed by his shop and saw something he didn't like and confronted Mr. Locke."

Henry's interest sharpened. "What was it?"

"I'm not sure. I was in here when it occurred, and though Mr. Norris grumbled about it when he returned, he never shared the details."

Had Norris suspected what Amelia had discovered from Mrs. Locke? That Randolph Locke was selling illegal antiquities?

Would that have been enough for Locke to decide Norris had to be silenced before he caused problems? If so, why had it taken a month for that to occur? And how had Norris ended up with the golden scarab?

"Did they ever seem to resolve their differences?" Henry asked nonchalantly.

Mr. Weston shook his head. "No. No, their relations remained quite chilly after that."

"Were any other shop owners involved in the dispute?"

"Not to my knowledge. Of course, Mr. Norris often stepped out without saying where he was going. He might have been visiting with others, or he might have gone elsewhere. I don't know."

"Are there any other details you can think of to help find who killed him? Anything which has occurred to you in the intervening time?" Henry hoped that once the clerk's shock had worn off, and he had time to consider the situation, something might come to mind. Something. Anything.

"Unfortunately, no." He shook his head. "All seemed like business as usual until I arrived that morning to find the door locked."

"Thank you for your time, Mr. Weston. You have been helpful."

Locke had failed to mention the severity of the argument to Henry, but it could also have been a situation in which the disagreement had bothered one party more than the other, in this case, Norris.

An argument didn't prove guilt. And thus far, Henry had no way to tie the golden scarab to Locke or Locke to Norris's murder.

That meant only one thing: he had to keep looking.

Eighteen

AMELIA RETURNED THOUGHTFULLY TO her fertilizer experiment after Henry's departure, carefully measuring the various ingredients to add to the pots of soil before planting the pea seeds.

She had high hopes for the crushed eggshells. Surely the additional calcium carbonate—in addition to other minerals—would strengthen the cell walls of the plants? If so, it would also make good use of the shells rather than simply tossing them in the rubbish. Amelia hated waste. Though perhaps the used tea leaves would be better—Mrs. Appleton often watered the house plants with leftover tea, and they seemed to be thriving. It would be interesting to see if it helped the soil, too. It was all part of the experiment.

Amelia had left one pot with only the soil and a seed, which would serve as her control pot. To the next, she added the eggshells and water, stirring the mixture into the soil before adding the seed. The next one received the tea leaves in water. Finally, she carefully measured the ammonium nitrate and added it to distilled water then stirred to dissolve it before adding it to the soil of the last pot. She labeled each one and documented her efforts.

After further consideration, she added both tea leaves and eggshells to one more pot to see if those results would double.

Pleased with her morning's efforts, she placed the pots in a wood tray and set them near the window. She would measure the water she added every few days, so all were treated the same, and wait impatiently for results. Hopefully what she discovered would benefit the entire household by growing healthier plants, especially in the garden.

As she tidied the work area, her thoughts returned to Henry and the case. The welcome distraction of an experiment, which required her full attention, helped to settle her more than reading or embroidery, or any other typical feminine pursuit. She had found that setting aside a problem for a brief time allowed her to view it more objectively.

While she had no desire to cause problems for Randolph and Victoria Locke, neither did she approve of them selling illegal artifacts—and if Mr. Norris had been killed because of something they were involved in, she had no regrets helping to put an end to it.

What bothered her the most was the question of whether Matthew had been doing something similar. The list of items she and Fernsby had found wedged in the drawer had been...alarming. If she or Henry had found it soon after Matthew's death, however, would they have thought twice about it? She didn't think she would have, especially not with the cloud of grief hanging over her.

The sound of the front door closing and voices in the hall had her listening more closely. With a smile she finished up, returned her apron to its place, then descended the stairs just as her Aunt Margaret was climbing them.

"Good morning, dear." Aunt Margaret's smile as she waited near the drawing room doorway warmed her.

"How lovely of you to call." Amelia hugged her, genuinely pleased to see her.

Margaret Baldwin was Amelia's mother's unmarried younger sister who had only recently moved to London. She had stayed with Amelia for several weeks before Christmas. The woman's usual adventurous spirit had faded into a restless one which had frustrated Amelia during her stay. Though she had yet to offer an excuse or explanation for her discontent, joining a church whose members worked to aid the mudlarks had helped. Finding a purpose seemed to have soothed her, though Amelia would still like to know the cause of her unhappiness.

Not that she was foolish enough to ask directly, of course...

"Fernsby mentioned that you were working in your laboratory," Aunt Margaret said as she followed Amelia into the drawing room.

"I'm conducting an experiment with the hope of improving our garden." After all, her aunt wasn't the only one who needed a purpose.

"That's quite industrious of you."

"A practical use of my time, I suppose. Mrs. Appleton is quite anxious to hear the results prior to planting the garden this spring."

They settled into chairs before the fire as Fernsby arrived to place more coal on it, offered to return with tea which Amelia agreed to, then departed.

"How have you been?" Amelia asked, pleased to see she looked more like her former self. It had been over two weeks since her last visit.

"Well enough. The ladies in the church have proven quite distracting."

The admission caught Amelia's curiosity. "Were you in need of a distraction?" The question had slipped her lips before she could halt it, though she already knew the answer—but hoped her aunt would finally admit it.

Aunt Margaret sat back in her chair, smoothing the skirts of her gown as she seemed to gather her thoughts. "I do believe I was."

Surprise stilled Amelia. That was more than her aunt had ever previously admitted. She waited, hoping she'd share more, allowing silence to grow between them. Henry's techniques for questioning suspects often worked in normal conversation as well.

Her aunt glanced toward the fire, and Amelia released a quiet sigh of disappointment. Apparently she wasn't yet ready to discuss it.

"I believe I owe you an apology."

The quiet words had Amelia watching her aunt closely, uncertain what to say. "Oh?"

"You may remember that I accused you of taking a lover during my stay here."

Amelia's cheeks heated. She remembered that very well, mainly because the accusation had involved Henry. He'd come to her house after being injured by a pair of men, one of whom had stabbed him to warn him off in the mudlark case. Her aunt had heard him, though not the details of their conversation nor the reason for his presence, and made the astonishing accusation the following day.

"I-I do." While Amelia might admit her growing feelings for Henry to herself, she would never do the same out loud. It was too soon, and she wasn't ready to talk about how she felt, if she ever managed to understand it.

"I suppose I suspected you of doing so because I did."

Amelia barely managed to smother a gasp of surprise even though she'd suspected as much.

Her aunt's eyes closed, her expression pained, which tugged at Amelia. Pain was something with which she was familiar. "Suffice it to say...that it didn't end well."

"I'm so sorry." Amelia's heart went out to her. While the older woman acted as if she embraced her spinsterhood, clearly that wasn't the case. Why shouldn't she have the same hopes and dreams as other women, much like Amelia herself?

Marriage wasn't for everyone, but who didn't long for companionship and connection—and possibly love? Amelia still did, despite losing Lily and Matthew.

"Is there hope of..." Amelia wasn't sure how to ask the question, "a future?"

"No. He has left England."

That sounded rather permanent. "How disappointing."

Aunt Margaret's smile was a sad one. "Probably for the best."

Amelia had so many questions. How did they meet? What had Aunt Margaret hoped for? Why had he decided to leave? But she held back, waiting to see what her aunt would share.

"I had thought we were of the same mind." The sigh Aunt Margaret heaved spoke volumes. "We had been seeing one another for several months, and we had much in common."

"No wonder your hopes were high." Their relationship sounded as if it had indeed been promising. To have one's dreams crushed, after such hopes, was not for the faint of heart.

"I suppose." She met Amelia's gaze. "Unfortunately, I lent him money. A rather substantial sum."

"Oh, dear." Amelia's heart ached for her. To feel taken advantage of made the situation even worse. "Are you in need of funds?"

"No, though I don't believe I will be taking any trips in the near future." She scowled, clearly annoyed. "Suffice it to say that it has been a hurtful and embarrassing experience."

"I can only imagine."

"And when I heard Inspector Field downstairs that evening, I couldn't help but fear the same thing might be happening to you."

Amelia nodded. "Understandable. I appreciate your concern." An idea came to mind. "What if I mention the problem to Henry to see if he can pursue the man?"

Aunt Margaret's mouth gaped, eyes going wide. "Truly?"

"Why should the blackguard escape without recompense?" The more Amelia thought about it, the more she warmed to the idea. Justice. She would have it, one way or another. "Your kindness and affection shouldn't be punished by having your money stolen."

Her aunt tapped a finger on her chin as she considered the idea. "Allow me to think it over. Imagine his surprise to learn he is wanted by the police." She smiled, a gleam shining in her eyes. "That would give him his just deserts."

"I can't promise anything, but I do believe it would be worth an inquiry." Amelia knew from experience that feeling like a victim was most unpleasant. Taking action would be a way for her aunt to regain her confidence, not to mention her joy in life—a quality that had been missing for weeks. And maybe her money would be returned.

"I haven't shared any of this with your mother," her aunt said after a long moment.

"I will keep your confidence." It wasn't up to her to say more. Her aunt was a grown woman capable of making her own decisions.

"Thank you." Aunt Margaret heaved another sigh. "I don't think she would approve, not of any of it—but I suppose I feared it was my only chance to truly explore love. I had to take it."

Amelia reached to squeeze her hand. "As would most others in your position." She liked to think she would have been brave enough to do so as well. "Life provides opportunities. Why wouldn't we take them?"

The tightness in her aunt's expression eased. "Thank you for your understanding, and for putting up with my poor mood while I was here."

"We are all entitled to them."

"Mine lasted longer than it should have. I need only look at you and how you have managed to not just endure, but make your way forward despite your losses."

"Thank you. It isn't easy," she admitted. "In fact, it is often a daily battle."

"Which is why it's even more impressive." Her aunt gave a decisive nod. "And should you decide to explore a new relationship, I hope it brings you happiness."

Amelia's eyes widened as surprise gripped her, once again uncertain what to say. "I...I appreciate that."

Never mind that Henry's tall form with those broad shoulders and his warm smile came to mind. Her cheeks heated at the image. Luckily, Fernsby arrived with the tea tray, providing the perfect distraction.

"Now, tell me what you have been doing, other than your experiment." Her aunt frowned as she took the cup Amelia offered. "You haven't been involved in another case with that Inspector Field, have you?"

Amelia supposed there was no point in keeping it secret. "Unfortunately, a man I knew was murdered. A man who had been well acquainted with Matthew."

"Dear heavens."

"He was in the same business. I saw him last in November, when I visited his shop. Needless to say, the news of his death was quite shocking." Amelia sipped the hot tea as she gathered her thoughts.

"I can't imagine. What happened?"

"He was shot in his home in Gravesend."

"Terrible." Her aunt shook her head in dismay. "Did he have family?"

"Not immediate, though I understand he had distant relatives."

Aunt Margaret lifted a brow. "And is Inspector Field investigating?"

It was a far too knowing question. "He is. Since he knew I was familiar with the man, he wanted to keep me apprised of the situation."

Though it was tempting to add that this case could be connected to Matthew's, she held back. She had yet to share that information with her parents and needed to tell them first before she told anyone. Though she'd written them only yesterday, she hadn't mentioned the murder or the possible connection to Matthew's. It would be so much easier to share the news after it had been solved.

"He seems more than competent. I hope you soon have news of an arrest."

"As do I." Amelia cleared her throat, ready to change the subject. "Are you able to stay for luncheon?"

"I would enjoy that very much. I spoke with Agnes and Pudge yesterday, and they asked me to extend a greeting to you."

After Amelia advised Fernsby of the additional guest for luncheon, her aunt continued, sharing an update about the two girls who were former mudlarks. To hear they were thriving in school warmed Amelia's heart. She would visit them soon to see them for herself.

But not even the topic of Agnes and Pudge kept her thoughts from returning to the troubling question of whether Matthew had been selling stolen artifacts, and whether that had been the reason for his murder.

And she could only think of one person who might know.

Nineteen

Upon Aunt Margaret's departure soon after luncheon, Amelia took a hansom cab to Threadneedle Street where she alighted and paid the driver.

"Shall I wait, ma'am?" the man asked with a tip of his hat.

Though tempted to say yes, she didn't know how long she'd be. A waiting cab might draw more attention, which she preferred to avoid. Besides, there was a cab stand a short distance away.

"No, thank you."

The driver dipped his head and flicked the reins, pulling away from the curb and leaving her to closely survey the area. Though she had yet to discover anyone watching her, she hadn't forgotten what Mrs. Drake had said.

"It is not the law I fear."

Henry wouldn't be pleased when he learned of her intended mission, but she felt certain more could be discovered along the street, especially from Randolph Locke. Her visit with his wife had convinced her even more of that.

Did Locke know whether Matthew had been dealing in stolen artifacts? She intended to ask—and she felt compelled to warn him of the danger, even if it seemed unlikely that he would listen. She would convince him—after all, he had a wife and young children to consider. Then again, so had Matthew. Had Lily's death somehow compelled him to flaunt the law? To dabble in illegal items for the money?

Or worse, for the thrill?

She wanted—needed—to know.

Amelia drew a deep breath, hoping to dispel the nerves fluttering in her stomach. She hadn't done anything wrong, she reminded herself. But it seemed Mr. Locke very well might have done. Right was on her side, and she wanted a few answers that might provide some peace and ease her grief.

She opened the shop door, the bell heralding her arrival. A heavy silence was her only greeting as she slowly walked forward. That was all right, she told herself. It would give her time to look around a little more. She would look for the crate she'd seen before, or any others marked with Sable Importers. This time, she would take a closer look if given the chance.

The thought had Amelia tightening her lips as disapproval swept through her, a welcome reprieve from her nerves. Something was afoot, and she would discover precisely what it was. She continued past the barrels of goods and paused again to listen, puzzled that neither Mr. Locke nor his clerk had emerged from the back to greet her.

"Hello?" She looked toward the back where the narrow curtain separated the rear of the store from the front. "Mr. Locke, are you here?"

A soft moan sent chills chasing down her spine. What was that? She glanced around, trying to determine where the sound had come from.

"Mr. Locke?" she tried again and moved to the counter. Heart pounding and mouth dry, wishing she could leave but knowing she could not, she stepped around the end of it to see if anyone was behind it. The space was empty.

The sound must have come from the rear of the shop.

With quick steps, Amelia walked toward the back and drew the curtain aside—only to be shoved hard.

"Out of my way," a man growled.

Amelia was sent careening into a nearby set of shelves, the corner of one catching her painfully in the ribs. Hands flailing, she managed to catch herself before tumbling to the floor. Side hurting like the devil, she blinked after the stranger who'd pushed her as he rushed out the front door, looked both ways, then ran down the street and out of sight.

Before she could even consider pursuit, another muffled groan sounded. She drew back the curtain with shaking hands to see—Randolph Locke. Randolph Locke sprawled on the floor, eyes closed, blood staining the front of the apron he wore.

"Mr. Locke!" Amelia rushed to kneel beside him. "Randolph." Her heart thundered as she tried to think of what to do—or how to help. "Dear heavens."

Blood pooled beneath him, shouting the severity of the wound.

"Hold on, Randolph." She gripped his shoulder, wanting to lend him strength and reassure him that someone was at his side. Her breath shuddered as fear threatened to take hold, and she gave herself a stern reprimand to think.

This was no time for emotion, but for action.

Her hands fluttered over his body as she tried to determine how best to aid him. With jerky movements, she folded the bottom of the apron into a pad of sorts to press against his stomach, hoping to staunch the bleeding.

Based on the blood pooling near her on the floor, she feared it might be too late.

"Randolph, can you hear me?" Amelia swallowed against the lump in her throat, eyes filling with tears.

His eyes opened briefly, his brow creasing as he seemed to recognize her. "M-Matthew..."

Amelia gasped as she continued to hold the apron against the wound. "Yes? What about Matthew?"

Locke's eyes drifted closed, and his head lolled to the side.

"Randolph!" She touched his cheek with a gloved hand but he didn't respond. His chest remained still even as a terrible knowledge swept over her.

He couldn't possibly be dead.

"I'm getting help," she told him and jerked to her feet.

She ran through the shop and out the door, hands covered with blood, filled with panic as she glanced up and down the street. "Help! Someone help, please!"

Twenty

THE FAINT SOUND OF someone shouting for help had Henry rising from where he sat at Norris's desk to rush toward the shop door.

This was an instinct he always heeded.

He'd spent the past hour looking through the desk and studying the ledger again, all with the hope of finding evidence or a clue now that he better knew what to look for. The clerk had departed some time ago, and Henry had been about to pause to find something to eat—when he heard the cry for help.

The desperation in the feminine call had him out the door in a thrice, glancing up and down the street, utterly stunned to see a terrified Amelia with bloody gloved hands raised before her a few shops away.

Fear threatened to choke him even as her gaze latched onto his. "Henry—Henry, come quick!" She gestured toward Locke's shop. Surely she hadn't been inside—

Henry ran to her even as he searched her form for an injury. "Are you all right?"

"Y-Yes. But L-Locke..." Her entire body trembled, eyes flickering between him and the door, clearly shocked by whatever had occurred.

Knees weak with relief, he put an arm around her to guide her back inside. Based on the amount of blood on her gloves, he had to assume the worst.

Thank goodness she appeared unharmed.

"Tell me what happened," he said as they entered the shop, already searching for the problem but not seeing anything that looked out of place.

"A man." She shook her head as if in disbelief. "H-He hurt R-Randolph." She pointed to the back. "There."

"Wait here." No point would be served in her seeing the injured man again when she was already upset, regardless of his condition.

Henry hurried to the back, moving aside the curtain to find an unmoving Locke on the floor, eyes closed, blood on his apron as well as in a large pool beside him. Henry knelt to check for a pulse but found none.

Damn.

"Is he truly...?" Amelia's quivering voice had him looking over his shoulder to see her staring at Locke's body, her eyes wide.

"Dead, I'm sorry to say."

His eyes raked over the man, noting the folded apron soaked with blood on his stomach. Obviously Amelia had done her best, fruitlessly, to stop the bleeding. Henry lifted it to see what appeared to be a stab wound, then lowered it before standing to block her view.

Shock had already taken hold and staring at the body wouldn't help Amelia. She still held her hands before her as if part of her was aware of the blood that covered them.

"What happened?" Henry asked, his voice calm and quiet as he reached to peel off her soiled gloves.

Her gaze darted about the room. "I-I came to speak with him. No one was in the shop, and I...I called out." She blinked several times, clearly attempting to gather her thoughts. "Someone m-moaned, and I followed the sound b-back here. When I drew back the curtain, a man shoved me and ran out."

Henry's blood chilled at the danger she'd been in. "You saw the man who did this?" He tossed the gloves aside and took her cold hands in his to warm them, offering what little comfort he could. Dear God, she had been so close to danger...

Amelia frowned and shook her head. "Not really. It happened so fast." Her breath came in shuddering gasps, lifting an elbow to glance at her side. "I fell into the shelves, so I didn't get a good look at him. Then he was gone."

"Can you describe him?"

After another shuddering breath, she said, "Brown hair. His face was tanned as if he spends time out of doors." She shook her head. "It was all just a blur—that's all I saw—I'm s-sorry, I—"

"Amelia." He gave in to the urge and wrapped her in his arms to hold her tight. "You must've been terrified."

She nodded against his shoulders, her uneven breathing making it clear she was holding back tears.

He rubbed a hand slowly over her back, hoping to lend her some of his strength.

After several seconds, she drew a shuddering breath and sniffed. "He...he was alive when I arrived."

Henry drew back to look at her but kept his hold. "Locke was?"

"Yes. Barely. I t-tried to staunch the bleeding."

"I see that. Amelia, there is nothing you could have done," he began, not wanting her to feel at fault for not saving him.

She nodded. "There was so much blood." She stared, unseeing, up at him, brown eyes swimming with tears. "He said Matthew's name."

Henry stilled, trying to understand. *Matthew.* "What else?"

"That was it. He just said 'Matthew' and then he was gone." She shook her head, a single tear running down her cheek as she swallowed. "I don't understand. What could he have meant?"

"I don't know." He could think of a few possibilities, though none of them boded well, and he wasn't about to share them with Amelia. Not now, at any rate.

She straightened as she glanced around the room as if in search of something. "Who would kill Randolph, and why?"

"I will do my best to answer both those questions."

Amelia drew another breath, this one steadier, as her attention returned to Henry. "His wife and children. Poor Victoria, she is going to be devastated."

Her empathy for the woman shouldn't surprise him, but it did. She was always thinking of others even though few could have endured what she herself had been through.

"I will call on her myself to tell her the news," he reassured her. Advising loved ones of their tragic loss was the least favorite part of his job, but he hoped he did it with empathy and respect. That was all he could offer in most cases.

"Thank you." Amelia nodded and straightened. "Should I find someone to fetch a constable?"

He hesitated, wanting only to see her home—but he couldn't leave Locke unattended, and Amelia couldn't be left with him after what she'd been through. Maybe she'd do better if she had a task on which to focus. "That would be helpful. If you feel up to it."

Her expression firmed as she nodded, which helped reassure him that she would be all right. She was stronger than he knew—than she knew.

"I will see what I can do." Her shoes tapped determinedly across the floor as she walked toward the door, the bell soon announcing her departure.

With a heavy sigh, Henry turned to more thoroughly examine the scene. Better that he focus on Locke's murder than his worry for Amelia.

He checked the man's stomach again, only finding one wound, but the knife had obviously struck vital organs. Locke's hands and face didn't show any sign of a struggle except for torn skin on one knuckle. Arthur would confirm the details once he completed his examination.

Finding the primary suspect of a murder investigation dead was a problem. A serious problem. It shook Henry's confidence in his own skills, a stark reminder that he was *not* a true Field.

Could he himself be at fault once again, at least indirectly? Had Randolph Locke been killed because, perhaps like Norris, someone had noted Henry's inquiries and thought the shop owner might tell him something incriminating?

It was a most disconcerting thought.

Henry rose and looked around the small space, hoping for a clue. A simple desk was tucked in one corner, and a worn, scarred table sat on the opposite side with several crates on it. The room was stacked with a few barrels and boxes on shelves. Whether the items awaited unpacking to be placed on the shop floor or were goods that were broken or hadn't sold, he didn't know.

In truth, it wasn't so different from Norris's back room and appeared to be equally unorganized, at least to Henry's eye. He looked over the items, but nothing stood out. None of the crates contained anything unusual from his cursory look. No items were near the body to provide a clue, either. No murder weapon—but the killer must have taken that with him.

The clerk was noticeably absent, but from what Locke had said, the man only worked part-time, the owner often working the shop by himself...and it would be easier to handle stolen artifacts without a witness.

Where had the crate gone that Amelia had seen? Another look around didn't reveal it, nor were any of the others stamped with Sable Importers.

The bell sounded once again, and he drew back the curtain to see Amelia returning.

"A lad is fetching a constable, though I don't know how long it might take."

"Thank you." Henry stepped out of the back, preferring to keep Amelia away so as not to worsen her distress. "Why don't we fetch a cab so you can return home?"

He'd prefer to escort her there himself, but that was unlikely to happen any time soon.

"I-I'd rather stay. At least for a little longer." She held his gaze, which helped to reassure him that she was regaining her balance. "I know you will be occupied, but I would prefer to remain with you for a while." Her brow puckered as she fought back her upset. "I-I suppose I'm not ready to return home where my thoughts might get the best of me."

He reached to squeeze her arm, touched to know she wanted to be with him. Then again, maybe she simply didn't want to be alone. Who would? "Of course. Just let me know when you're ready and I will help you find a cab."

"Thank you."

"I'm going to lock Norris's shop and will return directly. Then I intend to take a closer look around. Will you watch for the constable?" he asked.

"Of course."

Nearly ten minutes later, Henry looked up from the crate he had opened in the back of Locke's shop as Amelia called out. A constable approached.

He joined her to see a familiar form striding towards them. "It's Dannon." Henry nodded in relief. The man was good at his job and had proven helpful in the past. "Excuse me a moment." He stepped out to greet the constable and explain the situation.

"A stabbing on Threadneedle Street, in the middle of the day?" Dannon shook his head. "What is the world coming to?"

"Quite." Henry glanced through the window to see Amelia watching them. "You remember Mrs. Greystone?"

"Of course." The constable had the unfortunate experience of being struck on the head while keeping watch on the front steps of her house last November. He nodded and smiled to greet her through the window, an expression she returned.

"She had the poor luck of discovering the victim."

"As if she needs more challenges in her life." The constable's sympathetic gaze returned briefly to Amelia before he looked at Henry. "How can I help, sir?"

"We will need a dogcart to take the body to St. Thomas'."

"Of course. I'll find one then return to assist."

"Thank you."

Henry returned inside to take another look around the crime scene, leaving Amelia by the front door to keep watch once again, but he didn't find anything of note. The dogcart arrived in quick order, and though Henry suggested Amelia venture elsewhere while they hauled out the body, she declined.

He didn't quite know what to think of her. Did she hope to prove how strong she was? Did such circumstances no longer bother her? Or did she do it out of respect for Randolph Locke and to honor the friendship he and her late husband had shared?

Even as the questions ran through his mind, he knew the latter was the reason.

Amelia remained to honor both the Lockes and Mr. Greystone, even though no one but her would know. No one but her, and Henry.

He was touched as he watched her lips move as if in silent prayer as they carried Locke out of the shop. Despite the fact that he was helping to haul out the body, Henry said his own silent prayer—not for Locke, but the woman who looked on and the family the victim left behind.

The case was growing more dangerous by the moment, and he hated that Amelia was involved. If the killer decided she had recognized him, she was in even more danger now.

He would do everything in his power to protect her.

He only hoped that would be enough.

Twenty-One

As the afternoon waned, Amelia knew the time had come for her to go home. Fernsby would be wondering where she was, yet the idea of returning to her empty house was less than appealing—unbearable, in fact. She knew her thoughts would circle and result in a long, lonely evening and an even longer sleepless night.

Remaining in the shop allowed her to think she could be helpful. It prevented her from wondering what more she could have done to save Mr. Locke.

As she had several times before, Amelia closed her eyes, trying to remember the man who'd shoved her. She had been face-to-face with the killer yet could offer little to describe him. How could she be of assistance to Henry when she recalled so few details? What sort of detective's assistant—unofficial, of course—could she claim to be when she remembered next to nothing?

Amelia heaved a sigh of frustration as her efforts to picture the killer produced so little. Henry and Constable Dannon were in the back room, their voices a low, comforting murmur. The front door had been locked and the small wooden plaque turned to advise potential customers the shop was closed. With a glance around, she decided to try to make herself useful in some way.

The memory of the mysterious crate she'd noted during her earlier visit came to mind. She had already perused the shop without finding another crate, or anything that resembled the gold necklace she'd seen. Perhaps there was a list somewhere that cataloged the items? That might prove helpful.

Though it seemed more likely that any such list would be kept with the other records in the back, she couldn't bring herself to return there. Nor did she want to interrupt Henry and Constable Dannon. That left the front counter. Better that she lent ineffective aid than merely stood motionless, berating herself for what she hadn't done.

She moved around the end of the counter and walked along the length of it, searching for any papers that recorded inventory. Strange; the space wasn't so different from Matthew's. Though she hadn't spent significant time in her late husband's shop, Amelia remembered the layout and this one appeared similar.

The center of the long counter tended to be where important items were stowed to keep them safe, away from the prying eyes of shop patrons. She paused there and bent low to see several rows of narrow shelves which housed a ball of string, scissors, and brown paper to wrap wares. A few broken items from the shop floor were on another shelf. She kept looking and finally found several small stacks of papers.

She pulled them out and studied each one, disappointed to find they were invoices and correspondence but not for anything of interest. With a frustrated sigh, she bent down to search again, wondering if she'd missed a clue.

Methodically going through one shelf at a time, she continued the search, emptying each one before returning the contents to their place. A folded paper caught her eye, and she opened it to see a list of items that looked vaguely familiar.

It took a moment before she realized why. *Oh, goodness.* The list brought to mind the one she had found in Matthew's desk the previous day, mainly because the handwriting looked similar. The loops of the l, the curl of the g... And the descriptions of the items did as well.

A sinking sensation filled Amelia, weighing her down much like a stone thrown into a pond. She had to presume that Matthew had done something similar to Locke—selling what were most likely illicit artifacts.

How could she have been married to a man, shared a life including a child, but not known who he truly was or what he might be capable of?

Amelia closed her eyes. What a terrible wife she'd been. So distant, so withdrawn after Lily's death. In truth, she and Matthew had been growing apart even before then—but had her lack of awareness of how Matthew felt been part of the reason he'd chosen to pursue illegal activities? If she had been *more*—a better wife, a better lover, a better friend—would it have changed his choices?

More importantly, would it have saved his life?

The weight of that question pressed on Amelia's chest, making it impossible for her lungs to take in air. Panic took hold as the sensation worsened. She reached for the counter as the shop slowly darkened, her vision narrowing.

"Amelia?" Henry's voice pierced the fog smothering her. "Amelia, are you well?"

She couldn't move, couldn't respond, couldn't cry out. She was suffocating, drowning in her own body—

The feel of Henry's warm hand on her arm was welcome, yet still she couldn't draw a breath. The darkness surrounding her only deepened.

He pushed her head down. "Breathe," he demanded.

Blood rushed into her head, and the vise that had gripped her lungs loosened. She gasped like a swimmer coming up for air, and she took comfort in the feel of Henry's arms supporting her.

"That's it," he murmured. "Stay down and take another breath. Slower this time. As deeply as you can."

She did as he instructed, her head clearing. "Oh...oh dear," she said as Henry assisted her to straighten. "I don't know what happened." She pressed a hand to her still thudding heart, hoping to regain her wits as she continued several more deep breaths.

"It has been a trying day."

Amelia's face heated under his close regard. What must he think of her? "I suppose it has."

"You were so pale," Henry whispered, his brow furrowed with concern. "Are you sure you feel better?"

"Quite." She gave a single nod, as much to convince herself as him.

"Would you like to sit down?" He glanced around as if in search of a chair.

"No, I'm fine now." She didn't know the answers to her questions, but she would do what she could to find them. "And I found something."

"Oh?" He took the paper she offered and reviewed it. "This looks similar to—"

"Yes." She bit her lip as concern once again took hold. "What do you think it means?"

"That is a good question. Where did you find it?"

She pointed to the shelf. "There doesn't seem to be anything else of interest in them."

To her surprise, Henry's focus returned to her, his brown eyes dark with concern. "I am going to find you a cab—no arguments. It's time for you to go home and rest."

In truth, she did feel rather weak. "A cup of tea would be welcome."

"That is an excellent idea." He smiled, the empathy in his expression suggesting he didn't think less of her even though she'd nearly fainted. "Thank you for this." He put the paper in his pocket. "I shall compare it to the other one to see if it offers a clue."

"Good." She only hoped he would share the results.

"Dannon?" Henry called.

"Yes, sir?" The constable emerged from the rear of the shop.

"Mrs. Greystone is in need of a ride home, this very moment."

"Allow me to locate one."

In short order, Amelia was settled in a cab. Henry gave the driver her address and paid for her fare, a kind and unnecessary gesture she nonetheless appreciated.

"I will try to stop by after I'm done for the day to see how you're faring," Henry said as he held the door. "But if you need rest, retire for the evening. Don't wait for me."

"Please do come to call." Amelia was almost embarrassed by how quickly she latched onto the offer, but couldn't bring herself to care. "I would appreciate it." She managed a smile. "And bring Leopold if you can. We are looking forward to meeting him."

He reached into the cab to squeeze her hand. "I will do my best. I'll see you soon."

The ride home passed in a blur and soon she was alighting before her residence. It came as no surprise that her legs trembled as she walked up the front steps.

The door thankfully opened before she could reach for it.

"Madam, I was growing worried about you," Fernsby said urgently. After he closed the door behind her, he studied her face for a moment, brow creased. "Forgive me for mentioning it, but you look rather pale. Is all well?"

"No. Not really." She pressed a hand to her mouth as the events of the day came flooding back, bringing tears to her eyes. "Mr...Mr. Locke was killed in his shop today."

"Oh, no. How awful." Fernsby shook his head as he assisted her to remove her cloak and hat, his well-practiced hands a comfort to her.

"Indeed. Horrible."

The older man stilled. "You were nearby?"

"I was."

"Mrs. Greystone. That must've been terrifying." He watched her again, his obvious concern helping to warm her. "Would a hot bath be in order? Perhaps followed by a rest in the drawing room, and some strong tea?"

Amelia could already feel her shoulders relaxing at the very thought. "That sounds perfect, Fernsby. Thank you."

He dipped his head. "I will send Yvette up, and should you wish to speak further about the day, I would be pleased to hear it."

Amelia smiled, the ache in her heart easing. He always seemed to know the right thing to say. She was blessed to have him and the rest of the staff to lean on. "Thank you."

That evening she listened for a knock at the front door, but it didn't come until well after dinner. The sound was quiet, as was Henry's voice as he spoke with Fernsby. Had he thought she already retired for the night?

She might have been tempted to do so if not for his offer to come by. She was exhausted, despite having spent the remainder of the afternoon and evening with an unread book before the fire. Her side was bruised and sore from where she'd hit the shelves, but it could have been much worse. Not even spending time in her laboratory or working on her latest assignment for the periodical sounded appealing. Yet neither did she care for the constant replay of the day's events in her mind. She wanted to see but one man.

Amelia watched the doorway, anxious for Henry's solid presence, and released a relieved breath when he appeared.

"Good evening, Amelia." He came forward, hat in hand and still wearing his coat, clearly not intending to remain long.

The realization dimmed her joy at seeing him.

"Thank you for coming by." She didn't rise but gestured toward the chair near hers before the fire. "Please. Sit. You must be tired after such a long day."

He sank into the chair and nodded as he watched her. "It has been a challenging one."

She bit her lip, hating to ask but unable not to. "Did you...speak with Victoria Locke?"

"I did." His gaze shifted to the fire, making her wonder if he was trying to hide any hint of what happened in an effort to protect her. "Needless to say, she was shocked."

Amelia nodded even though he didn't look at her. She well remembered Henry delivering the news of Matthew's death as if it were yesterday. The terrible shock and disbelief she'd felt. How she had only understood half of what he had said. Henry had been so kind that day, going so far as to offer to tell her parents and Fernsby so she did not have to. Listening to his attempt to tell Maeve, the ravenkeeper's daughter, of her father's murder, had been painful as well, especially since the girl was deaf and mute. He was indeed a brave, honorable man.

"I don't know how you do it," she whispered, trying to rein in her emotions as the memories took hold.

"It is never easy."

"Did Victoria have any idea who might have done it?"

At that question, his focus returned to her—probably because she was the one who'd seen the man. "No. She was rather cross that we hadn't immediately caught whoever it was."

Amelia could well imagine Victoria being angry. That was how some people dealt with unfortunate news.

"I have tried to remember more," she said, feeling terrible that she couldn't. "But those moments were such a blur."

"Do you mind if we review the details? To see if a few questions might help?"

The kindness and respect in his tone made it impossible to refuse. "Please." Amelia clasped her hands in her lap to brace herself, knowing it would be unpleasant. "I want to help, however I can."

Henry slowly smiled, the approval in his brown eyes easing her upset. "You never fail to surprise me with your strength."

Her breath caught at the admiration in his eyes. She hadn't been strong earlier, and she did not feel particularly strong now, but she appreciated him not holding that against her.

"Now then. You heard a moan coming from the back of the shop. Is that right?" He waited until she nodded. "You moved in that direction."

"Yes. Then...then I reached for the curtain and the man rushed out, pushing me aside."

Henry stood and set his hat on the low table then offered his hand. "Do you mind?"

She took it and rose, wincing at her sore side, uncertain of what he intended, a flicker of unexpected disappointment searing through her when he released her.

"Do you think he was taller or shorter than me?"

Amelia studied Henry, noting the top of her head barely reached his chin. "Shorter." She held up a hand to where she thought the man had reached, about to Henry's nose.

"Good. And how was he dressed? Perhaps in a brown or black coat?"

"Brown. With a hat. A bit like yours but worn. A wool jacket, not a fine one but…"

"More working class."

"Yes."

"Did he wear spectacles?"

Amelia hesitated, but it was clearer now. "No. No, he had fine lines around his eyes and looked to be in his late thirties, early forties, perhaps?" Relief filled her that she'd remembered that much. It was much more than she'd been able to tell him earlier.

"Very good." Henry held out his arms from his sides. "Was he big? Fat? Or rather skinny?"

"Thickset, I suppose. Not fat but solid."

"Clean shaven?"

"Yes. I think that's why I noticed he looked almost tanned, though he could have been Italian or Spanish."

"Any scars or marks on his face? Anything that would distinguish him?"

She thought back, trying to remember. The vagueness of the image in her mind seemed to have filled in as Henry questioned her. "He had a small, hook-shaped scar just below the outside corner of his eye. Whiter than the rest of his face. Jagged looking. On the side closest to me."

"His right side."

"Yes. I...I think he did anyway." She hoped she wasn't imagining it. Was that possible, for the mind to fill in the gaps?

"Well done. That is all helpful." Henry paused, his gaze holding hers. "Did he say anything?"

"Something like, 'get out of my way.' Then he pushed me."

"Was his voice gruff, deep, or high-pitched?"

"Gruff, I think—though he kind of growled the words."

"Do you think you would recognize him if you saw him again?"

She closed her eyes, wishing she could say yes. "I don't know. I'm just not sure. I have more of an impression of him than an actual image, if that makes sense."

Henry took one of her hands in his. "Amelia, you must promise me not to return to Threadneedle Street."

"But I—"

"If there's the chance you could identify him, he might recognize you in turn. You could be in grave danger."

Amelia stared at Henry as fear crawled down her spine. For some reason, the idea hadn't occurred to her, perhaps because she didn't want it to be a possibility.

"I don't mean to frighten you," Henry continued, his gaze holding hers, "but I want you to take every precaution possible until we find him."

"Very well." She detested the idea of living in fear again as she had after Matthew had died. But she had endured it then, and again when the ravenkeeper's daughter had stayed with her, and could do so once more.

"I've already requested a constable to keep watch. Don't be alarmed if you see him outside."

"Thank you." She lifted her chin, not wanting him to worry. "We will remain vigilant."

"Good." Henry nodded as he released her hand. "I will have a word with Fernsby on my way out." He paused a moment. "Are you certain you feel up to dealing with Leopold?"

A meow echoed in the foyer as if the cat had heard its name.

The sound brought a smile to her face. "I am. I've been looking forward to meeting him."

"He seemed to immediately warm to Fernsby, and vice versa."

"I'm so pleased to hear that. And more than a little relieved," she said with another smile.

Henry leaned closer to whisper, "As was I."

Amelia laughed. "I will walk you out so I can be formally introduced." It would be nice to have extra company this evening, and the cat would be a welcome distraction.

She could only hope that the nightmares which had plagued her after Matthew's violent death would not return...

Twenty-Two

THE FOLLOWING MORNING HENRY provided an update to Director Reynolds, who was less than pleased to have another murder investigation on their hands. So was Henry, especially when he worried if he was once again to blame.

Luckily, the director hadn't jumped to that conclusion.

Yet Henry couldn't set aside the fact that he'd spent more time interviewing Locke than the other shopkeepers on the street...with the chilling exception of Norris. Had Henry's inquiries made both men targets? Or did their deaths have to do with the selling of illegal artifacts in which they were somehow entangled?

A collector might have taken offense to something Locke or Norris did, or the killer could be the person who provided them with the items, or something else entirely.

Was Locke's death connected to Norris's or Greystone's?

And most importantly, how could Henry protect Amelia? Having a constable keep watch didn't seem like enough, but there were hardly any men to spare.

Henry asked Reynolds if he knew anything about Edgarton, but the director couldn't add anything beyond what Inspector Duncan had already told him. How unfortunate.

"Field, you seem to be in a foul mood this morning." Perdy sidled up to Henry's desk as the latter tidied his files in preparation of leaving. "I see you met with Director Reynolds. Does that mean you are struggling on a case yet again?"

Henry held back an angry retort. He might be frustrated with the investigation as well as the way Perdy had handled the Douglas Grant case, but now wasn't the time to stir the pot. "All is as well as can be expected. What of you, Perdy?" Henry glanced about the mostly empty office. "You seem to be one of the few at a loose end. Are your skills not needed on any cases?"

The other man scowled. "I have plenty of cases. No need for you to worry." He leaned closer with a smirk. "Should the Director ask me to provide you with assistance a second time, I will do my best to do so, despite my workload."

Henry managed a brief smile. "No need to concern yourself. That won't happen after the disaster you caused on the ravenkeeper's case."

Perdy sputtered, filling Henry with grim satisfaction. "How was I to know the repairman wasn't who he claimed to be?"

Henry shook his head and reached for his hat. "I will allow you to think upon that further. Meanwhile, I have an investigation to conduct." He started to leave, only to turn back. Perhaps now was the perfect time to stir the pot, after all. "What do you remember about the Douglas Grant investigation?"

"Who?" Perdy frowned.

"Murder case about two years ago. The victim was shot in the temple."

The other inspector nodded slowly. "Can't imagine why you're bringing that one up." His scowl suggested he didn't like it. "Happened in a rookery. Hardly a place to find believable witnesses, and Grant was a convicted criminal with a long record of offenses."

"He was still a man who was murdered. The case was closed rather quickly, and without an arrest." Henry ignored the few other men in the office who had paused what they were doing to listen. He didn't care who heard the conversation.

Perdy's eyes narrowed even as his face reddened—whether that was a result of anger or embarrassment, Henry didn't know, nor did he care. "Got nothing better to do with your time than dig through my old files? Good. Maybe you can learn something."

Henry did his best to ignore the spurt of anger the comment caused. "The case might very well be related to my current investigation. I must say, I am puzzled as to why you made so few inquiries. Murder cases are usually pursued a little more thoroughly." Though he didn't expect a helpful response, he had to say it.

"Why bother wasting time on the death of a criminal?" Perdy started to turn away, clearly done with the conversation.

But Henry, as he put on his hat, was not. "Everyone deserves justice. Now it looks as if the killer has struck several times since then—an earlier arrest may have saved lives. And isn't it odd that Johnson had such difficulty finding the file?"

Perdy's expression tightened, anger glinting in his eyes. "What are you suggesting, Field?"

"I am not suggesting anything. I am saying you should do your job like the rest of us instead of lounging at your desk and flinging insults." With that he took his leave, only to see Director Reynolds watching from his office doorway.

Henry nodded at his superior, not caring if he had heard, though he couldn't deny a certain amount of relief not to be called into his office to discuss what had happened.

The moment he was out of Scotland Yard, he blew out a breath and rubbed a hand along his forehead, but it did little to ease his growing headache, especially after that conversation.

With a shift of his shoulders he adjusted his hat, done with Perdy as well as the questions that continued to circle in his mind.

No more questions. He needed answers.

His first stop was St. Thomas' to see what Arthur could offer. Hopefully by now, the surgeon had examined Locke's body. Though knowing the type of blade used didn't seem as if it would help, he wasn't about to ignore any evidence he could gather.

Luck seemed to be with him for a change as Arthur was in his office, working on a report rather than elbow-deep in blood.

"Morning, Henry." He gestured toward the nearby empty chair. "You've come by bright and early."

"Funny how having a second murder investigation does that to a person."

"Just the two?" Arthur put down his pencil and leaned back in his chair, half-joking based on his smile.

"Well, two recent—but four in total if you want to be specific." The pressure to solve them had Henry shifting in his seat.

"I can see they've put you in a less-than-dapper mood." Arthur offered a sympathetic look. "Understandable, when the bodies seem to keep piling up."

"Yes, sorry to be short. I confess that the investigation has proven frustrating when the only result thus far is another victim."

Arthur's eyes narrowed. "You think this one and the shooting are related?"

"I do, despite the difference in weapon choices. They might not be the same killer, but they are connected. I'm hoping you might have some sort of clue for me."

"I wish I did," Arthur sorted through several papers and pulled out one. "Based on the wound penetration, I would estimate a four-inch blade. The victim was facing his attacker who stabbed him in the abdomen, perforating the intestines, before drawing the blade upward."

"To do more damage?" Henry suggested.

Arthur nodded. "More than likely. It suggests a certain familiarity with the weapon. That move caused the blade to slice into the stomach and liver. The victim died from blood loss, though sadly organ failure would have quickly followed."

Henry nodded, wondering whether he should tell Amelia again that there was nothing she could've done to save Locke. He hoped she didn't still blame herself.

"I would add that there was little to no sign of struggle as you probably already noted yourself."

"Yes." Henry pondered the reason. "Makes me think the knife came as a surprise."

"He certainly appeared to be stabbed before he had time to react."

Henry could envision it. Men like Randolph Locke didn't seem the type to expect foul play. Not the murderous kind at any rate. They anticipated being able to discuss differences of opinion, to negotiate their way out of difficult situations. Henry tended to think Greystone and Norris had been of a similar mind as well.

"It speaks of a lack of patience on the killer's behalf," Henry mused. "He didn't like whatever Locke said, so killed him."

"That makes sense. I will send the report as soon as it's completed." Arthur lifted his hands, palms up, before returning them to his desk. "I don't have any other observations that might prove helpful."

"Unfortunately, neither do I." Henry stood. "Thank you for the information, Arthur. I appreciate it."

"Good luck. It sounds as if you will need it for this one."

Henry departed, deciding to stop by the Yard one more time to see if Fletcher was there and whether he was available to aid him.

As if he'd conjured the sergeant with his thoughts, he appeared from around a corner walking in Henry's direction, much to Henry's relief.

"Morning," Fletcher said when he joined Henry.

"Fletcher. Good to see you." Henry wondered if the man was alarmed by his enthusiastic greeting, but it didn't matter. He was more than happy to see the sergeant, who'd spent the previous day working with another inspector. "Are you occupied again today with other duties?"

"Not that I know of." He lifted a brow. "Do you have need of me?"

"I do." Henry paused to hold his friend's gaze. "Randolph Locke was killed yesterday."

"What? And here I thought he might be our man." Fletcher turned to accompany Henry down the street.

"As did I." Henry shared the circumstances, including Amelia's involvement.

"Poor Mrs. Greystone. How terrible for her." Fletcher shook his head.

"Needless to say, she was quite distraught." That she'd nearly fainted concerned him. Henry wasn't certain what had caused the moment. The only reason he could think of was her discovering the list that resembled the one she'd found in her late husband's desk. Why would that cause her upset when finding Locke and watching him die hadn't? Or had the events of the day finally caught up to her, suddenly becoming overwhelming?

"Was she able to describe the man?"

"Yes, but not until she had a chance to think about it." He shared the details which she'd told him. "It happened quickly, and the man shoved her before she got a good look. She's not certain if she'll be able to identify him."

"Unfortunate." Fletcher frowned. "It seems as if I missed all the excitement."

"I have the feeling more is yet to come." Henry could almost guarantee it, worse luck. "A constable is keeping watch over her home just in case."

"What is our plan to proceed with the investigation?"

"Return to Threadneedle Street to see if anyone recognizes the description Mrs. Greystone gave, for a start."

"Very well. What else?"

What else indeed? What else was there to do? "Another look at the crime scene. Somewhere there has to be evidence of the Egyptian artifacts he was selling. I want to know who sold them to Locke, as well as who Locke's customers were. Surely he'd keep a record of who bought what so he could contact them again if more items arrived?"

"Nothing found thus far?" Fletcher's eyes narrowed as if he considered other possibilities.

"One list of what might be artifacts, but it didn't have any names. I asked Constable Dannon to advise Locke's assistant of his death and have him come to the shop this morning. I just hope he knows something." Henry paused, catching Fletcher's gaze. "Mrs. Greystone found a similar list in her late husband's desk that appears to be in the same handwriting."

Fletcher's steps slowed, his surprise clear. "Truly?" At Henry's nod, he continued forward at a steady pace. "So Greystone was doing something similar before his death."

"It seems that could be the case."

"If so, how does Norris's murder fit in?"

Henry had given that question much thought during the night, which partly accounted for his headache. "Given the Egyptian scarab hidden in his chair, perhaps he found out about the illegal items. Joined them in their enterprise."

"Why did he have just the one? You would think that if he were involved, he would've had several artifacts. And why at his home?"

"Perhaps he took it from Locke and that was behind their disagreement." Henry shook his head. "But it doesn't make sense. The timing still seems off for that to be the case."

Fletcher watched a passing rider before looking back at Henry. "And it would suggest Locke killed Norris, which seems less likely now that Locke is dead."

Henry sighed, hating to admit that Fletcher was right. "I spoke briefly with Director Reynolds this morning. He's not happy about having another murder case." He could already feel more pressure to find the killer. "The constable who patrols near Spitalfields said the building I saw is now empty and no longer guarded."

"So maybe they moved the goods, or that location has nothing to do with any of this."

"Either could be true," Henry admitted.

Fletcher scoffed. "Or neither."

"Yes," Henry reluctantly agreed. Just when he thought they were gaining ground, it gave way beneath them. "Once again we seem to have more questions than answers."

"Isn't it funny how often that seems to be true?"

"I'm not certain funny is the right word." However, he appreciated the sergeant's attempt at levity. "Frustrating might better suit."

"True." His friend remained silent as they crossed a busy street. "Was Locke's widow able to offer any information?"

"Most definitely not. She seems only eager to find someone to blame."

"Understandable."

"Hmm." Henry couldn't help but compare how Amelia had dealt with the news of her husband's murder to Victoria Locke's reaction. The two were like night and day. "Definitely an angry widow."

"Everyone copes with such upset differently—though anger doesn't usually come until after some of the sadness passes."

"I will return for another visit with her either later today or tomorrow. There's always the chance she remembered something. And I want to look at her husband's study as well."

"Good idea. He had to have kept record of his activities somewhere."

Once they arrived at Threadneedle Street, they parted ways to question those who worked in the area, hoping someone knew of a man with a crescent-shaped scar. Henry knew it was too much to expect but was still disappointed that no one thought the description sounded familiar.

"Any luck?" Fletcher asked nearly an hour later.

Henry shook his head. "No. I'm trying to decide what that means."

His sergeant considered the question in his thoughtful way. "Maybe no one knew of him other than Locke."

"Possible. He could be the supplier of the Egyptian artifacts and took issue with something Locke did, and killed him for it."

"Logical." Fletcher nodded. "Based on Mrs. Greystone's impression that he didn't wear a fancy suit, it seems doubtful he was one of the collectors looking to purchase, which leaves us with the other end of the chain."

"Finding who brought the illegal artifacts into England is becoming more vital to the case."

The sergeant held his silence, leaving Henry to wonder at his thoughts.

"What is it?"

Fletcher sighed and met his gaze. "I have the sinking sensation that doing so will be a challenge."

Henry nodded. "It will more than likely involve customs officers. I will discuss the issue with Reynolds when we return to Scotland Yard."

"Don't do it while I'm there," Fletcher requested with a grimace. "The news will undoubtedly put him in a foul mood."

"It will indeed. Though in all honesty, it does so to me as well." The case had become an ever-widening spiral, involving even more criminals and victims than Henry had imagined. Surely further complexity—introducing another branch of the law—would only slow them down. "Let's return to Locke's shop and have another look, though I can't believe Dannon and I missed any clues after we spent several hours there yesterday."

"Often a little time away allows one to look at the scene with fresh eyes." Fletcher grinned. "A wise inspector once told me that."

Henry chuckled, touched the sergeant would remember him saying those very words. "Wise, indeed." Wise? He felt anything but that. Still, he appreciated the remark.

He led the way to Locke's shop, pulled out the keys he'd kept, and unlocked the door. A heaviness lingered in the air, but perhaps that was only in Henry's mind.

It was no wonder that Amelia had been upset. She had been shoved by a murderer then watched a man die before her eyes.

The fact that Locke had said her husband's name as his last breath had surely shaken her further.

It shook Henry as well. "I have yet to determine a reason for Locke to say Matthew Greystone's name before he died."

"As a warning?" Fletcher shook his head. "But why, when Greystone is already dead?"

"Could it have been a warning to tell Mrs. Greystone that she is in danger? I fear that is already the case since she saw the killer." Henry hoped she was taking his concern for her safety seriously. Should he have asked the watching constables for reports?

"Or was Locke telling her that Matthew had been doing the same thing he'd done?"

"That might be the case." Henry shook his head. "I only wish he had said a little more, so we knew for certain."

Fletcher glanced around the shop. "Where would you like me to start?"

"In the back where Locke was killed. That is where his desk is, as well."

"I assume nothing was in it?"

"Unfortunately not. The only possible clue was the list Mrs. Greystone discovered under the front counter."

"I suppose she has some familiarity with shops like these, eh?" Fletcher asked as he started toward the back.

"Yes." The thought had Henry moving to the counter, wondering if more could be discovered there—yet he had to think Amelia had already searched it thoroughly.

The shop door opened, and he turned to see Constable Dannon enter.

Henry frowned. The man was alone. "No luck with the shop clerk?"

"I stopped by his lodging house to tell him the bad news and request he meet you here." Dannon's lips tightened. "But he's gone."

"Gone?" Fletcher emerged from the rear of the shop to join them. "When is he expected back?"

"Apparently, he's not. According to his landlady he packed his things, paid the rent he owed, and left last night just after dark. No forwarding address."

Henry smothered a curse. "Did he provide any reason to the landlady?"

"He only said he'd been called away and didn't know when or if he might return. That she didn't need to hold his room." Dannon lifted a brow. "She said he acted nervous and was in an awful hurry, throwing his things in a trunk as if the hounds of hell were on his heels."

Henry met Fletcher's gaze. "Sounds as if he found out about Locke's death and felt threatened."

"As quick as he left, he must have believed he was in danger," Fletcher suggested.

"Which means he knew—or at the very least, suspected what was going on," Henry surmised with a heavy sigh.

"I asked the landlady where he was originally from and she thought it was Norfolk, though she couldn't say for certain. He had only been a tenant for a few months."

Henry's gaze shifted to Dannon. "Apparently he wants to put as much distance between him and whoever he's afraid of. More than likely, he left London. Check the train stations to see if you can discover any trace of him. Send a telegram to Norfolk—he might have decided to return home. We can only hope he's safe."

"Yes, sir. I will see what I can do." Dannon took his leave.

"Shall I have a word with the shops nearby to see if they know where else he might have gone?" Fletcher asked quietly.

"Good idea," Henry agreed. But somehow, he didn't think they would find the man. Not if he didn't want to be found.

Twenty-Three

AMELIA WAITED TWO DAYS before calling on Victoria Locke to pay her respects. In truth, she dreaded the visit but still wished to lend support, though she knew firsthand how feeble that offer was.

Nothing she said or did would take away the woman's grief and pain.

The dread tasted of those memories of her own first days as a widow, something she didn't wish to be thrust back into. Then again, she had already been reminded of that dark time since learning of Benjamin Norris's death.

She convinced the constable, who'd insisted on accompanying her, to wait in the cab. A wreath of boxwood adorned with black ribbon hung on the door, advising visitors that the house was in mourning. The familiar maid, now wearing a black armband, showed Amelia in. Grief struck her like an all-too-familiar heavy blow the moment she stepped inside the house.

"I will see if Mrs. Locke is receiving." The somber maid departed, leaving Amelia alone.

The drapes were all drawn as was customary, leaving the house in unmoving darkness. The gilt-framed mirror in the foyer was draped in black, preventing the deceased's spirit from becoming trapped within it. The elegant table which had been beneath it was gone. Amelia frowned at its absence, unable to think of a mourning custom that explained why it had been put away.

The maid returned almost silently. "Mrs. Locke will see you now." She led Amelia to the drawing room again.

The clock on the mantle had been stopped to match the time of death, as was expected, yet the room looked quite different from her previous visit. Several pieces of furniture had disappeared along with one of the Persian rugs. Nothing had taken their place, leaving the room rather bare.

Amelia had little time to glance around before the sound of footsteps and rustling fabric had her turning toward the doorway.

Victoria Locke, newly widowed, briefly paused to stare at her, expression unreadable, before slowly continuing forward. She looked like a pale, fragile shadow compared to the woman of Amelia's previous visit but days before. Her face was drawn, dark smudges ringing her eyes, and her mouth was pressed into a grim line.

"Victoria." Amelia walked forward with outstretched hands, taken aback when the new widow, attired in black bombazine and crepe, didn't reach for them but instead kept her hands clasped before her. "I...I am so terribly sorry for your loss."

"Randolph's burial is tomorrow morning." The woman's gaze held on a nearby candle. "Quite the irony, isn't it? Here I was feeling sorry for you only a few days ago." She met Amelia's eyes again, a sharp edge now in their depths. "And now the tables have turned."

"I'm so sorry." How many times had she heard the same inadequate words?

"I'm sure you are." Victoria turned aside, pressing a trembling pale hand to her forehead. "Everyone is." She gestured toward the room. "Except our creditors, of course. They descended like a flock of crows to peck apart the house."

Amelia looked about the room with a fresh understanding. Another term for the birds would be a 'murder of crows,' which was ironic given the circumstances. "How terrible."

"Yes. Well." Victoria lifted one shoulder in a half-hearted shrug. "It seems I was mistaken. Not all the updates were paid for. Those who extended credit weren't willing to wait to see if they would be paid."

The urge to apologize struck again, but Amelia held back. In truth, she didn't know what to say. As if losing one's husband, the father of her children, wasn't enough, having pieces of furniture taken added to the unfairness of the situation.

"The house?" Amelia couldn't help but ask even though it wasn't her affair.

"It appears we can keep it for a time."

The lack of certainty pinched Amelia's heart. That was one worry she hadn't had to face after Matthew died. But there had been other concerns instead.

"Amelia, I must know. Does Randolph's death have anything to do with you?" Victoria asked as her eyes filled with tears.

"Me?" Amelia stiffened in surprise. "No—why would you think so?"

"Everything was fine until you reappeared in our lives. One of the other shop owners came to pay his respects and told me he saw you there. That day. The day Randolph was...killed."

Amelia hesitated, uncertain what to say. *Yet how could she lie?* "I was." Her breath came in shallow gasps and she wished she could offer comfort along with what she had witnessed. Her only hope had been to prevent further pain. "I intended to ask if he knew anything about Matthew that he hadn't mentioned earlier."

"And?" Victoria took a step forward and gripped Amelia's hand as if she were a lifeline. "What did he say?"

"H-He had already been stabbed." She wanted to pull away but knew the painful squeeze of the widow's hand was a small price to pay for being there for Randolph's last moments.

Victoria's lips quivered and she barely held back tears. "Was he already gone?"

Amelia wished the grieving woman wouldn't have asked. Yet she understood the desire to know what happened during those final moments of life. How often had that yearning consumed her in the past year? What would she have given, to know that Matthew had not been alone in those final moments?

"No." Her voice trembled, and she cleared her throat, deciding not to mention that she'd seen the man who'd killed him. She would leave questions about the killer's identity for Henry to ask the widow. "I-I tried to stop the bleeding, but it was too late."

She wouldn't tell Victoria of his moaning or the pool of blood beneath him. She would spare her that.

"Did he say anything?"

Amelia used her free hand to ease Victoria's tight grip, uncertain how to answer, worried that the truth wouldn't bring her any respite. But neither would fabrications. "H-He said Matthew's name."

It took a moment for Victoria to react, then her brow furrowed as if she couldn't grasp the answer. "Matthew? Your Matthew—why? What exactly did he say?"

"Just his name, his first name. I don't know why. I can't imagine what he meant."

Victoria's eyes narrowed even as a snarl twisted her face. "My husband's last word was about *you*?" She spun away only to turn back, eyes glittering with anger. "Why couldn't you have left well enough alone? Why did you have to stir up the past?"

Amelia took a step back, shocked by the venom in her tone. "I only wanted to know if Mr. Norris's death had anything to do with Matthew's and to see if your husband knew what Matthew was doing. I never meant any harm to—"

"Never meant any harm?" Victoria's brittle laugh sent shivers down Amelia's spine. "Your selfishness cost my husband his life. It took my children's father from them—"

"Victoria Locke, I did not kill your husband." Amelia said the words quietly as she straightened, refusing to feel guilt for something she hadn't done.

Though frustration simmered within Amelia, sympathy won out. The poor woman didn't know what she was saying. She only lashed out in an attempt to relieve herself of her pain and grief. Would she have lashed out, if she'd been presented with a face to blame?

"Victoria, please." Amelia kept her tone gentle. "Do you know who Randolph was involved with? Who was providing the illegal artifacts?"

The couple had seemed close, and he might have confided some of the details.

"Illegal?" She scoffed, her movements jerky as she folded her arms before her. "You are casting stones when you know nothing about the situation."

Even now, her husband dead, she wouldn't admit the truth. Amelia gave herself a mental shake. That wasn't important at the moment. Perhaps Victoria needed time to process the facts.

What mattered was a name.

"Do you know who sold him the antiques?" Amelia asked again, her voice as gentle as she could make it. "That person could have something to do with his death."

"That won't bring Randolph back. Nothing can." Her lips clamped tight. "You only want to know because you hope it leads to Matthew's killer. As I said, so selfish."

"Victoria—" Amelia halted, at a loss for words to convince her to help even as guilt threatened.

Was her hostess right? Was Amelia only doing this for her own reasons?

No, that wasn't the case. Of course she wanted justice for Matthew, but she wanted it for Benjamin Norris and now Randolph Locke. Their deaths had to be connected; and whoever had killed the three men had to be stopped.

"You need to leave. Now," Victoria bit out.

Amelia held her ground. "Surely you can see that the murderer has to be found before he strikes again."

"I only know that you need to go."

"Very well." Amelia nodded reluctantly, sorry she had caused distress when that had been the last thing she wanted. "I wish you comfort during this difficult time."

With a last look at the woman she'd once thought of as a friend, Amelia walked out the door, realizing she'd made a mistake by coming there.

She only hoped she hadn't put Henry's investigation in jeopardy.

Twenty-Four

"How does one find a person who sells illegal artifacts?" Henry asked Fletcher with a heavy sigh as they waited for the meat pies they'd ordered at their usual locale.

It was a relief to sit inside the warm pub and out of the frigid breeze. They'd selected a table by the window which provided the added benefit of weak sunlight. Any sunshine was welcome, as far as Henry was concerned.

The sergeant lifted a brow. "If I knew that, the case might already be solved."

Henry waved a hand to dismiss the remark. "We are two logical, intelligent individuals. Surely we can make headway on the question." He stared out the window to the shops across the street, but his thoughts turned inward as he mulled over the possibilities. "If your life depended on securing an artifact, how would you go about it?"

Fletcher blew out a breath, clearly flummoxed by the question. "Do I have any friends with similar artifacts? If so, I might ask them."

Henry nodded, not wanting to break his train of thought. They had to think it through.

"I would ask at import-export shops. Just the ones that carry upscale items." The sergeant frowned. "Perhaps an auction house might be helpful as well. Or I might seek the advice of someone with expertise in the field. I suppose it could prove worthwhile to make a few discreet inquiries at museums with such things. Maybe not the British Museum as I doubt anyone there would be willing to say, but smaller museums display their own collections—and some of those must be Egyptian."

Henry stared at Fletcher as a spark struck. "Matthew Greystone's expert."

"Who?" Fletcher looked thoroughly confused, a reminder that he hadn't told his colleague about the man.

"I nearly forgot that Amelia—or rather, Mrs. Greystone—gave me the name of the expert her late husband used to verify the authenticity of antiques he purchased. Perhaps he knows how to obtain illicit antiquities."

"It would be worth asking him." Fletcher's moustache twitched, a telltale sign of doubt. "Though it seems unlikely he'd tell either of us since we're with the police. Many seem to suspect that, regardless of how we decide to dress."

"True." Henry's rush of excitement quickly fled.

"Unless..." Fletcher peered across the pub, clearly considering an idea.

"Unless what?" A sinking feeling found its way into the pit of Henry's stomach, and suddenly he knew exactly what the man was going to suggest. "No."

"I didn't even say it yet," the sergeant protested as he reached for his pint.

Henry shook his head. "I know what you intend to say, and the answer is no."

"You could ask."

"And she would agree without hesitation." Henry knew that beyond a doubt. Amelia was far too eager to aid the investigation in any way she could, even if her involvement came with great risk.

"But if she knows the man, and we were nearby, there might not be any true danger—"

Henry wanted to strangle Fletcher for his persistence. "I am not sure if she has ever met him. Either way, it's a very bad idea."

"Hmm." Fletcher's expression remained thoughtful, causing Henry to heave another sigh.

"I don't like it," he added. Yet had he any other ideas?

His thoughts were clearly transparent. "Unless you have a better suggestion, perhaps a nobleman with whom you are friendly who happens to collect Egyptian artifacts and knows a good smuggler." Fletcher sent him a knowing look.

Henry ignored him, trying to work through the potential advantages and disadvantages of Amelia risking a meeting with the man.

"She could take the Egyptian scarab with her to ask his opinion," his friend suggested, clearly dead set on this approach. "That would provide her with the opening to question whether other artifacts could be obtained."

"Showing him the scarab is out of the question. What if the man happens to be the one who helped obtain it?"

Fletcher nodded slowly with a grimace. "Blast. Good point. It might be best if she says that one of her late husband's customers contacted her and is interested in Egyptian artifacts. Perhaps similar to whatever is on the list she found in her husband's desk. Might as well make use of it."

Henry considered the idea for a long moment, reluctantly admitting it had some merit. "I still don't like it."

"Given that we have three murders on our hands and no suspects, I don't like a lot of it. But it might be worth the risk."

Henry briefly closed his eyes. "The reminder isn't helpful." He took a sip of his drink while his thoughts swirled. "We would have to make sure any meeting takes place in a location which allows us to ensure her safety."

"Absolutely."

"She might refuse." He almost hoped she did.

"She probably won't." Fletcher took another sip then wiped his moustache. "I have the impression she wants to solve her husband's murder almost as much as you do."

Henry knew that to be true—yet uncovering Greystone's activities before his death might prove very unsettling. She might *suspect* that her late husband had been involved in something unsavory but *knowing* it for certain was quite another matter.

Usually solving a case provided closure for the family. In this situation, it might not. Would the possibility of learning her husband had been neck-deep in illegal activities change her mind about how far she was willing to go to find who had murdered him? Would it place her financial position at risk? Would it end any feelings she might have for Henry?

The latter question pained him more than he was prepared to admit.

Once their luncheon arrived, they ate the steaming pies in silence. No matter how Henry looked at the situation, having Amelia speak with the expert seemed like the best option—or rather, the only option. There was of course the chance it might result in nothing.

But it might not.

After they'd finished their meal, Henry cleared his throat. Botheration. "I will call on her after work to see if she is willing to meet with the expert."

Fletcher nodded in approval. "Excellent. It is certainly worth trying—and if the man can't tell her anything, perhaps he can give us the name of someone who can."

That seemed to be the best they could hope for at the moment, given the lack of clues at the shops on Threadneedle Street.

"I am going to visit with Locke's widow again this afternoon to ask if I can have a look at his desk," Henry said as he stood. "Perhaps the shock has worn off and she's remembered something helpful."

"Let us hope so. I look forward to hearing what you and Mrs. Greystone decide." Fletcher rose and brushed the crumbs from his jacket. "If you don't mind, I'm going to check on the Sail and Anchor Public House where they were selling lottery tickets, see if there's any activity there."

"Perfect—but do take care not to be seen as it could be dangerous. I am sorry to say I nearly forgot Mr. Spencer with everything else that is happening."

"That's why there's two of us." Fletcher smiled as they walked out the door. "What one of us forgets, the other remembers."

Henry was grateful for that truth.

"I have nothing to tell you, Inspector." Victoria Locke barely looked at Henry, her focus hovering just over his shoulder.

"I thought perhaps you might have thought of something that could help us find who killed your husband. That is what we both want, after all." Henry knew he spoke bluntly, but he wanted to remind the widow that he was not the enemy. He was trying to help her.

She adjusted her position on the chair as if uncomfortable, making him think his message had been received, even if it was unwelcome.

"No. There's nothing."

"A man was seen in the vicinity." No good would result in the widow knowing the description had come from Amelia. "He has a hook-shaped scar beneath one eye. Does that sound familiar?"

Her brow puckered briefly as she considered the question. "No."

Henry looked about the room, certain she had to know more than what she'd said, and blinked. Nearly half of the furniture was gone from his previous visit when he'd given her the unfortunate news of her husband's passing. "Forgive me, but I cannot help but notice the...décor has changed since my last visit."

Mrs. Locke cast him a glare, clearly annoyed that he'd pointed it out. "Yes, well, apparently the recent changes to our home had not yet been paid for. The creditors came and retrieved a few of the items."

It looked like more than a few. "Do you have any knowledge about the increase in income your husband experienced?" Once again, Henry was pleased to already be aware of what the woman had told Amelia; otherwise, he wouldn't have known the truth.

She lifted her chin. "He had several clients willing to pay for his services."

"Services?" Henry was sorry for her loss, but he felt certain she knew more than she had shared thus far. "What did that entail?"

"He occasionally obtained unique antiques for clients who had specific wants."

"Such as?"

Mrs. Locke shook her head, hands clutched in her lap, pale against the black of her gown. "I was not directly involved in the business, so I couldn't say."

Henry leaned forward and held her gaze, hoping to make it clear how important this was. "Anything you could share might help. Did he have a desk here? Perhaps he kept records regarding those transactions. Those might point us to who murdered him."

Her face paled at his words. "Yes, he has a desk in his study. I'm sure I don't know what's in it. You...you can look in there if you must."

"I would appreciate that."

She heaved a sigh then slowly rose, her black gown rustling as she moved toward the bell pull. A long silence ensued until the maid appeared.

"Please show the Inspector to Mr. Locke's study," Mrs. Locke requested. "He is to examine anything he wishes."

The maid bobbed a curtsy. "Yes, madam."

Henry stood. "Thank you."

The widow only nodded, her lips pressed together in a thin line.

He followed the maid down to the first floor and along a corridor to the second door.

The maid opened it and stepped aside. "Just in here, sir."

"Thank you." Henry paused to look around the small, narrow room. Dark wood and stark décor suggested a masculine space. It was less impressive compared to some he'd been in, and certainly less so than the rest of the house before the furniture had been taken. Apparently the recent updates hadn't included his study. Had Locke felt compelled to deal in illegal artifacts to keep his wife happy?

The reason was less important than evidence. Henry strode to the window to pull aside the drapes, letting in light to see by, then sat at the desk to begin his search. He had to find something that would make it unnecessary to ask Amelia to speak with the expert.

Clearly any success Locke had gained was limited, given the missing furniture in the house. Henry had considered that he might have taken Greystone's place in the illicit artifact scheme, but more than a year had passed between their murders, making him uncertain.

Right. Evidence, not hunches.

The first desk drawer contained receipts and invoices, but they weren't for any items of interest from what he could tell. The next drawer was filled with blank paper and envelopes for correspondence. Nothing useful.

With a frustrated sigh, Henry moved to the other side of the desk. The top drawer held several letters, and he skimmed the contents one by one. Some were from family, others were business-related but clearly not relevant. The bottom one of the stack looked more promising as it was brief and written in a masculine hand.

Henry read it, excitement building as he noted the signature of M. Edgarton—the same name his contact in Spitalfields had shared. The one Duncan had said was dangerous.

Could it be the same Edgarton?

He reread it again. The language was vague yet threatening. But the letter wasn't proof of anything. It only mentioned the delivery of a shipment of goods which had gone missing, not what it was or where it came from. And had not Locke told Henry and Fletcher himself that a shipment was delayed? It was hardly a new clue.

Henry set it aside and continued the search. The last drawer contained a stack of bills for the furnishings, some of which Henry guessed had already been taken away. Locke must have planned on continuing to sell the illegal items and make a tidy profit, based on the amount he and his wife had spent decorating their home. He returned them to the drawer, hoping Mrs. Locke had someone to guide her in financial matters to clear any remaining debts. It would be a second devastation, for herself and their children to lose their home.

He glanced again at the Edgarton letter only to still, realizing the handwriting looked familiar.

The lists!

He needed to compare the letter to the lists Amelia had found in her husband's desk and Locke's shop, but he felt certain they matched. Now he needed to determine who M. Edgarton was—and exactly how he was involved in the illegal antiques.

"Are you quite done shuffling through my husband's things?"

Henry looked up to see Mrs. Locke standing in the open doorway, one hand fisted on her hip. He chose to ignore the impatient tone. The lady had lost her husband and couldn't be blamed if she sought a target to relieve her distress.

"I believe so." He stood and checked to make certain he had returned the papers where he'd found them with the exception of the letter. That, he carried with him to show Mrs. Locke. "Are you familiar with this person?"

She barely glanced at it. "No."

"It's signed by M. Edgarton," Henry persisted. This was too important to allow her to brush aside the question. "Do you recognize the name?"

"No." She sent him a lethal glare.

Henry waited a moment before saying, "I am doing all I can to find who killed him, but I need your help. Please think about it. Perhaps your husband mentioned the name at some point."

A visible wave of grief crossed her face as she at last seemed to give the question some thought. "No—not that I remember."

Henry nodded, despite his disappointment. Well, that would have been too easy. "If you do, please let me know. It could help us find the killer."

"Very well. Is that all?"

The fragile hollowness of her form tugged at him. This was only one of many difficult days ahead for both her and her children. For that, he was sorry. "I would like to take this letter with me."

She gave a single nod.

"Thank you for your time."

Twenty-Five

HENRY TOOK CARE AS he neared Amelia's that evening, perusing the street for any unusual activity. He couldn't allow his thoughts to distract him when he needed to remain on guard. The concern that his presence alone could place her in more danger than she already was continued to bother him, especially when he intended to ask her to risk even more.

The investigation was coming to a head, barreling toward a conclusion, one way or the other. He could feel it, though he wouldn't admit that aloud when he had no proof and three unsolved murders on his hands.

Edgarton had to be the key to the investigation but finding him was proving even more difficult than Henry had anticipated. Despite Inspector Duncan's remark that the man ran numerous businesses, most of which were illegal, Edgarton had always managed to avoid the attention of the police. Few of their records mentioned him. Of course, that didn't mean the man wasn't guilty, only that he hadn't been caught—not yet.

Reynolds made it clear he wanted results and soon. So did Henry. Unfortunately, he was running out of clues and leads, leaving him no choice but to ask Amelia for help. He rolled his shoulders to relieve the unease the thought brought. Reynolds would not be pleased with the plan, but that was a worry for another day—if his supervisor found out about it.

Given the possibility that she might agree, he had ventured to the Wexley House Museum after leaving the Locke residence, where Oscar Powell—Greystone's expert—acted as director. As the name implied, the place was situated in a large three-story house, converted into a museum in a quiet residential neighborhood.

During the brief period Henry observed, only a few visitors came and went. That had been somewhat reassuring, giving him hope they could minimize any potential danger if Amelia agreed to the plan.

He shivered, having become thoroughly chilled as he walked. The evening was cold and dark, with winter holding tight to January. His breath came in puffs as he sped his pace, both to keep warm and because he was in a hurry to speak with Amelia.

The constable keeping watch nearby reported that nothing of interest had occurred. After reminding him sternly to remain vigilant, Henry knocked on the door.

"Good evening, Inspector," the butler greeted him warmly.

"All is well, Fernsby?" Henry asked after stepping inside.

"It is, sir." The man reached for Henry's things, which he handed over after a moment's hesitation, uncertain how long he should stay.

Fernsby smiled as if reading Henry's mind. "I believe Mrs. Greystone was hoping you would stop by. She is in the drawing room."

"Thank you." Fernsby's remark made him curious. Surely nothing else had occurred? "How is Leopold?" he asked, equally curious about the adjustment for all involved, including the cat.

"Master Leopold has made himself quite at home, I am pleased to say. We are enjoying having him in the household."

"I'm happy to hear that." He liked to think of the cat keeping Amelia company, relieved that Fernsby and the rest of the household didn't seem to mind his presence.

Henry climbed the stairs and, as had become his habit, paused in the doorway only to find Amelia already at the sideboard, Leopold rubbing happily along her skirts.

She glanced at Henry with a smile. "Good evening, Henry. I thought I heard you and took the liberty of pouring us drinks."

"How kind of you." Henry couldn't resist bending down to pet the cat when he came slinking to him. "Hello, Master Leopold."

"He is a sweet thing and has already claimed his favorite chair." She gestured toward the one by the window.

"Fernsby doesn't mind him on the furniture?" Henry asked with surprise. The butler and his wife, Amelia's housekeeper, were quite particular about such things, from what he knew.

"Leopold meowed and rubbed against his leg, which rather seemed to end the debate. I wouldn't have guessed that Fernsby would give in so easily." Amelia shook her head, a smile on her face. "It is a cold evening, isn't it? Hopefully the whiskey will help warm you." She handed him the glass and led the way toward the chairs near the fire, a glass of sherry in hand.

"It is one of those nights that makes spring feel very far away." He sighed as he sat, taking time to enjoy the moment. A fire, a drink, and a lovely woman's company were a wonderful way to end the day. The cat settled on the rug before the fire and licked a paw.

"Indeed, it does." Amelia smiled again. This time, he could see the worry beneath it. No doubt the case—the cases were wearing on her, the danger impossible to forget when a constable watched the house. He detested seeing how it upset her.

She wore gray again this evening, and only then did he realize he hadn't seen her in anything else since he'd told her of Norris's death. Was that because learning about another murder brought thoughts of her late husband?

"Is something on your mind?" he asked quietly.

Better that they dealt with anything unpleasant with the hope of putting it behind them so they might enjoy a little conversation afterward—one that didn't involve the investigation. He looked forward to the day when they could speak of inconsequential things such as how they'd spent their day, rather than murder.

She briefly closed her eyes, which had him setting aside the glass as concern filled him.

"What is it?" he asked.

"I called on Victoria Locke earlier today to offer my condolences."

He nodded. He should have expected that of her. "How kind of you. I was there this afternoon as well. She is distraught, needless to say."

"She blamed me. She said that if I hadn't stirred up the past, her husband would still be alive."

Henry's gut twisted. "Surely, you don't believe that. Besides, I'm the one who dug into events again." If anyone was at fault, it was him.

"No one is to blame but the killer. Still, it was difficult to hear."

And hurtful, he was sure. "She was less than friendly toward me, too. I tend to think she is lashing out at anyone within reach."

Amelia nodded. "I have no doubt you are right. Did you notice the missing furniture?"

"Impossible not to. That must make the situation even worse."

She pressed two fingers to her temple. "How terrible is it that I am grateful that didn't happen to me?"

"Not terrible at all. The death of a husband is difficult enough without adding financial stress." Then again, Amelia had endured financial worry of a different sort, wondering where the extra money her husband left had come from—and whether she could keep it. Meanwhile it remained in her bank account with her spending little of it just in case from what she'd told him.

"Victoria was also displeased to learn that her husband said Matthew's name with his last breath."

"You were brave to tell her that." Henry didn't think he would've in her place.

"She asked a series of questions that made it impossible not to...and I didn't want to lie."

Amelia's distress had him shifting to the edge of his seat to touch her arm, compelled to offer comfort, no matter how small. "That must have been awful."

"It was." She briefly touched his hand where it rested on her sleeve, as if in appreciation of his support. "I didn't tell her that I saw the killer. I decided to leave that up to you."

"I asked if she knew a man with a scar—like the one you described—but she didn't."

"Not a surprise. He didn't look like someone with whom she would associate. At any rate, I don't think she and I will be furthering our friendship. I hope your visit with her went better than mine."

"It was interesting." Henry sat back in his chair, debating the wisdom of sharing any details in the ongoing investigation. Then again, Amelia was already deeply involved. What was the point in holding back? "Do you remember the list stuck in the desk drawer? And the one you found in Locke's shop?"

"Of course. What of them?"

"I discovered a letter in Locke's desk in his study from an M. Edgarton. Perhaps Monsier Edgarton?" He waited, hoping she might recognize it.

She shook her head, no familiarity in her eyes. "The name isn't familiar."

"The handwriting matches the lists." He'd compared the three closely when he returned to the Yard. There was no doubt.

"Finally a clue." Her eyes widened with interest. "I only wish I could be of more help as to who that is."

Henry hesitated, still wishing he didn't have to ask for this favor, but he needed to do all in his power to solve the case. That was the only way to end the danger to Amelia.

"There is one other lead I have yet to look into," he began, pausing to retrieve his glass and take a sip, his mouth suddenly dry.

"Oh?" Amelia waited, clearly intrigued by what he intended to say.

"We have reason to believe the antiquities expert your late husband used might be able to help us find whoever is selling the items, possibly Edgarton."

"Truly? If he can, do you think he will actually tell you?"

"Doubtful. If he is involved in something illegal, he would surely be less than eager to work with the police." Henry paused, still debating the wisdom of the plan. "Would you be willing to speak with him, to see what you can learn?"

"I will certainly try," she agreed without hesitation—just as he'd known she would. "What do you suggest?"

"Amelia." Henry hesitated, wanting to warn her it could be dangerous without frightening her. "He might very well have close ties to Edgarton, who is reputed to be a dangerous criminal. If so, speaking with him could cause you to become a target."

Amelia drew a slow breath, seeming to consider the situation. "I already am since the killer has to know I saw him—and if we don't find Edgarton, if he is truly the one behind it, this will never be over." The steadiness of her gaze and her voice made him admire her all the more. "How shall we proceed?"

We. If she only knew how much he appreciated her use of that word. It meant she understood that she wasn't alone, that they were in this together.

"My thought is that you call on him at the museum, tell him that a former client of your husband's contacted you and is interested in Egyptian artifacts. See where the conversation leads."

She nodded pensively. "That sounds simple enough, though I imagine he might deny that he can help. How persuasive should I be?"

"Not overly so," Henry said after giving it some thought. "We don't want him to become suspicious if you press too much."

"Very well. And what if he wants the name of the client?"

"Tell him the person insists on remaining anonymous."

"Is there a specific item this imaginary person is interested in obtaining?" Amelia smiled. Was it possible she was enjoying this?

He couldn't help but smile in return. She was a treasure, and he hoped to have the opportunity to tell her that one day. "I suppose we should think of several that would be appropriate."

"Gold and expensive, I would assume."

"Definitely. But not a scarab."

Her focus shifted to the fire, her expression tightening. "And will I meet him alone?"

"Fletcher and I will be nearby but out of sight. I looked at the building earlier this afternoon and think the plan should work. The museum doesn't seem to have many visitors which will help."

She drew a deep breath and nodded. Relieved, perhaps, to hear they would be nearby? "Should I send Mr. Powell a message tomorrow to request a meeting or do you think it better to stop by with the hope he's there?"

Henry weighed the options. "Perhaps stopping by with the idea of catching him off guard would be best." If the man was working with Edgarton, he wouldn't have the chance to tell him of Amelia's supposed interest ahead of time. "Hopefully he will have fewer questions that way."

It was logical to think the expert would reach out to his contact, potentially Edgarton, after Amelia spoke with him either with a message or in person. Hopefully that would allow Henry and Fletcher to follow and find whoever was bringing illicit artifacts into the country.

Of course, like any plan, there were numerous chances for mishaps; but Henry intended to do all he could to prepare for them.

"Act as if you think the antiques could be questionable but not necessarily illegal," he advised. "And that additional funds would be helpful to you."

"Very well. That should be easy enough."

"If you don't emerge after a reasonable time, I will come looking for you," he added. "If at any point you are uncomfortable, leave at once."

"All right." A long moment passed before she said, "There is one other item I wanted to mention." The wariness in her expression had his nerves growing taut.

"What is that?"

She smoothed a hand along the folds of her skirt. "I sent a letter to Mrs. Drake."

"What? Why?" He didn't want Amelia anywhere near the woman. From what Mrs. Drake had said during their conversation at the prison, and what she hadn't, she was playing games.

Dangerous ones.

Amelia sighed. "I can't release the idea that she knows who killed Matthew. My letter was one last request for her to tell me." She lifted a hand only to allow it to fall. "More than likely, it will come to nothing."

"As long as you're prepared for that outcome." Unfortunately, he thought that was exactly what would happen. The woman had no sense of right and wrong. Anything she said would have to be carefully considered and weighed.

Amelia met his gaze. "I had to try again."

As much as Henry understood, he detested it. That was all the more reason to move forward with their plan and hope it bore fruit. After all, Edgarton might very well be the one who had killed Matthew Greystone.

Twenty-Six

"This would be much easier if we knew what either Edgarton or Powell looked like," Fletcher said darkly as they walked along the street toward the Wexley House Museum the following morning.

"It would, but we shall do our best to prevail without that knowledge." Henry was trying to remain positive and stay focused on identifying who was supplying the illicit artifacts by the day's end.

Definitely not thinking about the worst that could happen.

He wanted Amelia out of danger, yet here he was, placing her at even greater risk. There was always the chance that Powell was legitimate and didn't deal in illegal items. This could be all for naught.

Or their efforts could end badly. The man might decide he took offense to what Amelia asked. He might refuse to help her. Powell could—

Henry cut off the barrage of concerns before his nerves got the better of him and he abandoned the whole scheme.

Amelia would arrive soon—but first, he wanted another look at the museum and to have a solid plan to ensure Amelia's safety.

The sergeant cleared his throat. "You remember I went by the pub yesterday, the one selling lottery tickets?"

"And?" He studied Fletcher's thoughtful expression and already knew the answer.

"I think they intend to start doing it again soon."

"Something occurred suggesting as much?"

"A few tables were being hauled inside, and a man I spoke to along the street said that usually meant they will soon hold a drawing."

"Excellent." They had waited weeks for news like this. Henry only wished it wasn't happening at the same time that the Norris and Locke investigations were heating up. "Reynolds approved the plan for us to raid the place when they do. A group of officers have been assigned to the task and remain on alert."

Fletcher nodded. "The constable in the area is keeping a close watch for the next couple of days. We will see what comes of it."

"What do you suppose the chances are of us having the majority of our cases tidied up within a week?" Henry was mostly jesting but couldn't deny how appealing the idea sounded. "We could have a holiday."

"Aren't you the optimistic one?" Fletcher chuckled. "We can only hope that proves true."

Henry slowed his stride to gesture toward the house across the street. "There it is."

The former mansion had a discreet plaque noting the name of the place. There were several similar museums in London, comprised of a wealthy individual's private collection the family often didn't know what to do with after their relative's death.

Why not create a museum and allow the public to view the items?

Of course, one needed enough wealth, thereby making it unnecessary for the house or the collection to be sold. A small fee was charged at some, but that was hardly enough to pay for the staff or the upkeep, from what Henry could tell.

"There are three entrances, but the back one that led to the garden appears to be bricked up," he advised Fletcher. "Why don't you go around the side of the house to watch that door, and I will keep an eye on the front?"

Fletcher nodded. "We should be able to see one another without any problem."

"Yes, I will signal you when Mrs. Greystone arrives. If she doesn't depart within a half hour, I'm going in after her."

"And if I see you leave your post, I'll follow."

Henry nodded, relieved to have Fletcher with him. "I expect Powell will be interested enough in what Mrs. Greystone shares, if he's actually involved in the scheme, that he will either send a message to the person supplying the artifacts or pay him a visit. Once Mrs. Greystone departs, we follow anyone who leaves the building."

"Understood."

Henry heaved a sigh as he stared at the large house with its numerous peaked gables. "It would be nice if everything went according to plan for once."

"I suppose stranger things have happened," Fletcher jested, then pointed to an alleyway. "I'll go through there with the hope no one pays me any attention."

That was asking much, given Fletcher's size and uniform. However, not many people were on the street, which was largely residential. Clearly the museum wasn't especially popular, at least not at this hour of the day.

"Let us hope all goes well." Henry's nerves were quickly getting the better of him, something which hadn't happened for some time.

"We will make sure of it." With that, Fletcher was off.

His friend's words were more reassuring than he knew.

Once the sergeant was in position, Henry took his own place across the street. He stood next to a tree and should only be visible from a few rooms of the museum thanks to the thick foliage blocking the view. Powell was unaware of Amelia's upcoming visit, so the man had no reason to watch the street.

The dim sunshine was deceiving, the air remaining cold. He didn't expect they would have to watch for too long so the chill wouldn't be an issue.

Within a quarter hour, a hansom cab rolled to a halt before the museum. Henry had advised Amelia to have the cab wait. Unfortunately, it blocked his view of her alighting. It took several moments before she appeared at the front door where she hesitated, seemingly torn about whether to knock.

She glanced around the street, allowing him a brief view of her. It was becoming more difficult to ignore the blooming sensation in his chest each time he saw her, even from this distance. An instinct to run over and enter with her was quashed firmly—and then she opened the door and stepped inside, disappearing from sight.

Henry raised his hand until Fletcher nodded then checked his watch. Now they need only wait. That was always the hardest part.

Amelia's entire body trembled as she entered the foyer of the museum, a chime somewhere in the house announcing her. She hadn't realized how anxious she would be for this meeting. Taking a firm hold of her nerves, she reminded herself that Henry and Sergeant Fletcher were outside, even though she hadn't seen them.

Besides, it was doubtful that she would face any danger. This was someone Matthew had most likely met on numerous occasions—and if Mr. Powell noted her nervousness, he would surely put it down to the unusual nature of her request.

It wasn't every day that one requested a meeting with an illegal antiquities dealer.

She distracted herself by focusing on her surroundings. This place wasn't so different from similar museums she'd visited that were housed in a former residence. Somehow, that familiarity did not add to her confidence.

The foyer was covered in dark wood paneling with small black and cream tiles laid in an intricate pattern on the floor. The house had a musty smell, probably a result of so many antiques in an enclosed space, but perhaps the museum simply needed a thorough cleaning. The staircase curved to the left, the newel post carved with flourishes. A knight's suit of armor stood in one corner with a sword at the ready, while the opposite corner held a large Chinese dragon sculpture with green eyes.

Footsteps had her turning to see an older gentleman descending the stairs. He was dressed in a fussy manner with a brightly striped waistcoat beneath a dark gold jacket and an intricately tied cravat. His gray hair was parted in the middle and slicked back with pomade. A neat, narrow moustache lined his upper lip.

"Good morning." He offered a polite smile. "Here to tour the museum?"

"Actually, I am looking for Mr. Powell."

One brow lifted. "I am Mr. Oscar Powell."

Amelia smiled brightly and drew nearer, hoping a little charm might help the meeting go more smoothly. "What a pleasure to meet you. I am Mrs. Amelia Greystone. I believe you were acquainted with my late husband, Matthew."

"Greystone?" Alarm flashed in his eyes so briefly that she wondered if she imagined it. "Oh, yes. I remember Mr. Greystone." A look of sympathy crossed his features. "I was terribly sorry to hear of his passing."

"Thank you." She pressed a gloved finger to her nose and sniffed, having already decided to play up the part of a bereaved widow, hence the reason she wore black from head to toe. "It...it has been a trying year since his death."

Guilt for the deception struck, but what she'd said wasn't truly a lie. If she was acting out of character, it was for Matthew's benefit—to help find his killer.

"I can only imagine." Mr. Powell paused, clearly undecided on how to proceed with the conversation. That made two of them. "May I inquire as to whether he...mentioned me by name?"

"Yes, he did. Many times." In truth, Matthew spoke of him only once when he was on his way to meet him.

Then again, she now realized there were many things he hadn't told her. And she hadn't asked.

"Oh? Oh, he did?" The man's eye twitched, suggesting he was alarmed by the news.

"Oh, yes—he praised your expertise on antiquities on many occasions and said he didn't know what he would do without you."

His unease appeared to smooth and he smiled, clearly flattered. "I am always pleased to be of assistance."

"To think you took time from your position here as..." She glanced about, wondering what exactly it was and hoping he'd share a few details...before she explained the reason for her visit.

Her false reason, in any case.

"As Director." He straightened, chest puffing out the striped waistcoat as he followed her gaze around the place. "It is a challenge to manage a collection like this one."

"I can't imagine. How many pieces are here?"

"Hundreds. Some more valuable than others, of course."

"Fascinating." She stepped forward for a closer look into the small reception room off the foyer to see it filled with paintings, statues, vases, and all manner of other items. "I wouldn't know where to begin."

"It takes years of training." Mr. Powell lifted his chin, not bothering to be modest. He was clearly quite proud of himself.

"Where did you study?" she asked as she turned back to face him.

He blinked, lips pursuing as if he resented the question. "I have worked in numerous museums over the years, learning from notable experts."

"Impressive."

He almost looked relieved by her praise. Amelia supposed some people had an affinity for such things. Those who had an interest in certain subjects tended to succeed if they pursued them professionally. She liked to think she did so with chemistry, though she would never consider herself a professional in the field.

"From what Matthew suggested, your specialty is in Egyptian artifacts?" she asked, hoping that was true.

The man inclined his head. "I have seen my fair share of them, and gained a reputation in sorting true artifacts from forged ones."

"It is incredibly generous of you to share that ability with others." She smiled even as she wondered how much he charged for sharing his opinion.

"Yes, well, I do what I can."

"Mr. Powell, I feel as if I already know you." It had been a long time since she'd attempted any sort of flirtatious behavior. Doing so felt terribly awkward and obvious, yet she needed some sort of bond with him before she took the next step in the investigation.

His warm smile suggested, much to her surprise, that he thought her efforts natural. "As do I, Mrs. Greystone. May I offer a...*personal* tour of the premises?"

"You are so kind." Amelia had no interest in his offer, but she smiled anyway. "However, in all honesty, I was hoping you could aid me with something." She dropped her gaze and tilted her head to the side, hoping he took the bait before catching his gaze again.

"Oh? What might that be?" His brows lifted as if intrigued.

"Much to my surprise, one of my late husband's former clients reached out."

"Who?" His eyes narrowed with a predatory gleam.

She offered a coy smile. "I am afraid I can't say. A gentleman of his...bloodline, shall we say, requires complete anonymity."

Mr. Powell nodded even as he sighed. "So many like to keep their desires private."

'Desires' was an odd way to describe the urge to collect illegal antiques. She pushed aside the thought. *This was not the time.* "He is beside himself that he hasn't made any new acquisitions, especially from the tombs of Egypt, and asked if I could help." She batted her lashes and leaned closer. "Needless to say, as a widow, I could use the extra funds any fee would provide."

"Of course." Mr. Powell's sympathetic expression suggested her instincts had guided her in the right direction. "I do hope Mr. Greystone...provided for you?"

She sighed. "Not enough, I'm afraid, which is why I immediately thought of you." She paused as if uncertain, which was easy, because she was. "Is there any chance you know of someone who could assist in providing items similar to what my husband offered in the past?" She held her breath as she waited for his answer.

"Hmm. That is a delicate question, madam." His greasy smile made her skin crawl.

"Is it?" She batted her eyes again. Was that too much? "I would hate to disappoint the client."

"As would I." He took a step closer. "You do realize it is illegal to bring items from tombs without the proper credentials, don't you?"

"I heard a rumor—but surely there are ways around that?" She knew that for a fact.

"How much is your client willing to pay?"

If only she and Henry had discussed this question. Her heart pounded as she tried to think of a reasonable answer. One that would keep his interest but not be outlandish.

What might that number be?

"He only said that the price was not an issue, though I suppose there is a limit." She held her breath, hoping that was enough of an answer.

"Very interesting." He nodded as he ran a finger over his thin moustache.

After a long moment, Amelia asked, "Do you think you could help?" She tried another smile. "I'm sure we could make it worth your while."

"I don't know." Mr. Powell looked across the room, seeming to consider her request. "I suppose I could reach out to one of my associates who might be willing to aid us."

She drew a slow breath of relief. "Oh?" She waited, heart pounding to see if he intended to commit. Though tempted to make another plea, she held back. As Henry had advised, she didn't want to appear too desperate. It took all her restraint not to fidget while he considered her request.

At last, the Director nodded. "I will attempt to assist you—but I make no promises," he declared.

"That is all I can ask." She clapped her gloved hands together in delight, no need to feign her exuberance when so much rode on his agreement.

"I will send word to you as to what happens once I learn more."

"Thank you, Mr. Powell. It means so much to me." And it truly did. Finding justice for Matthew depended on the Director aiding her. "I am so happy we had the chance to meet."

"As am I, madam." He bowed, one hand circling in the air pretentiously as he did so. "I will contact you soon."

Amelia took her leave with a light heart, knowing she had done all she could to further the investigation. Once again, she glanced around the quiet street but didn't see Henry or Fletcher.

It wasn't until she had settled in the cab again that the truth struck her—clearly Matthew *had* been dealing in illegal antiques. Mr. Powell had at no point questioned her request.

A wave of hurt and disappointment washed over her. The meeting served as proof that she hadn't truly known her husband. That truth not only shook the foundation of her marriage, but her belief in herself.

If she'd been completely unaware of what the man she shared a life with was capable of...how could she trust her own judgement or instincts when they were so clearly lacking? What else might she be wrong about?

Twenty-Seven

Henry heaved an impatient sigh, debating how much longer to wait. The thought of Amelia inside the museum with Powell, possibly in danger, was enough to drive him mad.

A glance at Fletcher showed him also shifting restlessly.

Perhaps he should see if the meeting was progressing as planned and if all was well. Yet he hesitated, worried that doing so might place everything they'd done thus far at risk—including Amelia's efforts.

The door opened at last. Seeing Amelia exit the museum and pause to look around filled him with such relief that his knees weakened in response.

Was she searching for him? Henry didn't dare give in to the urge to show himself. Instead he kept his place beside the tree, nearly out of sight.

Amelia stepped into the cab, and a moment later it slowly pulled away. Now he and Fletcher need only wait to see what Powell did, if anything. Was he involved in the scheme at all? Would he be eager enough to go himself to speak with his source, hopefully Edgarton? Or might he send a message? As long as the man took some form of action, they would have the next link in the chain they followed.

No purpose would be served in worrying about the outcome when it was out of his control. He could only react to what Powell did. Henry blew out a breath, hoping whatever the man decided to do was sooner rather than later. It was getting unpleasant, standing in the damp cold.

Thankfully it was only ten minutes later when Powell stepped out of the museum, hung a closed sign on the door, and then locked it, all to Henry's relief. After a glance around, the man walked down the street with quick strides.

Henry signaled Fletcher, and they started forward at the same time. Surely between them, they could keep the man in sight to see where he went. Henry remained on the opposite side of the street while his sergeant was on the same side as their quarry.

Powell hired a hansom cab at the next cab stand and was quickly off, leaving Henry searching for another. To his relief, Fletcher waved down one passing in the opposite direction and apparently explained the situation, pointing to his uniform.

Henry hurried to join him just as the driver was nodding in presumed agreement. Within a few minutes, they had turned around and were in pursuit of the other cab.

"You told him not to follow too closely?" Henry asked quietly.

"Yes." The sergeant looked out the front window in search of Powell's cab. "I just hope we can catch up."

So did Henry. He had no idea where the man might be going. If they lost him, all of Amelia's efforts would be for naught. Luckily their driver seemed to take his assignment seriously, and they moved along at a fast clip. Several minutes passed before the conveyance slowed to a more reasonable pace.

"That has to mean he spotted him." Fletcher craned his neck for a better view around the horse's head. "But I can't see it yet."

Henry also watched without success. The street became busier with more traffic the farther they went. "The driver must have a better view than we do."

"There—there it is," Fletcher declared a few minutes later before relaxing back against the seat. "With luck, we will soon know where Powell is going." He glanced at Henry. "What is our plan once we arrive?"

"I suppose it depends on the situation. If it's a business, we should be able to easily make inquiries to learn more. If it's a residence, the most we can do is note the address and wait to see what happens. We don't want Powell or the person he meets to suspect our presence. Better if we observe, take note of any details, and form a plan as we learn. We need evidence of some sort to prove what they are doing—the existence of the scarab isn't enough to confirm any crime."

Fletcher nodded. "Right. Proof. Proof would be helpful."

Required, in fact. But Henry didn't say that as Fletcher already knew as much.

They passed shops and other businesses without pausing. He studied the street as the cab slowed again. The neighborhood was a mix of smaller mansions and townhouses, with only a few shops in the area and a pub on the corner.

The cab slowed even further and the driver tapped on the small door, which Fletcher quickly opened. "The other driver pulled aside just ahead. Want me to do the same?"

"Yes," the sergeant advised.

The street had little traffic, so they would have to keep their distance if they didn't want to be seen.

Henry stepped out of the cab but remained alongside it, watching down the street as Powell opened a low iron garden gate and shut it behind him before walking up the steps to a house.

"We're too far away to tell which house he entered," Henry said to both Fletcher and the driver. "Take the cab and circle around to see if you can get the address."

Fletcher nodded, and the driver flicked the reins, leaving Henry to watch the house from where he stood. There weren't many trees nearby so he remained where he was, fairly certain he wasn't visible to anyone in the house. But he couldn't remain where he was for long, or the neighbors might note his presence. There was always someone watching when it *wasn't* useful to him. He need only think of Norris's neighbors to remember that.

Henry watched to make sure Powell didn't leave. If Fletcher couldn't determine which house the man had gone into, they would have a second chance when he left. One way or another, Henry wanted the address.

The cab returned a few minutes later.

"I have it," Fletcher advised.

"You're certain?" Henry asked as he hopped inside.

"Yes. Now we need only determine who lives there."

Henry hoped it was Edgarton. Learning where the man lived would be even better than discovering where his business was. If possible, Henry wanted to know both.

"Let's wait and see what happens once Powell leaves." He glanced around, all too aware that a cab sitting there for long could draw notice. Thus far, the street remained quiet.

"Do you want me to follow Powell?" Fletcher asked.

"I assume he'll return to the museum. Better that we see if whoever he is speaking with goes anywhere. If it is Edgarton, there's a chance he will venture to where he keeps the artifacts." Yet even to his own ears, Henry knew that was doubtful. It would take time for Powell to arrange another meeting with Amelia with details of available artifacts and how they would be delivered. No purpose would be served by getting the artifacts until then. The man Powell met with would likely not go anywhere after hearing about Amelia's request.

Somehow they needed to confirm who Powell was meeting with...but how?

Waiting was one of the most difficult parts of the job. Henry was a patient man, but even he tended to become restless when watching suspects in situations like this. The horse tugged on the reins, shifting its position as if it, too, was ready to leave.

A quarter of an hour passed at a snail's pace and still no sign of Powell or any other movement. The driver was the only one who seemed not to mind the wait—but then, he was paid either way.

At last, Powell emerged and walked down the steps. Henry held his breath as the man glanced up and down the street. Luckily, he paid them no mind, only stepped into his cab and pulled away.

"What if whoever lives there decides to leave from the rear of the house?" Fletcher asked with a frown. "Could be less conspicuous?"

Henry studied the nearby houses, trying to determine if any might have a carriage house in the back. "I will go check. Wait here and watch the front."

Fletcher grunted, and Henry smiled as he hopped out and walked down the street. Clearly his sergeant would've preferred to have a look himself.

At the next cross street, Henry turned to walk along the parallel one in search of an alleyway. He quickly found it, and with a glance about to make sure he hadn't been noticed, he entered.

No one else was in the alley, not even a servant or delivery man. The sound of traffic from a couple of streets away could be heard in the distance but otherwise, the silence was unnerving. The alley itself was packed dirt with a few ruts, the tracks suggesting some of the houses had carriages.

As he reached what he estimated could be the house Powell had visited, he slowed his pace, studying it. Three had similar tall, wrought-iron fences, and two had carriage houses, but he didn't know which was the correct house.

The scuff of a step behind him had Henry turning quickly to see a rough-looking man approaching.

"Here now—what're ye about?"

"Just out for a walk," Henry answered with what he hoped was an easy smile. He had no intention of announcing he was with the police—not unless he was forced to. "Visiting my sister who lives down the street."

The man, dressed in a tired black suit, frowned. "This is private. Move on."

"Happy to." Henry held up both hands with a shrug to show he meant no offense. "Do you work nearby?" He gestured toward the residences.

"What's it to ye?" His gaze narrowed.

Obviously the suspicious sort. "These are such fine houses. Must be nice to work in one."

"Nice enough." The man's gaze shifted to the center one. Was that where he worked?

"Hope the owner is as nice as the house." Henry stuffed his hands in his pockets, trying his best not to look like an inspector from Scotland Yard. It was not something he had a great deal of experience with.

The man scoffed. "I wouldn't say that. Got high expectations."

Henry looked at the structure again, hoping he could keep the man talking and learn a little more. "Is he nobility then, or does he work for a living like the rest of us?"

"You're awful curious."

Henry gave him another smile. "I wouldn't mind having a home like that. Just wondering what it might take to get one."

"He has several businesses. Calls himself diversified."

His interest perked even more. The description matched Edgarton. "Sounds industrious. What's his name?" The man hesitated, so Henry lifted one shoulder in a half-shrug. "Thought I could ask my sister if she knew him, being they're on the same street and all."

"Doubtful. Mr. Edgarton isn't the neighborly sort."

Satisfaction filled Henry. "Funny how often the successful ones are like that, eh?" He shared a knowing look with the man. "Keep to themselves."

"True." He glanced at the house again, then back at Henry. "He don't like snoopy people neither." The words were more menacing than the tone.

Henry nodded, pleased with what he'd learned. "I'll be on my way." He turned to go only to turn back. "I don't suppose he is hiring anyone." He tapped his chest. "I happen to be between jobs at the moment. Wouldn't mind working for someone so successful."

Again, the man considered the question a long moment, Henry's heart hammering. "He always seems to need more men at the shipping company. S'pose you could try there."

"What's it called?"

"Sable Importers." He provided the address with which Henry was already familiar.

Henry tugged the brim of his hat, careful not to show too much excitement. "Many thanks. I just might stop by there."

"Good luck."

With that, Henry walked back down the alley and along the street, eventually returning to the hansom cab. He glanced back once or twice to make certain the man hadn't decided to follow him, pleased not to see him.

"It's Edgarton's house," he announced to Fletcher as soon as he hopped in and closed the door. "And he is the owner of Sable Importers."

A glint of admiration shone in Fletcher's eyes. "Damn." He quickly grimaced. "Darn, I mean. Don't tell the missus I said that."

"Of course not." Henry grinned, still amused by the sergeant's attempt to curb his swearing to please his wife.

"How did you manage it?"

"Ran into one of his men in the back who warned me off."

"And instead of leaving like he asked, you interrogated him?"

"Not precisely." Henry shrugged. "Just did my best to keep the conversation going."

"Well done." His sergeant nodded in approval. "So are we knocking on his door next?"

Henry shook his head. "He would only deny any wrongdoing. Let us see what more we can dig up, now that we know where he lives and have confirmation of the name of his shipping company."

Somehow they needed to tie him to the illegal artifacts. That meant a visit to the shipping company—but only if they knew the artifacts would be there.

Though there was a great deal of work ahead of them, he was more than pleased to finally have clues to follow. Whether all this would result in an arrest for both Norris's and Locke's murders remained to be seen...but he had high hopes.

Twenty-Eight

Amelia paced the drawing room, wondering whether Mr. Powell had left to speak with his contact as they hoped. He had seemed intrigued by her request, but should she have said something different? Something more?

She sighed, stopping beside the chair near the window where Master Leopold was curled into a ball, content to nap in the faint sunlight. She scratched the cat's head, rewarded when he stretched then shifted into a more comfortable position before continuing his slumber. He seemed to be adjusting to his new home quite well. Amelia certainly appreciated his company.

Her thoughts continued to ricochet through various possible outcomes of her conversation with Mr. Powell. Had he thought her ridiculous? Been entirely taken in? Suspected her of something nefarious? Subterfuge was clearly not one of her talents. While she wanted to do her best to help Henry, she feared she wasn't a convincing enough actress to fool anyone, especially those who might be naturally suspicious. Surely Mr. Powell and whoever he might contact were both distrustful.

She glanced at the clock, wondering how long it would be before she heard from Henry. More than likely, it wouldn't be until this evening, if today.

With another sigh she returned to her pacing, needing a way to release her restlessness, only to hear voices in the foyer. Her breath caught as she rushed to the doorway to listen, but was quickly released in disappointment at the sound of the door closing and silence descending.

She had returned to her pacing when Fernsby appeared in the doorway, holding a silver tray. "A message arrived for you, madam."

"Oh?" She hurried forward, hoping it was from Henry, though it seemed far too soon to receive word of how events had transpired. "Thank you."

The familiar feminine script on the envelope had her stilling in surprise.

"Is all well?" Fernsby asked, his expression declaring that he clearly thought it was not.

Amelia glanced up at him, worry coursing through her. "I don't know. I do believe Mrs. Drake has written again."

The butler lifted a brow. "This time, it was sent as a message rather than through the post. A lad delivered it."

Amelia frowned. "How on earth did she manage that?" The possibilities were enough to make her shiver. "Clearly she has connections of a questionable sort. And it suggests a certain urgency, doesn't it?" With equal parts curiosity and reluctance, she opened the missive to read the brief note.

Dear Mrs. Greystone,

My fate is now clear. It is imperative we speak as soon as possible. I ask that you call on me one last time. Preferably today, as the matter is urgent and time limited.

Respectfully,

Elizabeth Drake (chemist)

With a deep breath, Amelia met Fernsby's gaze. "She wants me to visit her one last time. Today. She says it is imperative, that her fate is clear."

Fernsby said nothing, but his concern and disapproval were obvious.

"I have to wonder if she has decided to share the truth." Though she remained doubtful whether the woman would tell her what she so desperately wanted to know, she had to find out. "I don't think I could live with myself if I didn't see this through to the end."

"Do you think she has been convicted and sentenced?" he asked. "Is that what she means about her fate?"

"I don't know. I think Inspector Field would have mentioned it, or I would have read about it in the news sheet." She shook her head, uncertainty curling around her heart. "Then again, we have been quite busy of late. It's been several days since I read any news."

"True." Fernsby straightened, always prepared to support her in whatever way he could. "Shall we prepare for another trip to the prison?"

"Yes, I think we must." She only wished she could notify Henry in advance, but there simply wasn't time. Chances were he hadn't returned to Scotland Yard and wouldn't for some time.

"Very well. I will be ready in ten minutes." The butler started toward the door.

"Fernsby?"

The older man turned back to look at her. "Yes, madam?"

"Thank you." That she didn't have to ask him to accompany her when it would surely be an unpleasant visit for them both...that meant so much to her.

He smiled. "It is my honor, Mrs. Greystone." He dipped his head and departed.

She read the message again. *My fate is now clear.* The handwriting looked less smooth than the last letter, almost as if the woman had been shaken or rushed when she wrote it.

Amelia shook her head. More than likely, she was imagining such things. There could be numerous reasons for the unsteady handwriting. For all she knew, Mrs. Drake was toying with her. Amelia need only remember the knowing smirk the woman had worn during her last visit.

With a deep breath, she considered the various ways the conversation might go. All she knew for certain was that this would be the last one, regardless of the woman's future. Whether or not Mrs. Drake provided any helpful information regarding Matthew's death, Amelia didn't intend to see her again. The woman had sealed her own fate when she chose to kill children, and Amelia refused to feel sorry for her.

A half-hour later, she and Fernsby were in a cab riding toward Holloway Prison. She had advised the constable who continued to guard the house of their plan and asked that he continue at his post. The man hadn't liked her destination, nor that he was required to stay behind, but Amelia was firm in her request. Fernsby was enough protection, and Holloway was a prison filled with guards. They should be safe enough.

Once again she wore black, including her hat with the thick veil. She was much less anxious this time, knowing what to expect, but still the dreariness of the building as they rolled to a halt before it was impossible to deny, weighing on Amelia.

"Shall we, madam?" Fernsby asked, walking stick in hand.

"Yes." Dismayed to realize her nerves were returning, she took Fernsby's offered hand as he aided her to step down from the cab.

After the butler advised the driver to wait with the promise of additional payment, they repeated the same steps as before to enter the prison. A different warder sat at the desk but once again wrote their names and address on the list.

Surely it was only her imagination that the man stiffened when Fernsby gave her name?

Still, the moment added to her anxiousness as they waited to be escorted to the visiting room. It didn't take long before their names were called as they were the only visitors, and they followed another guard down the hallway to the familiar room.

Fernsby offered a reassuring nod before he took a position a short distance behind her as she lifted the netting covering her face. The silence while they waited for Mrs. Drake's arrival was heavy and stretched her nerves taut. At last, a key turned in the door and Mrs. Drake walked in, looking more disheveled than the last visit.

Her hair was matted and clearly in need of washing, though still drawn back into a bun. The gray gown she wore was dirty, a small hole visible near the neck.

Amelia remained seated, not bothering to politely greet the prisoner as she walked forward, her movements jerky as she pulled out a chair before slowly sinking into it.

"Thank you for coming," Mrs. Drake whispered with a wary glance over her shoulder at the guard.

"What is it you wish to tell me?" Amelia didn't bother with niceties, though a well of pity for the woman threatened.

How different this version was from the one who'd lectured at South Kensington Museum last autumn. She appeared...defeated. However, that could be nothing more than an act to gain sympathy. Amelia needed to remain on guard.

The woman's chin lifted, nostrils flaring, almost as though she were under duress. "It appears I am to die, by one means or another." She drew a breath, emotion evident in both the tremble of her voice and her movements.

Amelia didn't know how to respond, so she remained silent. What had Mrs. Drake expected? That somehow testing poison on innocent children would be overlooked because she claimed to have done it at the request of a government official for the benefit of England? That didn't justify murder.

"It has come to my attention that we have even more in common than we thought," she continued, a desperate note in her voice. "Both of us have been betrayed. By a man."

Amelia frowned, confused as to what she was speaking about. "How so?"

Impatience flickered across Mrs. Drake's face. "Your husband was doing things you didn't know about. Things you wouldn't approve of."

"Selling illicit antiquities?"

"Among other things."

Fear knotted in the pit of Amelia's stomach. "Other things?"

The woman nodded without breaking her stare.

Amelia couldn't imagine what that might be and couldn't bring herself to ask. A part of her didn't want to know. Already she felt guilty for distancing herself, especially after Lily's death. If she had been there for him, been the loving wife she had intended to be, that Matthew had needed...would it have made any difference?

"I have had the unique position of associating with equally powerful men on both sides of the law."

"Oh?" Once again, Amelia hardly knew what to say, though she wanted the woman to continue talking.

"Perhaps that's not quite true." Mrs. Drake's eyes narrowed as she stared across the small room. "One is undoubtedly more powerful, in every way." For the first time, she smiled, revealing a shadow of her former, confident self. "He and I were very close."

"How close?"

"As close as a man and woman can be." Mrs. Drake leaned closer. "You were married. A mother. I'm certain you know what I mean."

Lovers. That was the only word that came to mind.

What a life the woman had led. How unfortunate that it had come to this terrible conclusion, all because she had made the wrong choices, regardless of whether she was willing to admit it.

"Unfortunately he could have helped me but has chosen not to." Her gaze shifted to meet Amelia's as she lifted her chin. "I no longer owe him my loyalty."

Amelia leaned forward. "As one woman to another, I ask you again. Who killed my husband?" All of this meant nothing unless the woman said a name.

The guard cleared his throat, suggesting he didn't like the topic—or he didn't want the woman to answer.

Unease ran along Amelia's skin. Did the man she spoke of have contacts inside the prison, like the guard? Was that why Mrs. Drake seemed so nervous? Amelia studied the older man with his stout form, unkempt facial hair, large nose, and heavy jowls. Could he be associated with the man Mrs. Drake knew, or was she imagining things?

Again, the woman glanced over her shoulder at him before looking back at Amelia, her expression one of determination. "*Miles Edgarton*." She quickly shook her head. "Well, perhaps not him directly. I'm not certain. But one of his men did it, on his order."

Though the news wasn't a complete surprise, it still shook Amelia. Another blow to the memories of her husband, another doubt planted in her mind. But to have a name after all this time meant something, even if it brought forth grief and regret.

"Why?" Amelia wanted every possible detail, despite the well of emotion which threatened.

"From what Miles said, he became greedy." Her words were so faint that Amelia could hardly hear them. "He was selling illicit antiquities that Miles obtained to both their benefits—and then the two had a disagreement."

"Over what?"

Mrs. Drake scoffed. "Who knows? Men will be men. Their egos, perhaps. While Miles insisted your husband reached too far, it may well have been the other way around."

Amelia wanted more; information on exactly what had occurred and why. How Matthew had met Edgarton. Had it been through Mr. Powell? Why had her husband decided to take such a risk and sell illegal wares? But Mrs. Drake couldn't answer most of those questions. She could only speculate based on what she'd been told.

"I want to speak to him. How do I do that?" Amelia asked.

Mrs. Drake shook her head fiercely. "You can't. He would never permit such a meeting."

Frustration welled. "Can you tell me anything else?"

Again the guard cleared his throat, and Mrs. Drake glanced out of the corner of her eye at him. Why didn't he want his prisoner to say more?

"I gave you his name. What more do you want?" The woman's voice trembled. "Miles betrayed me. He promised to protect me, yet here I sit." Her eyes held Amelia's, lips pressed tight. "I am to be hung by the neck until dead, no matter that my intent was to aid England."

Amelia hardened her emotions, refusing to feel sympathy for such a woman. "You killed children. To me, who was once a mother, that is unforgiveable."

"They were *orphans*," Mrs. Drake protested, her expression one of disbelief. "They were nothing but a burden to our city. Some would believe I did them a favor by giving them a higher purpose."

"They were innocent and in need of protection. Not treated as if they were disposable." Amelia shook her head. "It is clear we will never agree on the matter. If you won't tell me how to find Edgarton, this meeting is over." She pushed back from the table, preparing to rise.

"Wait." Mrs. Drake lifted her chin, defiant to the last. "I've told you all I know, but beware. Do nothing rash—you would be in terrible danger if you confronted him."

Amelia's courage faltered. In truth, she wasn't prepared to face further danger, or worry what harm might befall her or those she cared for. But allowing Edgarton to escape unscathed would only prolong the danger. Matthew, Norris, Locke...how many more had to die? He couldn't be permitted to steal artifacts or continue to kill when crossed.

With a deep breath, she reminded herself that she had Henry on her side. That was all the reassurance she needed.

"Thank you for telling me." Amelia rose and turned to nod at Fernsby before looking back at Mrs. Drake. "I know someone who will find him. Find him, and make him pay for what he did."

Twenty-Nine

Henry and Fletcher returned to Scotland Yard and were told by Sergeant Johnson to report to Director Reynolds the moment they walked in the door.

"This can't be good," Fletcher muttered as they made their way to the director's office.

"Perhaps Locke's missing clerk has been found." That could prove helpful. Henry knocked on his superior's open door. "You wanted to see us, sir?"

"Yes." The director nodded as he leaned back in his chair, folding his arms over his chest. "Constable Walters reported in. The lottery ticket sales start this afternoon at the Sail and Anchor Public House at three o'clock."

"That is good news." Henry hoped they could catch the man Spencer's friend had told them about. This 'Richards' sounded like the most likely person to have interacted with Spencer, and possibly had something to do with his assumed death. Though they had no evidence, one of Richards' associates might be willing to tell them what happened if pressed. They just had to apply pressure in the right place.

"As previously discussed, we will time our arrival for after they have sold a few so we have proof of the scheme," Reynolds continued as he tapped a paper on his desk. "We should be able to quickly round up the majority of those involved."

Henry checked his watch. Three o'clock. That only left them an hour to prepare. He had already told Reynolds what he and Fletcher observed during their visit to the same pub two months ago. The challenge would be to ensure no one associated with the scheme slipped out the door. From what he and Fletcher had witnessed, several men were stationed throughout the place to act as guards. Those men would be difficult to spot, looking as they did much like regular customers.

"No one will be allowed to leave until we have cleared them," Henry confirmed. He and Reynolds had already gone through the plan at length in preparation for this opportunity.

"Right," Reynolds agreed. "We don't want anyone hurt. After all, we're doing this for the good of the community."

Fletcher cleared his throat. "I am not sure they will view it as such, sir, when most will only see us taking away a bit of their fun, along with their one and only chance for riches."

"I know you're not fond of Fleet Street," Henry began, holding the director's gaze, "but in this case, it might be worthwhile having at least one news source cover this if they're willing to share the full story, including the lottery's misleading claims about their prizes and how they're targeting those who can least afford to lose money. It might help."

Reynolds sighed as he considered the idea. "You're probably right. I will see if I can call in a favor with a reporter we could trust to tell the full truth. Leave it with me."

Henry nodded, relieved to hear it. "If that's all, sir, we will finalize arrangements."

"I look forward to hearing that it goes smoothly." The pointed look Reynolds sent them had Henry nodding.

On that, he fully agreed. He didn't like setting aside the other case when they were finally gaining momentum, but with luck, they wouldn't have to do so for long.

The next hour sped by as two patrol wagons were prepared and police constables were gathered. Henry quickly briefed them on their objective, with Reynolds looking on to add his authority to the plan. Perdy listened, clearly less than pleased to be working under Henry's supervision, however briefly. Henry was hardly happy about it; he could too easily imagine the other inspector doing something to deliberately sabotage the operation with the hope of making Henry appear inept.

But there wasn't time to worry about such things. Soon they were loading into the wagons and riding toward the pub with over a half-dozen men at a quarter after three o'clock.

The wagons pulled up before the Sail and Anchor Public House, effectively blocking traffic for the time being. Numerous people along the street paused to watch what all the ruckus was about.

Fletcher led an orderly charge inside the pub. Several officers had been assigned to block the exits while the remainder focused on restraining those obviously involved with the lottery. Any patrons who had come for the drawing were detained for questioning—anyone and everyone was a possible suspect, and at the very least, a witness.

Henry held back, searching for anyone who fit the description they had of Richards, and grinned as Fletcher came down the stairs with just such a man in cuffs.

Only one fight broke out when a man Perdy had restrained threw a punch, striking Perdy in the jaw. The inspector didn't take kindly to the blow and struck the member of the public back.

Henry rushed forward to lend assistance before matters got out of hand, grabbing the suspect's arm even as he placed a hand on Perdy, to keep him from striking the man again. "Why don't you cuff him?" he asked Perdy, unclear why the inspector hadn't done that to begin with.

"I don't need to be told what to do by the likes of you," Perdy countered, his glare adding heat to the words.

Henry dropped his hand. No need to try to assist someone who didn't want it, especially Perdy. Yet he couldn't let it go completely. "Try not to allow anyone else to get the upper hand on you, if you can?"

With that, Henry turned his attention elsewhere.

Another look at the man Fletcher had captured made Henry certain he'd seen him during their last visit to the place. A scar high on his cheek suggested it could be the man Spencer's friend had described to them. Hopefully a few questions would tell them for certain, but that would have to wait until they gathered all the men involved and took them to Scotland Yard. To that end, Henry strode through the place to ensure everyone was accounted for and no one escaped.

The operation took more time than he would've liked. The majority of the patrons needed to be released as soon as possible. Holding them any longer than necessary wouldn't improve the reputation of the police force, but they could hardly take each person at their word. A little verification needed to be completed with each detained person. Luckily, there were only a dozen or so.

At last they filled the wagons with those associated with the lottery drawing scheme and released the ones they thought to have been merely enjoying a pint. Only a few looked familiar to Henry. Then again, the men working might have changed since Henry's last visit to the pub.

They returned to Scotland Yard to begin sorting through those they detained. The process took time, especially since most weren't cooperative. Some refused to provide their name. Others gave false ones, obvious from the delay between when the question was asked and their answer. Henry was careful to keep the men apart so they couldn't create similar stories.

"This would be easier with a little cooperation, eh?" Fletcher muttered to Henry as they watched yet another man being taken into an interview room where one of the inspectors would question him.

"Indeed." Henry scowled. "At this rate, we could be here all night."

"Let us hope not." Fletcher rocked back on his heels, studying those who awaited questioning. "The wife is expecting me home for dinner as her parents are joining us."

"I hope to be done before that." Henry glanced at his friend, realizing he should have asked the question much sooner. There was no time like the present. "And when will I have the pleasure of meeting your wife?"

They had worked together over the last two years, but Henry had always kept his distance in an effort to remain professional. But the sergeant meant much to him, a friendship he had not sought but found, and that distance now seemed unnecessary. Hadn't Henry told himself to make more of an effort in the relationships in his life? That included Fletcher.

The man's brows shot upward. "I suppose something could be arranged, though she will insist on advance warning so as to properly prepare for it. You know how women are."

"No need to make a fuss on my account," Henry said warmly. "I only want the pleasure of meeting her."

His sergeant shook his head. "You must know a simple introduction won't do. She'll insist you come for dinner."

He couldn't help but smile. "I would be honored."

"Hmm." Fletcher's moustache twitched. "I will see what I can do."

"I look forward to it." Henry dipped his head. "Now let us have a word with Richards to see what he can tell us."

Thirty

Though Amelia didn't know if what Mrs. Drake had told her would be of any assistance, she wanted to speak with Henry about it as soon as possible. Waiting for him to call was not an option.

"Fernsby, I need to stop by Scotland Yard on the way home so I can advise Inspector Field of the results of my meeting with Mrs. Drake." And that was not even considering her desperation to know if anything had come of her meeting with Mr. Powell.

The butler frowned. "Do you think that wise, madam, given the warning Mrs. Drake shared during our previous visit?"

Amelia had already considered the possibility of placing herself in further danger by continuing her work with Henry but thought the threat no longer probable. That, or there were simply too many threats coming from all directions. "Anyone watching would already know I am involved with the police thanks to the constable stationed outside my home for the past few days."

"A logical observation," Fernsby agreed then opened the small hatch to advise the hansom cab driver of their new destination.

It didn't take long before the cab rolled to a halt at Whitehall Place where Scotland Yard was located. Amelia had driven past it before she had become acquainted with Henry, but now looked at it with fresh eyes. The two-story brick building with its arched doorway wasn't particularly large, from what she could see from the street. No wonder the police force had spilled into several neighboring addresses in the last few years.

"Why don't you take the cab and return home?" Amelia suggested to Fernsby compassionately. "I will be in safe hands at Scotland Yard." She knew he was anxious to return home to see to his duties. He never liked to be away long, and though a police officer was watching the house, Fernsby wouldn't relax until he was guarding it as well.

"I am happy to wait, madam."

"I don't know if Inspector Field will be here, but if he isn't, I would like to wait for him. The sooner I share what Mrs. Drake said, the better. It could be relevant to the case. There's no purpose in you waiting, too."

Fernsby lifted a brow. "Are you certain? I would be pleased to remain with you."

"No need. I would rather you checked on things at home." She leaned close. "I worry whether Master Leopold is behaving himself. I wouldn't want him to be a nuisance to Mrs. Fernsby."

"True." The butler nodded solemnly, seeming to share her concern. "You are quite sure?"

"Most definitely. If you would advise the constable at the house as to my whereabouts, I would appreciate it." She reached for the door handle. "I imagine Inspector Field will more than likely escort me home as his day should soon end."

"Very well. I will see you soon, Mrs. Greystone."

With that, she stepped out and entered Scotland Yard, well aware Fernsby observed her to make certain she did so without incident.

A mix of uniformed police officers and men in plain clothes were coming in and out of the building as she entered the small receiving area, some tipping their hats to her. Not another woman was in sight, which left her feeling decidedly out of place. She directed her attention to the desk where a uniformed man sat, a stack of files at his elbow.

He glanced up at her approach, then looked past her as if expecting her to have an escort. "May I help you?"

"I would like to speak with Inspector Field, please."

"Field?" The man leaned forward to look down a short hallway that led to a larger area where numerous men were visible. "He's here somewhere. It might take a moment to locate him as he has just recently returned."

That piqued her interest. Did it mean Powell had led him to Edgarton, or whoever was the source of the illegal antiquities?

"Who shall I say is inquiring?" the man asked as he rose from his desk.

"Mrs. Greystone."

He moved down the short hall, and Amelia couldn't resist following him to get a glimpse of where Henry worked. She remained in the hall while the man continued into the large office where rows of desks lined the space. The place buzzed with activity, but it was difficult to make sense of what was happening.

Nearly half a dozen rough-looking men stood scowling in handcuffs with uniformed policemen guarding them. One man sat at a desk with paper and pencil, taking down information from prisoners. The place was noisy with so many people speaking at once, and one or two were complaining in loud tones. A sour mix of sweat and fear tainted the air, stinging her nostrils.

It took her a moment to locate Henry, who was in the thick of things as he directed activities.

The man who had aided her approached him and apparently announced her arrival as Henry turned to look in her direction. Relief filled her as their gazes met, making her realize how pleased she was to see him. Then her breath caught. More than simple relief welled within her.

No. No, now was *not* the time to examine her feelings for the handsome inspector.

Worry darkened Henry's eyes before he turned to have a word with another man near him, then he moved away from the chaotic scene and strode toward her.

"Amelia—" He caught himself, glancing around as if to make certain no one had heard him use her given name. With the amount of noise in the room, that seemed unlikely. "Mrs. Greystone. What brings you by? Is all well?"

"I have come from another visit with Mrs. Drake." She braced herself for his disapproval, certain it would come.

It did, and swiftly. His lips tightened as if he bit back a protest. "That is...unexpected news."

"She sent a message soon after I returned home. It suggested her reluctance to give me a name had changed."

"And? Was that true or merely some odd game to summon you again?"

"Miles Edgarton. She says that is who...who killed Matthew. Or at least ordered his death." Saying it aloud was somehow much different than thinking it. Or perhaps it was saying it to Henry, or in this place, that caused her upset. In some way, it was like learning of her husband's death all over again, bringing feelings to the surface she wasn't prepared for, especially not while standing in a room full of policemen.

"I see." His gaze shifted to the side as he processed the news. "Interesting."

She drew a steadying breath, relieved to have told him. But now she wanted to think of something else, however briefly. "Did Mr. Powell lead you anywhere? Is Edgarton also behind the illegal antiques?"

"It seems so. Powell went directly to his home soon after you left the museum."

She drew a steadying breath and nodded. "So Matthew was working with Edgarton and apparently did something to anger him."

"Perhaps."

"And Norris, and Locke too...but we still need evidence. Thus far, all we have is hearsay."

Henry nodded, watching her closely as if concerned about how she was dealing with the news. "A name is helpful, but yes, we need more. That is, unless Mrs. Drake is willing to testify that Edgarton confessed to the murder."

"I think that is doubtful. They were involved in...a relationship." Amelia felt her cheeks heat at the word which was ridiculous when she was a widow. "Mrs. Drake still seems frightened by him."

"What made her decide to tell you? Did she say?"

"She said he betrayed her. That he promised to protect her but hadn't. She kept looking at the guard as she spoke, and he was less than pleased by what she was saying." Amelia looked at Henry, concern welling within her. "I should have found out what the guard's name was. I'm sorry I'm not a better assistant."

Henry smiled. "You are an excellent one, though I look forward to the day when you're not in the middle of a murder investigation. That has been happening far too frequently of late."

"Yes, it has." While she enjoyed helping Henry solve the puzzle of cases, she would rather not be so personally involved and definitely not in danger.

He glanced around. "Did the constable watching your home accompany you?"

"No, Fernsby did. We asked the constable to remain and watch over the house since we would be surrounded by guards at the prison."

"I am beginning to wonder how much protection that would actually provide you."

Her breath caught at his softly spoken admission. "Do you refer to the constable—or the guards?"

"The guards, if what you say is true. I hate to admit it, but there is a chance Edgarton has ties there." He shifted as his gaze swept the office. "I only hope it doesn't reach in here."

"Surely not." Amelia hated to think such a thing; yet she remembered that not long ago, corruption had been discovered within Scotland Yard, resulting in a restructuring of the entire department. Fleet Street had reveled in running the stories over and over again in their news sheets, covering the scandal most thoroughly.

"I would hope."

"What is our next step?" she asked.

His focus returned to her. "I will be needed here for a time as we have just made a significant arrest in another case. Until we have this sorted out, I would ask that you return home where I know you will be safe."

"Oh." Disappointment filled her. She'd hoped he might accompany her but based on the activity behind him, that clearly wasn't possible. "Very well. You're sure there's nothing more I can do while you are otherwise engaged?"

"No, thank you. We will need to carefully plan how to proceed with Edgarton. I will update Director Reynolds regarding the situation and decide our next steps."

Amelia nodded. In truth, she had a poor opinion of Henry's superior; he hadn't allowed Henry to investigate the mudlark deaths except in an unofficial capacity, which to her mind was criminal in itself. However, she wasn't about to share that with Henry—certainly not while she stood here.

"Is Fernsby waiting for you?" he asked.

"Actually, I sent him home in the cab." She didn't add that she had thought Henry would escort her home. It would only make her look foolish.

"Then I will help you find one." Henry took her elbow, but she remained in place.

"There is no need when you are so busy here." Matters had not calmed down in the brief time they'd been speaking; the rabble around them was, if possible, only growing louder.

"Yes, well, some are less than happy to have been arrested and are choosing to make their displeasure clear." He turned to glance at the prisoners, and Amelia did the same, her gaze flickering across faces she did not know. "We have only questioned a few at this point, though all insist they are innocent. They can wait."

"Why were so many arrested?" she asked as she studied the cuffed men.

"A lottery scheme."

The sight of one man in particular had her gasping is disbelief—and fear. She reached for Henry's arm, heart pounding as her attention held on the familiar face.

It couldn't be.

"What is it?" Henry asked, quickly shifting to block her view of the men.

She trembled as her gaze met Henry's. "H-He's there. The man w-who stabbed Locke."

"What? Are you certain?"

"Y-Yes." The urge to hide took hold, and Amelia hunched her shoulders even as she kept Henry between her and the man. "The scar beneath his eye is just as I remembered."

"Unbelievable." Henry's gaze darted about the room as if his thoughts were racing.

"What is?" She frowned, hurt by his response. "You don't believe me?"

"Of course I do." He looked back at her, eyes wide with surprise. "But that man is also suspected of killing another—the case of the missing man I have been working on since November."

She shivered at the thought. "How could he be guilty of both? That seems like too much of a coincidence."

"Unless..."

Amelia waited to allow him to put his thoughts in order, not certain what he might be thinking.

"Unless they're all connected," he finished quietly with a nod.

"How?" That seemed both impossible and illogical. How could one man be entangled in so much evil?

"We know Edgarton is involved in multiple businesses, mostly illegal. Perhaps one of them is the lottery scheme."

Amelia's skin went cold. "In addition to the illegal antiques?"

"Yes." He studied her, a glint of excitement in his eyes. Or was it admiration? Whatever the reason, the look brought heat to her cheeks. "I wouldn't have guessed if you hadn't made the connection."

"But I didn't." She refused to allow him to credit her when he was the one to spot the possibility. "You were the one who—"

"You recognized him, even when you thought you couldn't. Without you, I don't think I would have linked the details." He nodded again as if it all made sense. "I don't think any of those we captured would willingly provide the name of their boss. Now we can press them to confirm it."

"I am certain he is the one I saw that day." Though tempted to take another look to be certain, fear held Amelia in place.

For some odd reason, knowing that the killer she'd feared would come in search of her now stood in handcuffs in Scotland Yard didn't bring the relief she had expected. Surely it would once she wasn't in the same room as him.

"That is all I need to know for now." The steady reassurance in Henry's face had her unease calming. "Let us find you a cab." He glanced at a passing officer. "And a constable to escort you home."

"That isn't necessary," she said. Surely their presence was required here, based on the busyness of the place. "A constable will be on the street, waiting to see me inside once I arrive home."

He frowned. "Are you sure? I am happy to have someone accompany you—I only wish I could do so myself."

"The killer has been arrested." She straightened, reminding herself of that fact. *He was cuffed, and she was safe.* "Any danger has passed."

Henry nodded. "Very well. But I will find you a cab."

More than grateful that she didn't have to confront the man, she allowed Henry to escort her out of the building. The cold, damp air was unexpectedly welcome, after the stuffiness inside the police headquarters.

Daylight was already fading, nothing but a memory on the horizon. "I look forward to when the days grow longer."

"As do I," Henry agreed.

The brief warmth of his arm around her back helped settle her lingering nerves before he stepped to the street and waved at a nearby hansom cab parked a short distance away, which pulled forward, the driver nodding his head politely under his wide-brimmed hat.

"I hope you don't have to work too much longer." Amelia smiled up at him, pleased they had the brief moment of privacy together.

"As do I. Fletcher is anxious to be done as his in-laws are coming for dinner." Henry's eyes sparkled as if he found the idea amusing.

"All the more reason for you to return inside." She took his offered hand to help her into the cab. "Thank you, Henry. Have a good evening."

"And you, Amelia. Rest easy knowing you have helped to solve Locke's murder. I will be in touch soon." He closed the door, his voice muffled as he advised the driver of her address.

It was a relief to know the man who had killed Locke had been arrested, yet Amelia still couldn't shove away her uneasiness. Something still prickled in the back of her mind, warning her of danger.

No matter. She would soon be home and could put all of this behind her.

Thirty-One

HENRY WATCHED THE CAB pull away and move down the street, expecting to feel relief knowing that Amelia would soon be safely home.

Yet he didn't.

An unsettled feeling wrapped him in a tight, uncomfortable embrace and refused to let go.

He shrugged away the illogical sensation and turned to enter Scotland Yard—only to halt. A voice inside him insisted something was amiss. But what?

Something he had noticed. Something which had caused his mind to yell even has he had ignored it. Something important.

The driver. There had been something familiar about the man.

Then it struck him.

Dear God—he was the same one they'd questioned at Sable Importers several days ago.

Edgarton. He had to be behind this.

Henry spun to look down the street, but the cab had already disappeared. Fear knotted in the pit of his stomach and froze his thoughts. He had to—

"Director Reynolds wants an update on what we learned from Richards." Fletcher's voice sounded as if it came from far away. "I thought you would prefer to tell him yourself that Richards insists he never met Spencer." The sergeant frowned at Henry. "What is it?"

Henry could hardly manage to say it, his lips numb. "The—the cab. The one that took Amelia—Mrs. Greystone." He gestured to where the conveyance had been only moments ago, hating the helpless feeling that weakened his limbs and clouded his thoughts. "The driver—he was the man we questioned at Sable Importers."

The sergeant stilled. "Are you certain?"

"Yes." Henry groaned as he ran a hand over the back of his neck, nearly beside himself. "Fletcher, I just handed her over to a criminal!"

"How could he possibly have known where she was?"

"She stopped here after seeing Mrs. Drake at the prison—where the woman told her that Edgarton killed Mr. Greystone. The guard in the prison, he must have got word out—the driver must have followed her, waiting for an opportunity."

"Where could he be taking her?" Fletcher asked, eyes dark with worry.

Henry couldn't think. No thought was possible; he could only see Amelia smiling as the cab pulled away.

The feel of Fletcher gripping his arm brought him back to his senses as his sergeant said urgently, "Think. Think, man. Where might he take her?"

"To Edgarton, I assume." He shook his head. "But where would that be?"

"Surely not his home," Fletcher said slowly.

"You're right. Sable Importers is the only other place we know of where he might be." Henry's stomach dipped. What if he was wrong? They already knew Edgarton had other businesses—but they didn't know where the rest were located.

"Say the word, sir. Wherever your gut tells us to go, we will go." Fletcher nodded, his gaze steady, his belief in Henry humbling.

Again, Henry stared down the street, trying to sort through the options. The house, the warehouse, spending time asking other officers if they recalled any other places connected with the criminal...yet all he could think was that he was wasting precious time. "Sable Importers."

"I'll round up some men." Fletcher turned and hurried inside.

Henry prayed he was right as he followed him.

Amelia stared out the cab window as it rumbled along the street. She could hardly believe that Locke's killer had been at Scotland Yard right when she had been there to identify him. The timing could not have been more perfect.

What a relief to know he was already arrested and no longer a threat. Upon arriving home, she would advise the constable he wasn't needed to guard the house since she wasn't in danger anymore. Fernsby would be delighted.

Her thoughts returned to what Mrs. Drake had told her about Matthew.

"Your husband was doing things you didn't know about. Things you wouldn't approve of."

"Selling illicit antiquities?"

"Among other things."

To think that he had been embroiled in an illegal scheme of any sort was truly disheartening. Her marriage, her husband hadn't been what she thought he was, even if she were partly to blame. A new wave of grief threatened, and she drew a shaky breath to hold it back. Her upset would have to wait until she returned to the privacy of her home.

She blinked to clear her thoughts and noted the passing scenery—only to frown. The street wasn't familiar. The driver must have taken a wrong turn somewhere while she'd been lost in her ruminations. It was easily done; half of these streets looked identical to the others.

"Sir?" She turned and reached for the hatch to speak with the driver, but it was fastened shut. She rapped on it. "Sir."

The man did not respond to her call.

Concern took hold, though Amelia told herself he would soon either realize he was going the wrong way or hear her attempts to alert him to the problem. Yet she couldn't halt the unease spreading over her. She was paranoid, after everything which had happened this last week, that was surely it.

But what if it wasn't?

"Sir!" She knocked on the hatch even harder but still didn't receive a response. The cab was traveling too quickly for her to try to alight. The only other thing she could think to do was to open the door. That would surely gain the man's attention.

"Hey," he hollered when she opened it. "Close the door!"

"You are going the wrong way," she called out. If she could hear him, logically he must be able to hear her.

To her dismay he paid her no attention, and the cab continued on its way.

Frustrated, she left the door open wide, allowing it to crash against the side of the carriage, thinking he might halt to shut it himself. The cold breeze quickly chilled her, and she tightened her cloak, fear clenching her chest, making it difficult to breathe.

This felt terribly wrong.

The neighborhood they drove through had to be fairly close to the docks, based on the number of warehouses and the scent of the Thames in the air, though it was difficult to tell in the fading light.

Tension gripped her as she acknowledged to herself that something was most definitely wrong. Locke's murderer was in handcuffs at Scotland Yard, but that was now little comfort. It didn't eliminate the sense of impending doom crashing over her.

Edgarton. Could this have something to do with him? Possibly because of her visit to Mrs. Drake at the prison? Given how fearful the woman seemed to be about her former lover, Amelia needed to assume the worst and prepare for it.

But how?

Once again, she was in danger, but this time, she didn't have the comfort of hoping Henry was on his way to rescue her. Fernsby wasn't expecting her home at any particular time, and Henry surely believed she was safely on her way there. Neither of them would come looking for her—and they would have the entirety of London to comb through.

She was on her own, and had to find a way out of the situation as quickly as possible.

Amelia pushed aside the fear which made it nearly impossible to think. Action was needed, and the sooner the better. The moment the cab slowed, she would jump. Her skirts might hamper her, but if she took care, she could manage it. The driver would be busy with the cab and horse, so wouldn't pursue her. At least, not immediately.

With a nod to confirm the plan, if only to herself, Amelia tightly looped the straps of her reticule over one wrist, gathered her skirts in one hand, and shifted as close to the open door as she could manage.

A few minutes later, the cab reduced its speed to round a corner, then slowed even more. Her chance was coming. Warehouses lined the deserted street and looked like less than a promising haven, but she was offered little choice. She waited another moment as the conveyance started to come to a halt then leapt out the door, stumbled, but managed to remain on her feet.

"Come back here!" the driver shouted.

Amelia ignored him and ran in the opposite direction, heart pounding. A glance about did little to help her get her bearings in the dusky light. Where should she go? Most buildings were unlit, and it wouldn't do to run along the pavement when the driver could easily follow her.

Hide, hide—but where?

The sight of a faint light coming from a nearby building gave her hope, and she quickened her pace to reach it—but a different door opened as she passed, the outline of a man filling it with the glow of a lantern behind him.

Relief weakened Amelia's knees. "Help! Please, help me!"

The tall man took another step closer. She couldn't see his face with the light in her eyes. "What is it?" he asked gruffly.

"I need assistance—please." She glanced frantically over her shoulder.

The driver had halted the cab, secured the brake, and hopped down from his perch as if he was in no hurry at all as he stepped nearer. "As requested, sir."

Amelia looked between the two, unable to understand what was happening. A small plaque beside the door where the stranger stood caught her notice.

Sable Importers.

Dear heaven. She had stepped directly into the hornet's nest.

"Mrs. Greystone, I presume." The man's knowing smile, barely visible, sent ice through her veins.

Without a second thought, she shoved him with both hands using all her might and ran.

"Hey!" the driver shouted.

A muttered oath caught her ears and Amelia quickened her pace. There had to be someone else nearby willing to aid her—someone, anyone. "Help!" she shouted again. Most buildings along the street were already dark, apparently closed for the night. Closed, and empty of those who might assist her.

There! Just ahead was a light in a window.

Hope burned bright as she reached the door, only to be jerked back.

"You're coming with me."

Amelia screamed, the grip on her shoulder painful but the shock far more to blame for the noise. The sound was cut short by a hand over her mouth as she was hauled backward bodily toward the shipping office. Twisting, she bit the hand and screamed again. This time, whoever held her struck her on the side of the head and pain spiraled through her.

"Shut up."

Dazed, Amelia continued to struggle but was no match for her opponent who dragged her to the open door. It wasn't until they were inside that she managed a well-placed elbow into the man's side then stomped on his foot, spinning away from his loosened grip.

"Ouch! Damn, woman." The driver reached for her again.

"Enough!" A sharp tone made the driver quit his efforts.

Amelia looked at the large man she'd shoved. While they had never met, she could easily guess who he was. She lifted her chin and glared at him as imperiously as she could muster. "Mr. Edgarton, *I presume*?"

Thirty-Two

WITHIN TEN MINUTES Henry and Fletcher had gathered half a dozen police officers, advised them of the situation, and prepared the two wagons still parked nearby. The trip to Sable Importers wouldn't take long, but every minute was an eternity when Henry knew Amelia was in danger.

Darkness had fallen in full, and the lanterns on the wagons did little to penetrate it. Gas lights along the streets offered some relief.

Fletcher shifted on the bench beside him as they lumbered toward the docks. "What could he want with Mrs. Greystone?" the sergeant asked quietly. "Why would he care if she visited Mrs. Drake at the prison?"

Something niggled in the back of Henry's mind, something Amelia had told him from her first visit. She'd said that Mrs. Drake had almost said a name. 'My'...or perhaps she had meant 'Mi' for Miles, as in Miles Edgarton. "I believe Mrs. Drake and Edgarton had a...romantic relationship."

Fletcher's eyes widened in clear surprise. "Interesting—but I still don't understand why he took Mrs. Greystone."

"Perhaps to confirm what Mrs. Drake told her?" He met his friend's gaze. "Mrs. Greystone came by Scotland Yard to tell me that Mrs. Drake said Edgarton and her late husband worked together to sell illegal antiquities. They had a disagreement, so Edgarton either killed him or had him killed. At least, that's what Mrs. Drake claims Edgarton told her."

"Which could mean he also killed Norris," Fletcher suggested. "And Locke?"

"Yes. Or rather ordered one of his men to kill Locke. My concern is that he intends to silence Mrs. Greystone now since she knows the truth. After all, Mrs. Drake will likely hang for her crimes. That would eliminate the two loose ends." He couldn't bear to think of Amelia as a loose end. If something happened to her—

"Oh no." The horror in Fletcher's voice didn't come close to matching how Henry felt.

"Mrs. Greystone also identified Richards as Locke's killer while she was at the Yard, and I would be willing to wager that he is employed by Edgarton." Impatience simmered through Henry as he glanced about to gauge how much longer it would take to reach the warehouse. How could he have been so stupid to let her attempt the journey home alone?

"Edgarton is leaving a trail of bodies in his wake." Fletcher frowned. "How long did he expect to escape our notice?"

"He obviously hasn't been worried about getting caught. Not for years." That realization concerned Henry.

"Not only is the blaggard bringing illegal antiques into the country and killing those who cross him, but he runs a fixed lottery scheme." The sergeant shook his head. "How many illegal enterprises can one man be involved in?"

"Numerous, apparently, just as Inspector Duncan suspected." The situation seemed too fantastic to believe, yet it also made a terrible sense.

"Then Edgarton is our target when we arrive—although we don't yet know what he looks like." Fletcher's moustache twitched in the glow of a lantern's light as it swung on the side of the wagon.

"Our priority is Amelia—Mrs. Greystone's safety," Henry advised, trying to still the panic in his lungs. "Arresting Edgarton and those working for him is secondary." Just the thought of her in the criminal's hands terrified him, but he had to set aside his emotions and focus on his job.

Clear thinking was needed now more than ever.

"Pull over here," Henry ordered minutes later when they neared the warehouse, keeping his voice quiet. The element of surprise would be on their side if they could enter without notice. He'd already advised them that Amelia might be in danger, and that Edgarton should be treated with caution.

The officers hopped off the wagon, many with batons in hand, all prepared to follow Henry's orders. Thank goodness he had managed to leave Perdy behind.

"I will meet you inside." Henry glanced at Fletcher for confirmation.

"Right. I'll find the rear entrance as quick as I can. Mrs. Greystone will be safe and sound shortly." With a nod at one of the constables who held a lantern, Fletcher led the way toward the back with another in tow.

Henry didn't wait for Fletcher and his two men to move into place but waved for the other three to follow him to the front door.

There wasn't a moment to lose.

The grimy window just about managed to reveal light from within. The glow reassured him; he had chosen the correct location to search. *Please let that be true.*

Drawing a deep breath, Henry turned the knob, relieved to find it unlocked. Apparently Edgarton wasn't worried about the police or anyone else arriving. He opened the door wide to find the small receiving area empty, looking much like he remembered.

Indistinguishable voices echoed from the rear of the building. Henry gestured for the officers to follow him, moving slowly and silently in case someone stood guard—since Edgarton seemed to employ more men than the City of London.

He reached a second door, this one partially open. Heart pounding and mouth dry, he eased forward enough to try to catch a glimpse of what was happening, holding back the urge to rush into the room. First, he needed to know where Amelia was—if she was there—and how many men were inside.

"—so imagine my surprise when I heard your name not once, but twice in one day," an unfamiliar masculine voice said.

"Oh? I didn't realize I had gained such notoriety." The sound of Amelia's voice, sharpened with annoyance, threatened to buckle his knees.

Thank God he was right. How terrible that he'd had to be.

"First from Powell, and then from another regarding Mrs. Drake. Needless to say, you have become a thorn in my side. One I can no longer tolerate."

"Is it not enough that you killed my husband? Now you intend to do the same to me?"

Though disbelief now colored her tone, Henry knew her well enough to recognize her fear. He held in place, aware of the officers waiting behind him. If there was any chance Edgarton, assuming that was who she spoke with, would admit to Matthew Greystone's murder, Henry wanted to hear it—perhaps nearly as much as Amelia.

The man laughed. "I spoke with your husband numerous times, but he never mentioned what a delight you were."

Henry could well imagine Amelia being taken aback to hear the casual mention of the men's relationship. His own fists were clenching.

"And exactly what were the two of you involved in?" Amelia asked lightly.

Henry couldn't help but admire her pluck to question Edgarton. She seemed determined to find out all she could while ignoring the danger she was in. He hoped she could keep the man talking.

"You didn't think he left you those funds because of his skill in selling run-of-the-mill trinkets in his shop, did you?" Edgarton's voice asked with derision.

Henry shifted to gain a better view of the room, spotting numerous shelves and crates but neither Edgarton nor Amelia, much to his dismay. In fact, no one was visible from his narrow view—yet the discreet clearing of a throat suggested someone stood on the other side of the door.

"You stole items from other countries and Matthew sold them," Amelia stated, her voice flat, disappointment in her husband—and Edgarton—clear.

"Such antiquities do no good if left in the hands of thieves. They would've stolen them, regardless of my interference. Better that they are sold to someone who can appreciate them and line my pockets at the same time."

Henry could imagine Amelia biting her tongue to keep from protesting as a long moment of silence ensued.

"What happened?" The tremble in her voice struck Henry to the core. "Why—why did you kill him?"

Henry continued to wait, wanting her to have the answer with the hope it would bring her peace, though he worried it wouldn't.

"I've answered enough of your questions. I had one to ask of you, regarding your visit with Elizabeth Drake—but from what you said, I already have the answer. She told you something she shouldn't have. Unfortunately, that is poor news for not only her, but you."

The thinly veiled threat was enough to have Henry shoving open the door. He'd heard enough. "Police! Stay where you are."

The man standing on the other side of the door pushed against it in a failed attempt to keep them out to no avail. Henry waved a hand to direct the officer behind him to restrain the man, and a scuffle ensued.

A quick glance around revealed four other men in the room. Edgarton was easy to spot, based on his demeanor and elevated attire compared to the others, but Henry looked past him until he locked gazes with Amelia, whose eyes went wide in surprise—and relief.

Edgarton stood next to her, immediately grabbed her arm and jerked her before him.

"Release her," Henry demanded as he drew nearer, his focus on her captor.

"Stay back." The man who had to be Edgarton, a bull of a man with brown hair and cold, dark eyes who appeared to be in his forties, didn't look worried in the least by the arrival of the police.

"Miles Edgarton?" Henry asked, aware of the officers spreading out to restrain the remaining men, two putting up quite a fight.

Edgarton didn't bother to respond, but Henry continued anyway. "You are under arrest for the murders of Matthew Greystone, Benjamin Norris, and Randolph Locke." He might not have all the evidence he needed as of yet, but he had enough to make an arrest—to take this dangerous man off the street.

The criminal mastermind scoffed as he watched his men struggle with the officers. "You can't be serious."

"You will also face charges for the sale of illicit antiquities and illegal lottery drawings," Henry added for good measure.

A flash of surprise shone in Edgarton's eyes but was quickly replaced by a hard glint of determination as he quickly pulled a knife from a pocket and placed it at Amelia's throat. "But I'm not going anywhere."

"You are only making matters worse for yourself." Henry kept his voice calm, despite the fear surging through him. "Release Mrs. Greystone. Now."

"Stay back." Edgarton glanced over his shoulder and drew her backward, one step at a time.

Amelia visibly stiffened as she clutched at the man's arm, wincing as the blade caught. A trickle of blood became visible on her throat above the knife.

Henry stilled, though panic threatened. "It's no use. We have you outnumbered."

"And yet I have the lady *and* the upper hand." Edgarton's confident smile chilled him. The man eased steadily backward, and Henry could only guess he thought to escape through a rear door. Hopefully, Fletcher had found it and would be there to greet him.

Another of the officers, a newer constable named Peters, moved slowly toward Edgarton, and to Henry's surprise the brute didn't protest. In fact, he paid him little attention.

Just as Henry opened his mouth to order the constable back, pounding echoed from the rear door.

That had to be Fletcher.

The sound startled Edgarton, and he loosened his hold on Amelia just enough for her to pull his arm—and the knife—away from her throat before ramming her elbow into his stomach.

The man groaned as Henry ran forward and grabbed Edgarton's wrist, wrenching it down and away from Amelia, who quickly escaped his clutches. A rush of anger flooded Henry, and before he could stop himself, he had punched Edgarton in the jaw and then again in the stomach, the knife clattering to the floor.

Someone must have unlocked the rear door, for a moment later Fletcher was grabbing Edgarton while another officer placed cuffs on him.

"Perfect timing," Henry told Fletcher before he moved toward Amelia.

"You have no proof—you'll regret this night!" Edgarton glared at Henry as he attempted to jerk free of Fletcher's hold without success. "This will be the end of your career with Scotland Yard."

The threat sent unease crawling along Henry's spine, but he reminded himself those were the empty words of a criminal.

"Once again, I missed all the fun." Fletcher grinned before glancing about the room. "Load them into the wagons," he directed the officers.

As if sensing his words had hit its target, Edgarton continued to look at Henry. "This isn't over, Inspector Field."

That he knew Henry's name, when no one had said it since their arrival, caused concern—but it would have to wait until later.

"Are you all right?" Henry studied the nick on Amelia's throat as she touched the spot, smearing the thin line of blood.

"I'm fine." She closed her eyes briefly. "Though it might take a little while to recover from my fright." She met his gaze, emotion swirling in the depths of her brown eyes. "I can't believe you realized what happened or where I was."

He couldn't resist reaching for her arm—to reassure himself that she was well, as much to offer support. "I almost didn't.

It wasn't until after you left that I realized the driver looked familiar. Fletcher and I spoke with him when we followed Locke here."

"How fortuitous." She placed a hand on her chest as if to help calm her heart. "Thank you."

He nodded, though there was so much more he wanted to say. "Allow me a few minutes to see to things here, and then I will escort you home."

"I would be happy to assist, sir," Constable Peters said as he drew near, a friendly smile on his face as he nodded at Amelia. "If the lady would like."

"No need, Peters." Henry didn't intend to trust Amelia's care to anyone else, not again. "I will take care of it."

Within minutes, all those in the room had been handcuffed and loaded into the wagons, including Edgarton. Fletcher sent an officer to find a hansom cab for Henry and Amelia, and just five minutes later, they departed for her home at the same time the wagons left.

"Thank you again, Henry." Amelia offered a weak smile. "I do believe I owe you my life."

"I am happy to have helped, since I was the one who quite literally handed you over to Edgarton." He shook his head at the terrible mistake. Amelia wasn't the only one who needed time to recover from a fright.

"We had no reason to suspect any such thing would happen." She sighed, her hands still trembling in her lap. "I...I can hardly believe Matthew's killer has been arrested, though I worry if what Mrs. Drake told me is enough evidence to convict him."

As did he. Whether Edgarton's arrest truly solved her late husband's death in a court of law remained to be seen. Henry felt certain Edgarton was to blame, but *feelings* weren't enough. He needed evidence, and information supplied by a condemned prisoner was dubious at best. Nor had he forgotten what Duncan had said—that Edgarton had a way of escaping punishment.

"It is a start," he said. "We will dig until we discover what we need." He didn't want her worrying about Edgarton being a threat any longer. Amelia not worrying was fast becoming his greatest goal.

The answer seemed to satisfy her as she nodded.

It was difficult to believe the case that had eluded him for over a year had now been solved. He had stumbled upon the killer almost by chance, which left him far from confident about his skills.

But he would have to worry about those concerns another time. For now, his focus was Amelia.

"Can you tell me what happened?" Henry hoped her speaking of it would keep her from dwelling on the events later. She would need to provide an official statement, but that could wait until the following day.

She shared the details, answering his few questions as well, until he had a good idea of what had occurred.

"You are certain you're all right?" he asked once they neared her home. "I don't like the thought of leaving you, but duty calls. I must return to the Yard."

"Of course. The Fernsbys will take care of me." She smiled. "And young Master Leopold is proving to be an excellent distraction."

Only then did he realize that the final thread that connected them might now be cut, and he wouldn't have a reason to see her in the coming weeks or months.

That was, unless he created one.

He helped her alight, then bid the driver to wait while he saw her inside, his thoughts unsettled. The door opened before they reached the steps, a frantic Fernsby greeting them.

"Mrs. Greystone! Thank goodness you've returned." He glanced between them, nerves clearly wrought. "I sent a message to Scotland Yard to advise Inspector Field of your worrisome delay but wasn't certain what else to do."

"It has been quite an evening," Amelia told the servant with a weak smile.

Henry left it to her to give a brief overview of the evening while he listened, noting the shadows beneath her eyes and the tremble of her movements. He hoped having some answers about her late husband's death would provide her peace, once she had time to absorb them.

Aware of the passing of time and that he was needed at the Yard, Henry cleared his throat. "Once again, Mrs. Greystone has proven herself a heroine."

Amelia smiled as she reached to touch his arm, the contact tightening his chest. "Since you were the one to rescue me, that makes you the hero of the evening."

Her words touched him, even though he knew they weren't true.

"And you will no doubt be happy to be rid of your unwanted assistant," she continued. Before he could protest or say how much he would miss time with her, she added, "Henry, I can't thank you enough for not giving up on Matthew's case."

Was this truly the end? Her way of saying goodbye? He supposed so; he no longer had a reason to stop by to see her.

"I will continue to press until Edgarton's convicted of his numerous crimes." He held her gaze, hoping she understood the promise, and he wished he could add just how relieved he was that she was all right and how much he admired her courage.

One day soon, he hoped those words could be spoken—and would be well received.

Epilogue

One month later...

AMELIA SMILED AND TOOK Henry's offered arm as they walked from a hansom cab toward the arched entrance of the Criterion Restaurant in Picadilly Circus. "Won't this be a treat?" she asked. "My editor says it comes highly recommended."

Gas lamps flanked the entrance, casting a warm glow over the grand Italianate façade with its decorative columns and carved stonework. Though it had been open for a decade and was still popular, she hadn't dined there or at many other restaurants, for that matter, for a very long time.

The moment made her realize, once again, how small her life had grown. Relief at knowing the man who had killed Matthew was behind bars helped convince her that she needed to move forward with her life. They'd found justice for Matthew, and she hoped his spirit could rest easier. But now it was her turn. If she'd learned anything in the last few years it was that life was short. She lifted her chin. The time had come to venture out more, starting now.

They weren't the only ones enjoying an evening out. Numerous carriages and cabs lined the street with well-dressed couples coming and going.

Henry's invitation to dinner had been welcome, though she wasn't yet certain of his intention. Did he wish to discuss the case...or was this a more personal endeavor?

The uncertainty made her anxious, but she told herself to simply enjoy the evening and worry about such things later.

After all, she would know soon enough.

"I am pleased our first dining experience here is together." He smiled as he opened the door of the restaurant for her.

The lavish, golden interior of the restaurant had Amelia glancing about in admiration. Gold mosaics decorated the ceiling and glittered with light from gas lamps and candles below. Dark wood furnishings, marble paneled walls, and elegant moldings gave the place a rich, exotic atmosphere.

She was pleased she had worn her purple gown and admired Henry's evening attire. He looked handsome, with his hair neatly trimmed and brushed to the side. For a moment, she almost thought she caught the scent of cologne—but decided she must be mistaken.

Do not get ahead of yourself, Amelia Greystone.

They were shown to the table Henry had reserved, with a crisp white tablecloth and plush, upholstered chairs waiting for them. Henry held her chair and she couldn't help but look around after she was seated, appreciating the tall, gilt-framed mirrors that allowed her to study the décor and its other occupants without being too obvious.

Though she worried how expensive the restaurant was, she put aside the concern. If Henry had invited her as his guest, he surely already knew and was comfortable with it.

A waiter greeted them and, with Amelia's agreement, Henry ordered a white wine for her and a small brandy for him.

From what Henry had told her on the ride over, the past few weeks had been spent untangling Edgarton's activities. Amelia had provided a formal statement to confirm that she had seen Richards leaving the scene of Locke's fatal stabbing and that Edgarton had held her against her will, as well as what Elizabeth Drake had revealed. The woman had been sentenced to death, and the punishment carried out a mere week ago. Amelia had mixed feelings about her death, but then, Mrs. Drake had made terrible choices in the name of science. Choices which could not be undone.

Richards had admitted to being ordered to kill Locke by Edgarton, in exchange for a lighter sentence. Henry had said investigating Edgarton's activities revealed more questions than answers; his criminal network was more complicated and widespread than thought, and he seemed to be able to block them at every turn—even from inside prison.

"And how is Sergeant Fletcher?" Amelia asked, eager for more news of Henry's work.

"He is well and asked me to give his regards. His cousin was recently promoted to Inspector and has moved to London to work at Scotland Yard." A frown briefly marred his brow, making her wonder at the cause.

"That's exciting."

"Indeed. How is Leopold?" Henry asked after their drinks were served and they'd given their orders.

"Master Leopold is ruling the house," she said with a laugh, fingering the stem of her wine glass. "Mrs. Fernsby threatens to evict him at least once a week while spoiling him rotten."

Henry's smile had her heart beating a little faster. "I can imagine it perfectly."

The conversation continued, and Henry steered clear of the case and his work. She wasn't sure whether to be pleased or disappointed. What was this invitation for?

"May I say how lovely you look this evening, Amelia?" The admiration in his brown eyes had her cheeks heating.

"Thank you. You—you look handsome, as well." She caught her breath, worrying that had been too forward.

The first course arrived, a consommé printanier of clear seasoned broth with finely chopped vegetables and freshly baked rolls served warm.

Henry asked after her parents, followed by her aunt, and though her aunt hadn't decided whether to pursue the money she'd lent her former gentleman friend, Amelia mentioned it to Henry.

"We can certainly put out the word for the police to watch for his return to England," he advised. "Let me know if she would like to pursue it."

"Thank you. I will share that with her." The conversation moved on to his parents, along with a letter Amelia had received from Maeve's aunt, and an update on Agnes and Pudge. Their lives had so closely intertwined in the last few months.

The next course of sole fillets poached in wine with mushrooms was delicious and served with small potatoes and asparagus. Then came the entrée of a slice of roasted mutton with rich gravy and a dollop of sweetness in the form of redcurrant jelly. The course was served with glazed carrots, mashed potatoes, and a lovely Bordeaux.

Amelia felt completely spoiled, enjoying the evening immensely, thanks to Henry's company. They had much to speak of given the cases and those involved with them, but it was not the food that caught her attention. It was the company she was keeping.

Just as Amelia wondered how she was going to manage two more courses, she saw someone rushing toward their table, causing gasps and heads to turn in his wake. A uniformed constable drew to a halt beside them, clearly out of breath from his efforts.

"Inspector Field. Madam." He nodded at Amelia. "Terribly sorry to disturb you, but we have a problem."

"This better be of the utmost importance, if you're interrupting our dinner." Henry's lips tightened, clearly displeased to be disturbed. "What is it?"

"Director Reynolds sent me to fetch you. It's about Edgarton. He's escaped."

Amelia gasped as her gaze met Henry's, who appeared as surprised as she was. To think, she had finally been adjusting to the nightmare of Matthew's murder being over—and now it seemed another might be beginning.

"Escaped?" she breathed, hardly able to believe it.

Almost as though he did so without thought, Henry reached across the table and took her hand, squeezing it in welcome reassurance. "We will find him. And soon."

Amelia squeezed back despite the worry coursing through her. Thank goodness she could rely on Henry to do everything in his power to resolve the matter—and perhaps, once again, she could lend him aid.

Ready for the next Field & Greystone adventure? Look for The Rookery Killer.

A murdered prison guard, a dangerous fugitive, and missing evidence all point to one thing—the shadows of corruption are brewing within Scotland Yard...

Inspector Henry Field is under pressure to track down an escaped prisoner—a man suspected of murder in a cold case that Henry is desperate to put behind him. When a prison guard turns up dead, it seems obvious the fugitive is to blame. But as Henry delves deeper, the evidence twists into something far more sinister, leading him to a chilling realization: the true threat is lurking closer than he ever imagined.

Amelia Greystone never intended to become entangled in yet another murder investigation, but danger finds her once again. And the suspect is the very same man accused of killing her husband—someone who clearly wants her silenced.

As deception tightens its grip and danger closes in, Henry and Amelia must navigate a treacherous web of lies. Can they unmask the killer and expose the corruption before one of them becomes the next victim?

Order your copy of The Rookery Killer today!

Author's Notes

Thank you for reading *The Gravesend Murder*. I hope you're enjoying Amelia and Henry's adventures. I thought I would share a few historical notes that I found interesting while researching this book.

Gravesend is a town in Kent, England, near London, founded in 1268 with a port on the River Thames. It was originally noted as Gravesham in the Domesday Book of 1068 and has one of the oldest surviving markets in England. It was developed as a watering place and became an industrial center in the 1800s with paper mills, cement works, and ship repair businesses. It also has a chantry still standing, dating from the 14th century. Pocahontas, a First American woman from the Powhatan people, died there after falling ill at the start of a voyage bound for the Commonwealth of Virginia.

The Cats' Meat Men or Women sold meat (usually horsemeat) from barrows (handcarts) during the 19th and 20th centuries, with each tradesperson working a particular route that served several hundred households. Mewing cats announced their approach, allowing those in need of cat meat to purchase some. Cats were also commonly fed oatmeal porridge or bread soaked in milk. Boiled "lights" which are lungs, were thought to be better than horsemeat but were not always available. Fish was also recommended.

Threadneedle Street is an actual street in London. The idea of needles and pins being made by hand is intriguing with wire being redrawn, straightened, cut, and one end sharpened. Straight pins were used frequently and are still found by mudlarks along the River Thames. Needle makers were located in London during the 16th century, but most moved to Redditch near Birmingham in the 18th century, and a museum there shares the history of the trade.

Thank you again for reading this story. Reviews are much appreciated. Watch for the next book in the Field & Greystone series, *The Rookery Killer*.

Other Books by Lana Williams

The Field & Greystone Series

The Ravenkeeper's Daughter, Book 1
The Mudlark Murders, Book 2
The Gravesend Murder, Book 3
The Rookery Killer, Book 4

The Mayfair Literary League

A Matter of Convenience, Book 1
A Pretend Betrothal, Book 2
A Mistaken Identity, Book 3
A Simple Favor, Book 4
A Christmastide Kiss, Book 5
A Perilous Desire, Book 6
A Sweet Obsession, Book 7
The Wallflower Wager, a novella connected to The Mayfair Literary League and the Revenge of the Wallflowers series
A Secret Seduction, Book 8

The Wicked Widows Collection

To Bargain with a Rogue, a novella

The Duke's Lost Treasures:

Once Upon a Duke's Wish, Book 1
A Kiss from the Marquess, Book 2
If Not for the Duke, Book 3

The Seven Curses of London Series

Trusting the Wolfe, a Novella, Book .5
Loving the Hawke, Book I
Charming the Scholar, Book II
Rescuing the Earl, Book III
Dancing Under the Mistletoe, a Novella, Book IV
Tempting the Scoundrel, a Novella, Book V
Romancing the Rogue, A Regency Prequel
Falling For the Viscount, Book VI
Daring the Duke, Book VII
Wishing Upon A Christmas Star, a Novella, Book VIII
Ruby's Gamble, a Novella
Gambling for the Governess, Book IX
Redeeming the Lady, Book X
Enchanting the Duke, Book XI

The Seven Curses of London Boxset (Books 1-3)

The Secret Trilogy

Unraveling Secrets, Book I
Passionate Secrets, Book II
Shattered Secrets, Book III

The Secret Trilogy Boxset (Books 1-3)

The Rogue Chronicles

Romancing the Rogue, Book 1
A Rogue's Reputation, a Novella, Book 2
A Rogue No More, Book 3
A Rogue to the Rescue, Book 4
A Rogue and Some Mistletoe, a Novella, Book 5
To Dare A Rogue, Book 6
A Rogue Meets His Match, Book 7
The Rogue's Autumn Bride, Book 8
A Rogue's Christmas Kiss, a Novella, Book 9
A Rogue's Redemption, a short story, Book 10

A Match Made in the Highlands, a Novella

Falling for A Knight Series

A Knight's Christmas Wish, Novella, Book .5
A Knight's Quest, Book 1 (Also available in Audio)
A Knight's Temptation, Book 2 (Also available in Audio)

A Knight's Captive, Book 3 (Also available in Audio)

The Vengeance Trilogy

A Vow To Keep, Book I
A Knight's Kiss, Novella, Book 1.5
Trust In Me, Book II
Believe In Me, Book III

Contemporary Romances

Yours for the Weekend, a Novella

If you enjoyed this story, I invite you to sign up to my newsletter to find out when the next one is released. I'd be honored if you'd consider writing a review!

About the Author

Lana Williams is a USA Today Bestselling Author with over 50 historical fiction novels filled with mystery, romance, adventure, and sometimes, a pinch of paranormal to stir things up. Her latest venture is with historical mysteries.

She spends her days in Victorian, Regency, and Medieval times, depending on her mood and current deadline. Lana calls the Rocky Mountains of Colorado home where she lives with her husband and a spoiled rescue dog named Sadie. Connect with her at https://lanawilliams.net/.

Printed in Great Britain
by Amazon